TIFFANY

A WITHDRAWN

FLOOD

OF

POSIES

ISBN Print 978-1-64548-026-6
ISBN Ebook 978-1-64548-027-3

Cover Design and Interior Formatting
by Qamber Designs and Media

Published by Black Spot Books,
An imprint of Vesuvian Media Group

PRAISE FOR
A FLOOD OF POSIES

"Bewitching debut....this is a promising first outing from Meuret."
—*Publishers Weekly*

"With its unforgettable imagery, *Posies* is a phenomenal novel set at the edge of an unforeseen apocalypse." —*Foreword Reviews*

"Meuret's examination is as much upon changing relationships and human endeavors as on the face of world-changing disaster....*A Flood of Posies* is highly recommended reading for readers of fantasy and women's literature who look for more in their world-ending and world-building studies than an action-packed survival saga alone." —*Midwest Book Review*

To my Grandmother, who upon reading this book from her hospital bed told me, "The ending needs work."
May she rest in peace.

CHAPTER ONE

THE AFTER

SESTRA WORKED HER arms through the endless ocean, sinking them into the blue. Every inch of her body dripped from the salty spray and sweat. She'd been paddling atop an old door for hours now and the sun stood at high noon. It had still been dark when she left.

She wasn't sure where she was going. She knew what she was looking for, just not where it was, exactly. So she paddled and swam, just like she did every day, a combination of swimming and floating and swimming again. After the flood, that's all there was to do.

The water was calm and she moved with the tide, letting it lead her. She'd dipped in and out of consciousness due to fatigue more than once. The beast she sought was everywhere, always, except now, when she wanted to find it. She couldn't help but feel watched; the idea that it was spying on her from somewhere deep below was insidious and uncomfortable. How long would it wait? Would it lurk beneath the water until her body withered to a shell, then pluck her like an appetizer from a tray? She was growing weaker by the moment, infection and dehydration and starvation all culminating into an effective and deadly flourish.

Perhaps that was the point.

It was difficult to gauge how long she'd been searching and floating, floating and searching. Her limbs dangled in the water, her body barely afloat on the flimsy sheet of old wood. She might have stayed that way forever, drifting into an unending sleep, her body a feast for whatever still lived, but then a throb of water swelled around her. It nearly sunk her—the pulse of something big coming to life. Sestra peered into the water, an adrenaline spike threatening to end her where she lay.

Even though she hadn't caught sight of it yet, the thump from below was enough to let her know she'd found it—or rather, it had found her. After all this time, she and the beast were finally face to face, nothing but blinding fury and a plank of wood to separate them. Just when she'd become content in paddling and being thirsty until she either died of dehydration or drowned, there it was.

Fucking things had a nasty way of showing up just when she'd almost forgotten about them. Nasty posies. Rob had named them—Poseidons of the sea, angry creatures full of malice and vengeance. Sestra shortened it to posy, because who wanted to bother with three syllables when two would do? Not even the end of the world could stamp out the human love of shortcuts.

Aside from the basic functions of trying to not die, Sestra had spent the past year running from posies and praying they wouldn't take her too. That she wouldn't be stolen into the water like so many others, never to be seen again. As if the earth-ending flood of biblical proportions wasn't enough, of course there had to be monsters too.

She was tired now yet couldn't stop flexing her fists. The feral instincts of her old life were hard to shake. Hard to imagine the old life could be measured away in mere months. Bored and anxious, Sestra had decided last night she was going to hop overboard and find one of the fuckers haunting her. It had waited for her, behind her, underneath her. And now she'd found it.

She'd slit her wrists for a needle right now. The entire ceremony of tying off, tapping her shriveled-up veins and finding that perfect one, coaxing it out of hiding just to stab it with the beautiful, beautiful poison. Heroin would make all of this better. But all the heroin of the world lay somewhere lost underneath millions of gallons of water, down below with the old world and all its ghosts—pressurized like an opioid diamond.

Sestra faced the eerie calm of the water. Just one pulse for the posy to let her know it was there, and nothing more. The surface was slick as glass now; how long had she been sitting there thinking of heroin? Smooth water never stopped unsettling her, not with knowing the monsters that lurked just below. Things that horrible shouldn't be allowed to be so damned stealthy.

Willing it to show itself, willing it to leave, hoping and terrified and ready to vomit, Sestra carefully leaned over the edge of her raft so as not to upset her precarious balance and send herself over the edge. She stared into the water. The sun penetrated just a few inches, but it was enough. Her raft bobbed as she settled onto her stomach, and then again as something thick and silvery shot underneath her. The thing was thicker than her torso, and that was just one of the tentacles that she could see. There were more—nobody was sure how many—all attached to a massive body hiding deeper than the light could penetrate.

She was out of options, not that there were ever many to choose from.

Scooting to the edge, Sestra slid into the water headfirst and swam.

CHAPTER TWO
THE FLOOD

DORIS SAT IN her kitchen drinking tea and dragging a thumb over the leather of her husband's wallet. James had forgotten it and conspicuously not called to ask if she could look for it. He'd probably already cancelled the cards in hopes she'd never notice. The last place he ever wanted her to look was his wallet. It was less of an inconvenience to simply have it stolen.

The morning pounded down on her from above—rain in all directions for the foreseeable future. The sky was heavy with the bleary gray of a storm. If she believed the weather app on her phone, it was bound to be one for the ages; it was only nine in the morning and small pockets of water already pooled in the recesses of her yard.

Not that there was much she could do for it, even if she'd had the urge to bother (which she did not). Physical therapy was a slow process—slow and painful and limited in effectiveness. She was a tuning fork for pain, and every flinch, sneeze, or heavy sigh set her body ringing with it. Years, they said. Years, and there was no guarantee she would ever regain her former strength.

A petrichor musk rose up from the oak planks of her floor; the smell of wet earth mixed well with her green tea. She propped the wallet against the tall glass vase centering her kitchen table.

James screwed so many lilies into it that they burst out the top like fireworks. He bought them because they were her favorite, and they were her favorite because they looked so damn mean.

Work gnawed at her. More than one deadline today for more than one client. Copywriting was brainless work. She'd done it for so long now that she often didn't remember what she wrote immediately after sending it, like arriving at home and not being able to recall the drive. Her brain deleted the words from her memory, needing the space for more strenuous activities, like staring out windows.

Turning away from the window, Doris glanced at the phone in her hand. Eight missed calls. Thirteen text messages. She'd silenced all notifications this morning for this very reason, predicting a panic equal to the storm.

Rain. Oh God, the rain. And she without a caregiver.

Tossing it aside, Doris dragged her fingers along the keyboard of her laptop, feeling exhausted at the thought of doing anything. Nothing enticed her, but there was only so much television she could watch before she wanted to scream, only so many books to read before they all began to sound the same. Copywriting forced her into a routine, and while the money was poor, it was money nonetheless. She still couldn't work a regular job in her state, and even extended bouts at a computer were too much—pain like lightning radiated against her spine after only an hour. The computer screen itself was also an enemy, causing migraines after so little as thirty minutes of uninterrupted work, which prior to the accident had never been an issue.

As tends to happen when a person is faced with an excessive amount of time to think, all the items around the house that needed tending to populated her mind at inconvenient times. Things like the weather stripping under the front door that had peeled off, leaking puddles of water into the house after heavy rain. Rain like today's rain. Soon enough, the hardwood would warp from the moisture, and considering she never remembered to take care of it until it was too late, she was resigned to stuffing towels beneath it until the wood gave up the goose completely.

Thinking better of working at the kitchen table, Doris decided to retreat to her office near the front of the house. James had set up an automatic lift chair in there, and while she resented the hell out of having to use it, it was extremely helpful and more comfortable than she'd ever admit. Plus, she could watch for James's return. She hated being surprised by his arrival.

The walk there was slow and shuffling, but not as bad as usual. She'd placed her laptop and phone in a small tote, having learned the hard way what happened when she was forced to bend over and retrieve them after dropping them. Bending was the most painful process in her new repertoire of discomfort—an act most don't consider until the ease of it is swept away. It felt like a car radio on the loudest volume, shocking her eardrums in surprise as the ignition turned over, but instead of her eardrums, it was her entire body. Instead of noise, it was pain. And instead of the shock fading away by the end of the drive, it lingered forever until the thought of bending made her want to vomit.

The front yard seemed to hold up better than the already-flooding back. Small puddles formed in the pockets of the yard with blades of grass peeking through like rheumy swamp reeds, but that was all. Good. It could use a good soak anyway.

She was a silver-lining kind of person.

Although Doris's phone pelted her incessantly, demanding attention, she left it in her bag and settled into her raised chair in preparation for the roller-coaster ride that was small business copywriting. James had initially tried to move her office into the living room, for her comfort and ease (he claimed), but Doris balked, furious that he'd dared.

He'd just been trying to be nice, her mother had explained. James probably *thought* he was being considerate, even as he chose to ignore the glaring insult of it. It never occurred to him how much of her personal autonomy had been stolen, and now he wanted to take even more? As if she couldn't be trusted to exist alone in a space for a few hours without dying in misery? James felt compelled to keep her under his thumb for her own good, willfully ignoring all prior evidence to the contrary. But it was for her own good, and of course, she must understand that. Her physical therapist seemed to think so. So did her mother. So did everyone. It seemed that the only person they didn't consult was her.

Obviously, Doris just couldn't be trusted to make up her own damn mind on the matter.

Their house sat on the bulb-end of a cul-de-sac, street sloping toward her so that all the loose pieces of her neighbors' recycling bins always collected around her mailbox. Rain *thock-thock-thocked* against the roof; the lazy storm had grown comfortable and decided to stay awhile. Doris hated the weather and being stuck inside her house. Her last memory of rain was just after the accident. She'd wandered into the street as water pelted her and cried. Out in the wet, nobody could tell she was crying, so she'd kept doing it until her husband had discovered her, ushering her to the house like a flight attendant's cart on a cheap airliner.

It wasn't really the water she hated.

There was something about being cold that didn't suit her. Cold infected down to the bone. It was something that clung to her like a parasite, impossible to peel away. Doris preferred the stinging heat of summer and the way it slapped at her skin. She imagined it often on cold days like today—the heat reaching out to her, striking her like a match, bringing her back to life, sweaty and out of breath from jogging. Like all normal people, she hated to jog, but now it was one of her therapy goals, so she thought of it often. It was this incendiary hope of recovery that kept her going most days, stopping her from leaving her kettle on the stove until the whole place burned to the ground.

Discordant with her sour mood, the laptop pinged cheerfully. *Good morning, human. I am awake!*

She had four emails—two from a client and two from her mother. It'd become instinct to simply delete anything sent from her mom, but today she happened to glance at the subject line.

THEA

In all caps, of course.

"Great," she said to no one. Then she remembered her phone and all those missed calls. Just great.

Three more missed calls from James. Five from her mother. Ten additional texts from a combination of them both.

Was this it? The thought crossed her mind every time her mother called. Was this it? Even after Doris decided she no longer cared, that she was done with Thea, she couldn't stop the thought and the hike of her blood pressure whenever her sister's name was mentioned. She tried ignoring Ma's calls, but then the emails started. No matter where Doris went, so too went Thea.

IS THE HOUSE FLOODED?
DO I NEED TO COME HOME?
SORRY FORGOT TO GET WEATHER STRIPPING AGAIN.
CALL ME.
CALL ME.
CALL ME CALL ME CALL ME CALL ME.

Her gut stopped churning, her worst fear still unrealized.

It's just a little rain. Jesus Christ.

Tossing her phone back into her tote, Doris resolved to meet her deadline, make some money, and forget about all of them for an afternoon.

Minutes later, the email still open on her laptop, she realized that this would be impossible. If it were possible, she'd be far away from here. Another state. Another country. She'd have disappeared into the mist and never looked back.

Something tethered her here, and that something happened to be Thea, her younger sister. Doris could pretend it was noble a gesture done out of love, but that would be a lie. It was fury that kept her here, and an overwhelming urge to be vindicated, that bound her even more tightly to Thea than her current predicament.

Outside, the storm raged in turn. No doubt that Thea sat at its center, manipulating the wind and rain to suit her whims.

Doris returned to her work.

———

Thea shoved her belongings into a backpack. Turns out hospitality was null and void when the houseguest passed out in the hallway with a needle still stuck in her arm. Lots of tut-tutting and sad looks that Thea couldn't stand anyway, so it was just as well. It didn't take her long to pack, as all she owned was an empty pack of gum and a bag of roasted almonds that she'd stolen from the Circle K across the street. She didn't even have any cigarettes left.

She and Megan had gone to school together since they were fourteen, so Megan hadn't batted an eye when Thea had shown up at her doorstep looking for a place to crash. Megan somehow had gotten her shit together after the clusterfuck that was her high school career, got herself an apartment and a nice boyfriend/fiancé (depending on whether he was within earshot). She waitressed at a dump of a café a few blocks over that teetered on county closure on a constant basis. Thea only knew this because she'd shot up in that bathroom on more than one occasion, often right after stealing some tip money left on one of the corner booths, and witnessed the disapproving rotation of alphabet letters indicating the café's health inspection status: *C, B, C, CLOSED, C* again.

Somehow that yellowing half-apron gave Megan license to shake her head, pretend to cry, and stare like a feral cat whenever

Thea came into the room. Her friend had always maintained lofty opinions of herself.

Thea left without saying goodbye. The second-floor apartment opened to a narrow walkway with stairs that dropped into the parking lot below. Thea tripped in a pothole while dragging her hungover ass through the complex toward Union Avenue. Water sloshed against her ankle. Only then did she realize that it was raining.

God, was Union Avenue a sight for sore eyes. She'd spent more than one night on the bus-stop bench on the corner after being kicked out of a long list of friends' and family's homes, laundromats, and back seats of unlocked cars from the night-shift crew at the grocery store.

Most bus stops were a gamble. Aside from vicious competition from other urban loafers, they were heavily monitored in this area. Not the best place, honestly, but just nice enough that when vagrants like her started collecting en masse, they set police officials to the task of removing them. Set in front of a post office, tucked against the busy intersection of Union and Nineteenth, the bench was untouchable before ten p.m. Then everything just stopped. There was nothing so destitute as an after-hours government facility. To Thea, it was the only peace she knew.

Judging by the fringes of her high and the ferocity of her hangover, she figured it was between eight and ten in the morning. She needed heroin. Pills or heroin or even some heroin. Her fucking feet were soaked, her shoes ridden with holes and burns from ash and dropped lighters and that time she'd tried to light one on fire because she was bored and curious and high. By the looks of the street it must have been raining all night and showed no indication of stopping.

People huddled under the bus-stop overhang, hoping to avoid the weather while waiting for public transportation to haul them off to work. Cars zipped by, huge wings of water spraying up in their wake. Thea trudged in the mud to avoid their assault on the sidewalk.

Thea rubbed the inside of her elbow where the needle had bent as she'd passed out in Megan's apartment. Though she was covered in bruises, that was all that hurt. The vein throbbed. She hugged herself to hide her trembling. She was fine, really. A blood-sugar issue. She hadn't had a real meal in weeks, living off potato chips and cigarettes, and she was always a bit hypoglycemic. Doctors said she should have outgrown it by now. Doctors also claimed her way of living was incompatible with life. At least, that was what the last GP her mother had dragged her to had said while running gloved fingers up her arm. Thea had nearly spat in his face, but Ma had warned upfront that she'd not pay her the money she'd promised if she "cussed, spit, or broke anything."

Instead, Thea had yanked her arm back toward her chest and said, "You think?" She'd demanded the cash right there and then. Ma had given it to her wordlessly, knowing that if she refused, the next time she saw her daughter might be in a morgue.

It wasn't an easy pull, often laced with Ma's emotional baggage and turmoil, so Thea only played the card when she was most desperate for cash.

But she wasn't going to die. Well she might die, obviously, just as well as anyone might—hit by a bus, cancer, stabbed by a transient under the Union Avenue overpass, overdose, hepatitis, HIV, a bad deal, terrorists—there were endless opportunities for people to ruin themselves. So she *might* die, sure, but it wasn't something she thought much about. She didn't have to—her mother had that paranoia locked up.

Cutting though the grocery store parking lot, Thea weaved through the cars looking for opportunity—unlocked doors, purses, cell phones, anything left behind and worth having. Slim pickings in the rain. Doors and windows were shut tight in bad weather as people seemed to fear a slick of water more than an opiate-powered thief. She didn't expect much, but looking gave her something to do.

Stopping just short of the industrial white lights vomiting from the automatic doors of the store, Thea spun around to leave just as a large white truck caught her attention. Parked at an angle, it not only consumed the handicapped space but also the space next to it. Ford. Pristine. Nice rims and locking lid over the long bed. Thea circled it, watching over her shoulder for witnesses. The grocery doors remained vacant, and the few shoppers scuttling through the parking lot were too wet and too rushed to bother caring about what she might be up to, as long as she wasn't anywhere near them.

No handicapped tags. She was sure to look long and hard. Prick.

Practiced with a knife, she stabbed at the front driver's side tire. But rubber on a tire this big was thick and she was tired. She thought she heard a hiss from a puncture. Not enough. It was the kind of leak that the driver would find the next morning parked safely in their driveway. Not enough.

She hit it again, but her hand bounced off the rubber, twisting her wrist. The knife splashed in a puddle at her feet. *Bloop*. It was gone. Shit.

Shit shit shit.

She kicked the tire. The car alarm sounded. *Wheeeeooooo wheeeeooooo wah wah wah.*

Shit.

Fuck it. The car sirens pinged against the rain, softened by the desolation of the parking lot. An alarm didn't change anything. A prick was still a prick was still a prick, and she felt obliged to teach him a lesson—one prick to another. Also, his wallet in the front cup holder looked mighty healthy.

A toppled cart lay in the gravel embankment a few cars down. Thea grabbed it, heaving it out of the mud—*whoop whoop*

whoop—and hurled it at the truck. It clattered uselessly against the driver's door, but it was enough to start a spidery crack in the window. Praying her jacket would protect her, she finished off the glass with a smack, but cut her arm as she pulled it back through.

Despite the truck's squalling, the parking lot remained empty. So she snatched the wallet and fled, not stopping for two or three blocks. Good to stay clear of rampaging dudebros whose cars just got wrecked in the rain.

With each step, the adrenaline that carried her waned. Unable to run any longer, Thea receded into the shadows when at all possible, arms crossed to hide her injury now bleeding through her jacket. The jacket hadn't been enough to protect her, and she spent the better part of twenty minutes picking tiny, invisible shards of glass out of fabric and skin.

She needed a hit. She couldn't call anyone, as she'd sold her cell phone for heroin. She'd hocked anything worth hocking for drugs. She'd sell her jacket in a snowstorm for heroin. Stopping to rest against a dumpster behind a Jack in the Box, Thea thought about food and counted her cash. Twenty-three whole dollars and some loose change.

Water chilled right through her, pooling around her boots and siphoning up her leg through the hole near her big toe. Her lucky shoes—she'd never considered replacing them. It would be easy to lift another pair. The Walmart a few blocks south was notoriously lax. She even knew the security guard by name—Ralph. He was over eighty and felt sorry for her because she looked just like his little daughter who'd died decades ago from polio. But even though she'd stolen just about anything else, she refused to replace her shoes. They'd run when she ran. They'd carried her. They'd been there, glued to her feet, when nothing else was. Perhaps because all she did was run. Maybe it was because of the drugs and the stealing, or maybe it was because she was just that pathetic to have no one rooting for her but a single pair of busted shoes.

She needed a phone, and without thinking, she followed her feet on their automatic path northward. It was a familiar trek, one she'd taken a thousand times before. She'd lived in the plaza most of her adult life—either bumming on couches or sleeping under streetlights, but just north of there was where her sister lived. The two were currently on terrible terms—Doris had cut off all contact, and Thea wasn't terribly eager to resume it herself. But whenever Thea found herself at a crossroads, she simply started off toward Doris on instinct, assuming she'd figure out something before she ever reached her sister's house (the house she'd crashed at so many times and now was no longer welcome to visit). Most of the time, she never even made it to her street. There was always something ready to beg her attention—a purse left unattended for the briefest of moments, a busy parking lot perfect for hustling (Sir? Madam? Do you have a buck or two for the bus?), or even another tweaker further gone than she was ripe for the pickings.

Thea made a conscious choice to avoid punching down whenever possible—she stayed away from kids and others that just looked rough. It wasn't anything scientific, but there was a glint in their eyes, a certain twinge to their mouths, that revealed all that turmoil boiling around inside. Thea understood it well and tried her best to leave those people alone. Some just looked sick or whatever, and she wasn't going to be the one to fuck up their day even more. Her favorite picks were the Karens—the self-righteous bobbed-haired bitches that made it their life's mission to ruin as many people's days as possible. And Doris's neighborhood was fucking full of them, a point heavily lobbed against her when she and James bought that house.

"How long before you ask to see the manager for not letting you bring your chihuahua into the dentist's office?" Thea would tease.

Doris would shrug and ask her how long until the HOA

would file a complaint against her and James because Thea was passed out drunk in their driveway.

Those were the good(ish) days. Those were the days when Doris was still speaking to her. Those were the days of pills and booze, when she was just a rowdy kid preparing to mature into something responsible, before she graduated to the grown-up disaster she was today.

Union Avenue faded at her back as Thea crossed the threshold between poverty and suburbia. Every now and then a car would pass by overhead as it ran through the water, slick like a buzz saw. A few other unlucky wanderers huddled near the top of the concrete embankment of the underpass, threatening her with their silence. This was their space. They must have been there since before the rain, waiting it out. They were dry and hungry-looking. Thea hitched up her backpack, clutching her injured arm against her stomach. Not that it did any good. The front of her was stained watercolor red, her injury smeared like a scrolling marquee: *Hey, I'm injured. Come and get me.*

Up. North. It was an association she'd never quite shaken from childhood. North was up on the rose compass, and her mind followed that path ever since. Orienting herself to the actual geography of land was difficult and unsettling, and even though she knew the path she took now was northward, it felt down—south. She got lost often, mixing up streets that she'd grown up on. Once, when their family cat got sick, Thea was volunteered to take it to the vet after school. She'd ended up being late as she drove up and down and up again Fifty-Ninth Avenue looking for the right building, which was actually located on Sixty-Seventh Avenue.

Directions were never her strong suit, and because of it, she was ill-suited to street life. Good thing was that one didn't give much of a shit about being suited for anything once there. If she wasn't high or trying to get high or coming down from a high, she was thinking about getting high and walking in a big circle around Union Avenue, hoping to run into some heroin along the way.

The Greyhound station and CASH NOW Loans faded into a ritzy bank with a solar-paneled car park and a gourmet donut shop.

Thea was not going to see her sister. No, she was not. She just needed an easy score. Maybe needed to stop inside an urgent care for stitches (a joke, of course). All sorts of reasons for her to be near Doris's house after being explicitly told to never come there again. Or something like that. What Doris had actually said was, "Just leave."

The thing with her older sister was that it never mattered what she said, but what she didn't say. It exhausted Thea just to be in her presence; the constant duality and double-speak was too much for her. Just say what you mean or say nothing at all, she believed, and if she asked her sister, Doris would probably say that she subscribed to the same policy. But that wasn't true. Doris was the loudest fucking person Thea had ever known. She screamed at people through clenched teeth and smiles, effortless in her disdain for them and everything they stood for.

She and Doris never quite clicked as sisters. They never had a conversation, just a childhood of cymbal clashes. They existed next to each other, measured side by side, and Thea was always found lacking beside her sister's glow. Doris the scholar, Doris the beauty, Doris the chosen one with her honorary name (after their mother's favorite triple threat, Doris Day). Doris had been planned, wanted.

Thea was the afterthought, the whoops. She joked, mostly to herself, that they simply started to write *The Accident* on the birth certificate but lacked the fortitude to finish even that, much like her upbringing. She'd never say it aloud, on the off chance her parents might confirm it true.

Poor her. Poor ugly little sister. It was a nasty hole, and

she'd spent a lifetime scratching her way out of it. But no matter how long she ran, she always managed to circle back here, feet plodding onward toward the one person who hated her most. Thea's comeuppance.

The rain had picked up. It was difficult to walk against the slanting sheets. Little droplets pinged her like needles. Bleeding, with a ripped jacket, she wandered until a sliding noise and then a long hissing whine exploded behind her. A squeal and a crunch and a slide—metal on metal—grabbed her out of her thoughts. A silver sedan with Oregon plates hydroplaned on the road and slammed into a Prius. The road churned with muddy brown water. It ran southward, against her, pulling away from the sky that dropped it. Fucking morons thinking they could drive on roads like that, let alone pass someone. The driver of the Prius popped out immediately, circling his car, shielding his eyes against the rain. The people in the sedan never so much as cracked their door. Thea recognized the glow of a cell phone.

The weather was nasty. Something ominous sank into her bones. She needed to get out of the rain, away from the road. Thea had the sudden idea that she wasn't safe out here. Sensing bad shit coming was a highly attuned sixth sense of hers. Her lifestyle lent itself to shit going wrong often.

But this was *bad* bad. She trembled all over, unable to stop her limbs from clattering together. Her adrenaline spike faded, replaced by the grip of hunger and nausea all rolled up into one gelatinous lump of shit.

She pressed the wound on her arm harder to try and slow the bleeding, but it didn't help. Red poured into puddles at her feet and adrenaline spiked her legs into longer strides. She felt the sudden urge to hurry, a feeling of being watched that she couldn't shake or outrun. Thea had learned enough times to obey that instinct when she recognized it, as if some ancient, primal receptors were picking up on a threat her mind was too slow and stupid to see. And whenever that happened, there was only one person to which she thought to turn, no matter how much they might hate her.

Doris.

Trying to forget about the rain, about her blood spatter trailing her path like breadcrumbs, Thea tunneled toward the only solution she had to all her current problems.

Whether she would be allowed beyond the front stoop remained a mystery, but once the idea was there, it beat against her skull until she listened. It was a way. Not the best way, but a way, and critical thinking beyond that simply annoyed and exhausted her.

Thea went to her sister.

CHAPTER THREE
THE FLOOD

DORIS IGNORED HER phone as it buzzed in her tote. Every time it growled for her attention, she would stop writing, posture drawn up like a dancer in her chair, and try to pretend it wasn't annoying the hell out of her. She did this for an hour, until it buzzed more often than it didn't. Her music did little to drown it out. She felt it ringing in her bones.

She threw her headphones off her ears, whipping them to the floor in a disjointed heap. Jesus Christ, *this day*. It was just a little rain. Without bothering to read or listen to any of her messages, she texted James before his panicked head exploded.

WATER IS ONLY UP TO MY KNEES. WILL CALL ONCE REACHES MY NECK PROVIDED I CAN STILL MANAGE TO OPERATE A TELEPHONE.

Heat slapped her cheeks. She could just feel James's indignance radiating at her through the phone.

"Is anybody ever allowed to worry about you?" he'd asked her during one of their rotating arguments. "I get that you don't need me. You've made that perfectly clear, but do you *want* me anymore? Have you ever?"

Doris hadn't answered him. There hadn't been an answer to give, not one that would make him feel better. His question was a

21

can of compressed snakes disguised as peanuts. She could say yes, which would be a lie. But no wasn't any closer to the truth.

They hadn't spoken more than a few icy pleasantries in more than a week because of it, but not even that stopped him from refilling the vase on the table. Sometimes Doris wished he would just stop. It'd become more of a taunt now, whether he meant it to be or not. *He* still cared. *He* was trying.

She could just leave him. No. She wouldn't give any of them the satisfaction.

The storm had picked up during the torrent of nauseating worry attacking her phone. The walls shuddered. Thunder shook the house from the ground up, jostling something in the attic so that it hit the ceiling with a thud.

Tink tink tink. Little tinny pings emerged behind her. The roof was leaking, a wet spot on the ceiling near the front door pooling in the center and dropping water onto the picture frame holding their wedding photo. She really ought to deal with it, dry the frame and leave a bucket under the leak, but the thought of standing up and bending to get a bucket and bending again to lay it down and peeling the photo free of the metal frame brackets and drying it so that it didn't warp—simply the *thought* of all that sparked an exhaustive panic.

But she couldn't focus. Starting and stopping and erasing and starting again. Nothing worked. None of her words were right. A fog settled over her brain. Everything became sticky.

Then came the dread, knotting her insides like the ends of a string being pulled tighter and tighter in opposite directions. The fuzzy unknown of it, something primal screamed at her, *You're in trouble. Something is wrong.*

It came and went all afternoon. Panic, then a moment of rationalization and a scan around the rooms to convince herself she was crazy. Just a little rain. Just another shitty day. Times like these, she enjoyed going out onto the back porch with a cup of herbal tea, but the water crept dangerously near the lip of her patio, and honestly, she didn't want to open any of the doors. But it wasn't because of the rain. It was something else.

Her mind instantly went to James, and she again checked her phone. Nothing since her last text. Quiet. Her words had obviously hit their mark. But even so, James couldn't not dictate his every move to her. If he was coming home, he'd have said so.

Her mother, perhaps. No, she hated the rain. She hated driving. Her mother would not come here today, which Doris learned to treasure as the only positive to a weather most despised.

There was only one other, and as soon as she thought it, Doris knew it to be correct. A sixth sense she'd picked up after years of a permanent state of unease. T. H. E. A. Four letters in an email. Doris could smell her, feel the weight of her sister's presence in her chest. A mixture of doom, guilt, fury, and sadness, she felt a tug toward her sister as reliable as the drip of the leaky roof. The sensations thrummed in unison, each drip another step closer. Another step, another step, another drip.

Stopping her typing, Doris folded her hands in her lap and waited. God damn it. Thea probably needed cash, or a couch to crash on just long enough to reach her dealer. The last time the two of them had sat across from one another, Doris had restrained herself from slapping Thea across her chapped, junkie face. Despite this control, Thea had balked, slamming the front door and breaking the lock as she showed herself out.

She grabbed her phone and dialed. A line trilled, and for some reason this surprised her. With the water beating down and the thunder and the loudness and shaking, she'd just expected the phone to be a dead brick of cold circuits. But it worked and she waited for James to pick up.

He didn't. He was at work. She knew he was at work. His wallet was just where she'd left it on the kitchen table, soggy with credit cards and a punch card for the sub shop by his office, the only item he might transfer from the old wallet to the new one. She dialed James again, hating that she needed him, but if Thea was on her way—and considering this monumental deluge and Thea's penchant for lingering on Union Avenue just a few blocks south, she *was* on her way here—Doris needed backup. In her current state, she couldn't stop Thea from ransacking the place, forcing Doris to pay attendance to her own robbery.

Her calls continued unanswered, for how long she didn't keep track. The clouds overhead cast shadows through the room, and the air was thick with moisture and the scent of an old library. She chastened herself as her frustration mounted.

He was at work. He was busy. He was at work.

And she didn't really want to talk to him.

She was probably being paranoid anyway. Thea would have to be insane to come here begging. She dialed again.

Like it or not, it just wasn't like James to not get back to her. Peering through the window, she scanned the yard. For what? For James? For Thea? Doris didn't even know what she wanted to see.

The yard was empty, though there wasn't much relief in it. Water climbed suspiciously high. Her pretend swamp reeds were gone, swallowed under the mounting tide. It was many inches high, and while she couldn't see everything without painfully straining, she figured it was high enough to reach over the front porch to the front door missing its weather stripping. Shit.

But then she saw something. Or thought she saw something. The cul-de-sac she lived in was dark under the storm, the streetlights not cued on at this time of day. In the very corners of her windows was a shiver of movement—the type of jerky fluttering of a ghost in the periphery. Then it was gone, disappeared into the gloom. Her stomach pooled into her chair as recognition set in.

She knew that movement. She'd seen it a hundred times as a kid, but never here. Never here at her home. Never.

What the hell was *it* doing here?

"No," she said aloud. "Impossible." Obviously, this was no more than a trick of the eye. A flickering of her imagination produced by her growing sense of unease.

That's when she heard water gurgling somewhere off in the distance. No—wait. *In* her living room. It was a subtle, slow sound, like that of a bathtub draining.

There was nothing to be done for it now; she had to get up and check it out. Hoisting herself free with a grunt, Doris startled as her feet hit the hallway with a splash.

Water oozed through the cracks in the door. A slick of it gleamed atop her oak floors. The rug under the coffee table squished as she moved over it.

It was quick—seconds—between that realization and the first surge of the flood. One moment she was thinking about how badly the wood was going to warp, and in the next instant, water crawled up her walls, roared, and splintered pressboard and drywall and glass. *Whoosh*—it stole her away, colliding against her like a truck. She toppled and was overcome, breathing it in. Slammed against the opposite wall, Doris dug her nails into the drywall and clawed for purchase. She rose, gasping and choking, barely able to hold her chin above water. If she could stand, it'd only be up to her thigh. Panic severed a line connecting her brain to her limbs and everything rebelled.

But she could swim. A far cry from the controlled swim therapy of the rehabilitation center, but she managed.

Or she thought she could, but the rush was too much and water was everywhere and *fuck* her legs would not cooperate. Her grip was too slick. There was nothing close in which to steady herself.

The water was too strong.

Not able to discern one sensation from the next, Doris didn't recognize the pull of someone's arms yanking her up by the hair. It could have been a toppled-over bookcase or a magazine or a chair or a barstool or even God reaching down to take her. Everything was a swirl of water and chaos, and it was killing her.

Hair ripped up by the root, she screamed and gagged as blood poured down her forehead, dripping off her nose. The hands caught her again, a clump of her hair plopping onto the surface of the water, twirling away in the eddies.

The owner of the hands spoke in grunts, struggling to heft Doris's weight above water and keep it there.

Not even a flood could wash the scent of her sister away.

"Thea," said Doris between gasps.

"Doris."

Thea returned the deadpan pleasantry like any proper debutante dragging the useless body of her sister might.

A garage sale copy of *I, Robot* floated past. One of many copies. It was the first science fiction she had ever read.

Adrenaline shocked Doris into a freeze, her body trembling from the cold while her sister pinned her up by her armpits.

"Fuck, you're heavy. Can you stand?"

She honestly didn't know if she could. Pain would have doubled her if it didn't hurt even more to bend that way. She wanted to curl on the floor and vomit, but the water was rising. God, it was rising so quickly, and Thea couldn't hold her much longer.

"I can't hold you. Can you stand? Can you walk?"

Doris vomited in response, curling on the floor turning out to be a completely unnecessary step in the process. The heaving motion of it racked her body—it felt like she might snap in half, like her bones were wrenched apart from the force of it. Then she went limp, sliding down the wall that Thea failed to hold her against like a decommissioned robot—one section at a time. Dripping to her knees, Doris screamed as every fiber of recovering muscle ripped and tore all over again.

For a while, everything was white. Noise, vision, everything.

The water called her back.

Nerves enraged, they sparked and lit against these new sensations. It was as if her body had completely rebelled, throbbing in all sorts of uncomfortable ways, but then she focused on the water; the way it eddied around her, lifting the hem of her shirt away from her body, a gentle reprieve to its earlier show of force.

"Open your eyes! Doris!"

Thea snatched her by the cheeks, squeezing until Doris had no choice but to wince in acknowledgment.

"Good, you're awake. We have to move."

Thea had saved her. She might have drowned. She might have died, but as Doris gazed into her little sister's sunken face, all she could think to say was, "Why were you hiding in my yard, Thea?"

A familiar look scribbled onto her sister's face, one Doris recognized as the precursor to explosion. It meant a dozen things, all of which were easier swallowed in a gaze rather than in words.

"I wasn't hiding anywhere. I was fucking running!" she shouted at Doris as furniture floated by.

"I saw you—you were out front in the shadows. You were moving weird. Are you high?"

"Can we not? Like, really, can we not?"

"You're high."

"And you're about to drown. Let's go."

The sensation of Thea's hands on her sent a fresh batch of vomit to the back of her throat, but the water was coming so fast, and there was so much of it, and she didn't have much choice but to grimace through it and go. Arm slung over her sister's shoulders, Doris hobbled toward the kitchen.

Water lapped against the white cabinetry, and a layer of gray grime already clung to it. The initial surge settled, choosing a devious, slow rise over the powerful punch of its entrance.

Thea heaved Doris toward the countertop nearest the kitchen

sink. "Can you climb?"

Doris snorted, exhausted and not sure that she could. They both knew it, yet Thea didn't dare set her hands on her again without permission. Instead, her gaze fixated on the window overlooking the backyard while Doris decided whether she wanted to ask for help.

"What is it?" Doris asked.

"Nothing."

"You see something—what do you see?"

"I can't see shit. It's nothing but water, sis. Water everywhere. We have to get out of here."

She couldn't help but notice the way Thea trembled. She'd say it was from the cold, but they both knew the truth. "Where do you expect me to go? I can hardly move. Out there I'll just . . ." The rest of that sentence refused to materialize.

"Up, then. You can't stay here."

Doris didn't want to think about that now. It would stop soon; it had to stop. This was just a flash flood, something to enrage her homeowner's insurer and physical therapist alike, but nothing more. It just didn't rain like this here. It would stop.

Doris reached a hand toward Thea, past her, and latched onto the sink faucet, struggling to hurl her upper half onto the counter. Thea held back a supportive hand. Doris didn't want it, any more than she wanted to explain why she didn't want it.

The faucet bent, and with a guttural clunk below the countertop, it popped free of its setting just as she'd made a little headway. Thea caught her before she fell entirely, pushing her upright before removing her hands.

"You want help?"

"No."

Thea leaned against the faucetless sink as if this were some kind of business brunch and not a weather-induced disaster. "This shit again?"

"What is that supposed to mean?"

"You said yourself that you can't move."

Doris bristled. "I can move enough."

"Enough to get out of here?"

"And go where, Thea?" Doris gripped the edge of the countertop, willing herself to stay upright. "Out there to get swept away?"

"Better than in here to drown."

"It's going to stop eventually." Eventually, sure. But before she drowned? That part remained to be seen.

Thea shrugged, scanning the room.

"What are you doing?" Doris asked.

"Thinking," Thea said.

"You're getting at something. What is it?"

"I'm *thinking*."

"Don't treat me like a mark. What do you *want*?"

Thea cocked her head to the side as if Doris was pitifully dumb, which was the instant she understood.

"No," she said.

"They don't send people as injured as you home without something good."

"I didn't fill the prescription."

"Maybe you didn't, but I bet James did."

She was right. James filled every prescription the doctor gave her. Doris had taken a few of them in moments of agony—she wasn't the addict, so what was the harm? But even then, she knew what would happen. She feared it every day those pills sat in her medicine cabinet. It's part of the reason she'd told Thea to never come back (a small part, but a part nonetheless). Thea would come for them, and then what would happen? As much as she hated her sister sometimes, she couldn't bear to be the reason she overdosed. Doris couldn't live with herself if she let that happen, and now here they were, doing exactly what she'd dreaded for months.

"I threw them in the toilet."

Thea slammed a hand on the Formica, shit-eating grin morphed into something far more sinister. "You're going to do this now? Now, Doris? Fuck, look at your house! Look at *us*!"

Water rushed against her thighs, climbing higher as the moments passed. It just kept coming, as if bubbling up through the floor from an oozing geyser.

"Now is not the time to cling to your principles."

"Oh no?" Doris returned her fury. "Now is the exact time to cling to my principles. What good are they otherwise?"

Thea took a moment to consider this, then sneered in a way that sent her insides spiraling. "Go ahead and stop me, if you're so fucking good."

And then she was off, tearing open the upper cabinets with manic speed. Water dragged her back on occasion, slowing her fury with its weight and accompanying debris, but she remained undeterred.

"Where'd you hide them?" Thea asked as she tried and failed to pry open the refrigerator. Instead it slid against the floor, buoyed by water. "Not in an easy place, I bet. You figured I'd come looking eventually, didn't you?"

Doris stared at her, unable to do anything. The water alone threatened to swallow her, and Thea was unhinged. God only knew what she'd do if Doris tried to intervene. In this state it'd probably end with them both dead.

Then Thea stopped. "They aren't in the kitchen. You'd never leave them anyplace I might find myself unattended. Be right back."

Doris didn't bother saying anything. She couldn't stop her sister, and nothing she could say would stop Thea once she sniffed out a high. And by the looks of her—a missing tooth, ghostly white skin, and a gash on her arm Doris only just noticed as she fled the room—Thea hadn't been doing much with her time but getting high.

The water was surging again, as if whipped into the same

frenzy as her sister. Doris's hands slipped against the counter as she struggled to hold herself up. It wouldn't be much longer before her strength gave out and she'd be sucked under. Who knew if Thea could find her then? Or if she'd even bother?

She had to get out of this water. Her table, a sturdy oak that had to be assembled in pieces, lifted off the tile, swirling toward her with enough speed to pin her against her cabinetry. With little time to consider the consequences to her body, she jumped up, using the table for purchase as she flopped herself onto the counter.

Just as Doris's vision clouded white again, Thea rounded the corner, a shadowy image swirling behind her. Then it all melted away to pain.

Doris shouted at her. To her. Words she forgot as soon as she spoke them. Hands crawled over her—whose hands?

But it was Thea. "So you *can* climb."

"There's someone behind you."

"There's no one here but us." She gripped a square, plastic case in one hand.

The room sounded like the inside of a washing machine, rumbles and roars and splashes congealed into a singular gray noise.

"What are you doing here anyway? Why did you come?" Doris said, staring out her kitchen window at a scene much worse than she could have predicted. Her yard was nothing more than a swampy brown river.

"I was hoping to crash on your couch."

Doris covered her mouth, coughed, and ignored her as the dining table eased against the wall.

"Where's James?" Thea asked.

Doris snapped her attention to her sister. "Not here."

"Have you spoken to him? Where is he?"

Doris stared at her, jaw clenched and jutting slightly to the left.

"Fine," she said, then unfurled her palm to expose small, pink squares inside the clear plastic case.

"What are those?" She knew what they were. She did not know that James had filled the prescription.

"So, you don't know?"

"Know what?"

Thea yanked them away as Doris looked closer. "This is ketamine, sis. I didn't even know they prescribed this shit like this."

Doris tried sitting up, but the surface was slippery, and she was weak. Thea held out a hand, stuffing the ketamine in her back pocket before she did.

Finally upright, Doris leaned against the wall. "Where did you get that?"

"From James's bedside table. Lucky for us it was in this handy case, or else it'd have dissolved."

"James wouldn't have ketamine. Why would he have ketamine?"

"You'd have to ask him."

The two were silent a moment, Doris boiling with an emotion she couldn't quite articulate.

"Where'd you really get it, Thea?" She couldn't believe it was just sitting here in her own house like that. James knew how she felt about it.

"I told you—"

"Bullshit." Doris snatched at Thea's arm, thumbing purposefully at a fresh welt. "Then what's this?"

"An iron deficiency," she said, and jerked her arm away.

"You're shaking."

"I didn't come here to get high." Thea covered her arms protectively.

Thunder rattled the windows. The sisters paused. Water had risen noticeable inches since Thea had returned, and it was still coming. This was bad, and it was going to get worse.

A river pounded against the wooden fencing of the backyard, uprooted it like saplings. There was nothing left of the manicured perfection of Doris's garden. Nothing but water coming from everywhere, coming to swallow them up.

Thea tapped the porcelain of the sink like she had a nervous tic. Doris couldn't help but gape at the wreckage of it all.

"Do you have an attic?" Thea asked.

"We can't go into the attic."

"Why not?"

"There aren't any windows. If the water keeps rising, we'll drown in there."

"Okay then. I'll just grab my motorboat out of my pocket, and we'll be off. Where the fuck else do you plan to go?"

Turning away, Doris settled her gaze out the window over the sink. There were options, just not many for her. Thea could run, she could swim, she could float away. Doris could go into the fucking attic or sit on the counter and pray the rain to stop.

"Do you want to die?" Thea asked, toeing the line between sympathy and annoyance.

"Nobody is going to die." Doris said it matter-of-factly, like she said everything.

It was enough to get Thea to her feet, colliding with the floor in an angry splash. "Where is it?"

Doris pointed. The house was nothing more than a few small rooms connected by decorative archways. Through the arch from the living room was the kitchen, and beyond that a hallway that contained a laundry closet truncated by an add-on den. Thea spotted the swinging chain of a pull-down entrance to the attic dangling from the ceiling just inside the hallway.

It didn't budge as she yanked at it.

Stuck. She pulled again, harder. It groaned and somewhere above her, wood snapped and splintered, but still she couldn't force it free. Her hands were wet and kept slipping.

This only made her fight harder until—*pop*—the door shot down like a loaded cork. The collapsible stairs were slick on their rails and careened at her face. Slamming into the water, they stopped short of completely unfolding, buoyed by the water.

Thea turned to Doris. "Your Majesty."

Doris glanced at her, then at the wobbly stairs, then back at Thea. A distinct trickle of water flowed down the stairs.

"I think the roof has a leak," she said.

Thea fingered the liquid running down as if it might be anything but water. Then she gripped the slide rails and let the trickle of water glide over her hands. "Yup, it's more water."

"Just go check the roof."

Thea did, slipping out of sight only a moment. Doris couldn't help the flex of her chest as her sister disappeared. Part of her didn't believe she'd come back.

"How bad is it?" Doris said.

"Like someone dropped a bowling ball through the ceiling."

"I guess we have a way out, if we need it." Little fuses lit with each word she spoke. She had to get out. They had to get out. They had to go up. God help them if they needed to get any higher than that.

"Well, let's go, then," Thea said, leaping into the flood and waiting.

———

Thea hated the way her sister looked at her, sizing up everything. Sizing up *her*. Eyelids lowered, mouth pulled into a knot, Thea assumed that all had been found wanting, as usual.

"Fuck, Doris. At least up there the water is running down." Thea didn't even know why she was trying so hard. It's not like Doris cared. It's not like they were really sisters. More like two strangers that happened upon the same biological parents. Why did Thea care when no one else ever seemed to? It spoke little to her hedonistic, narcissistic nature; there wasn't an altruistic bone in her body. Everything she did, she did for her. So why was she doing this?

"I swear to God, Doris. I'll drag you if I must. I will not just sit here and watch you drown."

At this, Doris scoffed. She looked at the water the same way their old family tabby, Cid, used to stare at the fish tank. Finding whatever it was she was looking for, Doris dropped herself into the water more inelegantly than she'd probably have hoped.

Thea knew better than to wade into the water to retrieve her, and she waited at the stairs while Doris waded indelicately through the carnage. Pain distorted her features into an expression Thea knew and understood with alarming clarity. She'd also been around enough druggies and tweakers to know to stay the fuck away from a person making that face.

It was a short distance to cover, fifteen feet maybe, but the first leap and subsequent crash left Doris gasping. Thea outstretched an arm, palming the door leading to the garage, and sucked in a sudden bout of nausea threatening to explode. Clutching her body together in a ball, she waited from above. The ketamine in her pocket burned a hole in her ass. Pop a couple of those suckers under her tongue and she'd be just fine. But first, she had to get her stubborn mule of a sister to a place where she wouldn't drown unattended.

Seconds passed. Minutes. Thea stared at her feet to keep from hurling. She didn't know what Doris was doing, but she wasn't moving.

"Doris?"

She didn't respond.

Shit, Doris. God, please don't make me open my mouth again. She had enough of a time keeping her nonsense from falling out on a good day. So she peeked, catching sight of her sister at the top of her vision.

Doris had gone stiff.

"What's wrong?" Thea asked, risking it.

But then she heard splashing, and Doris let her know she'd arrived by grabbing Thea's shoe, probably more by accident than intention, as she let go as if scorched once she saw what she'd done.

"Move," she said.

Thea moved, slinking up a few more steps.

Water mushed the pressboard planks, and the steps began to peel around the edges. Doris worked her way up five of the nine steps before pausing to rest and gape at the hole in the roof. It looked like it'd been pierced by a cannonball. The storm raged from above, leering at the sisters through the hole like Sauron's eye.

Thea wanted to shout at Doris to hurry the fuck up. It was all she could do to not tear into the case right now, but she had to show some sort of restraint—at least enough to get Doris up a few more steps.

But she'd stopped moving again, her feet still dangling in the water. Thea wasn't sure whether her sister was exhausted or just pissed off or both, but her patience was waning. Maybe she should say something.

"Come on," she said. "You can do it. Almost there."

Doris snapped her gaze toward Thea with withering intensity. "Don't talk to me like I'm a dog."

She should *not* have said something. But Thea was as well versed in this game of insult ping-pong as Doris. She stuck out her hand. "Then hurry the fuck up."

Thankfully, Doris accepted.

The attic was small, and Thea curled into herself just under the hole, relentlessly pounded with rain. There wasn't anyplace to go that wasn't being pounded with rain, but Doris managed to flop herself along a row of boxes that provided a small reprieve.

The sisters breathed and listened, listened and breathed. All Thea heard was the roar of the sky cracking in two. When she finally tore her eyes away from the sight of it, she saw the water below creeping and creeping. Fourth step now. It'd only been ten minutes, maybe. Or not. There wasn't any way to tell.

"Do you have a phone?" Doris asked.

Thea didn't respond. Her body shivered violently, trying and failing to buck off the throes of withdrawal. Freeing the case from her pocket, she held it out for Doris to see.

"If you're going to do it, at least turn around. I don't want to watch you."

But Thea sidled closer, careful to keep the case just out of Doris's reach. "We're both going to do it."

"Fuck off, Thea."

"No, you listen for once." She seized her by the shoulder, unsure if the resulting grimace was due to pain or simply because of Thea's presence. "You're fucked, Doris. We're fucked. You can't move and I'm moments away from something you do not want to fucking see. I can feel the shivering already. Hate it, hate *me*, whatever you want, but this at least gives us a chance."

"That's not mine." It was a question more than an answer.

"I didn't get it for him, if that's what you're thinking," Thea said.

"Would you have, if he'd asked?"

Thea considered lying, but why bother? "Yeah, probably."

Christ, she was infuriating. "But you need to take it with me. You're barely holding on as it is."

For a moment, Thea thought Doris was considering it. "The physical therapist mentioned it. You can go get infusions or whatever, through an IV, but I said no. These things, troches or whatever they're called, were just approved. Not as effective, lower dose. I said no again. James conveniently must not have heard me."

"That's a great story. Open wide." Perhaps it was because her brain was full of holes from all the drugs or because she was tired and desperate, but Thea thought she would just be able to slip a piece right into her sister's mouth, like a junkie mama bird. This is not what happened.

Doris slapped it away—pink ketamine flying out of reach and down the stairs where it disappeared into the slush.

"What the *fuck*, Doris!"

"We aren't doing that shit, Thea. You can try and moralize it all you want."

Thea clutched the remaining ketamine in a tight fist, probably crushing it a little. "Do what you want, then. Die down here with your morals if that's what keeps you warm and fuzzy and comfortable. I don't have time for this shit."

She was about to storm an entire three feet away, but Doris stopped her with a hand, snagging the shredded hem of her jeans with thin fingers. "This isn't about comfort. Believe me."

And she did believe her. One look at the ragged thing that was her sister, Queen Doris, perfect Doris. The sister Thea outgrew by six inches yet always seemed so tall, the bright star the family orbited for fear of shriveling in her shadow; Thea saw what she was just then—a frail and tired wraith, clinging to the only feature of herself still whole. Her righteousness and sense of duty were all she had, and boy, if Thea didn't relate to it. If anyone understood what it was like to watch oneself unpeel layer by layer, it was her. And yet the empathy would not come. That part of her burned and fizzled long ago.

"If being right is worth dying for, then I guess there's nothing left to discuss." She knelt next to Doris. "But here. If you decide not to be an ass, here's one square. Put it under your tongue. Or throw it in the water. I don't care what you do, but I'm done arguing about it."

Thea popped one in her own mouth, closing the plastic case over the rest of them with an authoritative snap.

She made a point to look anywhere other than at Doris. Her gaze instead traveled through the gash in the roof. Water tumbled through it, drenching her from every direction. She couldn't even make out the sky between the rain and the dark, as if that was all that existed now. No clouds, no earth, no trees or birds, just punishment. Trying not to think about it, she tongued the ketamine against her cheek.

God damn, it couldn't come soon enough. Her nerves itched with anticipation, the wait almost being more unbearable than the withdrawal. She chuckled to herself and patted her pocket. Of course, that wasn't true. There was nothing worse than withdrawal, something Doris would never understand. No amount of morals or judgment or superiority or hatred could be worse than what Thea's own, dumb body could dish out on a bad day.

"You never answered me," Doris said, shocking Thea out of her satisfied stupor.

"About what?"

"Do you have a phone or not?"

"I left it in my Ferrari."

It was a stupid question. Everything of value Thea owned was inevitably shot up her arm. She wouldn't have a phone unless she'd stolen one and hadn't yet had a chance to sell it for drugs.

It dawned on her then, as she tried to think of some other smart-ass remark, that the outside was eerily quiet. Besides the whir and rumble of the storm, there were no helicopters. No sirens. No screams. No anything but water and more water. It was as if they were the only two people left on earth.

No one was coming for them. Not yet, anyway. Not for a while. Perhaps not before they drowned. The pair were in sorry shape. A losing bet, these two.

Lightning ripped at the seams of the black clouds, casting oily shadows across the attic floor. Thunder rocked the floorboards. Thea glared toward the sky as splashes of rain haloed her head.

"Jesus," Doris said. "It's almost up the stairs."

The entire kitchen was under water, the surface threatening to spill over onto the countertops. Bulky shapes bobbed around in the brown muck. Clothes and some mail and an oven mitt flushed out the shattered back door.

"We have to get out of here," Thea said, again turning her gaze upward. "We have to get on the roof."

Doris didn't answer her. She didn't say much at all, opting instead to twist her wedding ring around her finger. Her eyes glazed over as if she was deep in thought. Thea had seen her like this before, and it usually meant she was one loud sneeze away from a meltdown. Hers never looked the way one might expect a meltdown to look, though. Doris swallowed everything, bricked herself up stone by stone. The ring twisting was the small crack in the dam that preceded collapse, and no way did Thea want to be around when those walls finally caved in.

Which was the very moment that her own began to wobble.

"Fucking shit," Thea said.

"Look at this shit. Fuck. Fuckfuckfuck!"

She kicked and thrashed, an unbearable edge creeping into her veins. It happened so suddenly, more so than she was used to. Something in her snapped and she just couldn't take it anymore. This was too much, all of it too much. What was she supposed to do? If it was just her, she'd dive headfirst into a k-hole and let Mother Nature do its work, but it *wasn't* just her. And as much as she liked to convince herself that she didn't give a shit about anyone, she did.

Her body spasmed, not even sure what the hell it wanted, and Thea spun her limbs, hoping to hurt something, someone, anything. Even herself. By the time the throb of exhaustion had caught up to her, she'd made a nice little natural disaster in the middle of the attic, consuming the storm in her fury.

Doris hadn't said a word. Just watched and spun her ring.

By the time she finally dared a glance, Thea was pushing, throwing, heaving shit into the center of the attic, just under the hole in the roof—a Christmas wreath; old clothes; a box of childhood stuffed animals, bloated like a dead body and ripping at the seams—toppling them in a heap.

"Why do you even have all this stuff?" Thea said, scoffing while standing up, indignant despite sending another box forward with a good kick. "This isn't going to work." Then she grabbed another. And another and another. Pieces of an old bed frame, a garden hose, any old shit that was easy enough to move.

Thea sank her feet into the pile. The detritus of Doris's life clung to her shoes as she squashed through the rubble for a decent foothold. After a few near falls, she finally managed to swing her elbows onto the roof and pull her head up.

One, two, three seconds, and she was down again.

What she'd seen had sucked the rage right out of her, hollowing out her insides. "You never prepared me for this, sister," she said.

Doris let her ring drop to the floor. "I know."

Saying nothing else, the sisters got to work.

CHAPTER FOUR

THE AFTER

NOBODY TELLS YOU about the boredom. There isn't much to do after the terror and shock subsides. Just floating and sitting and getting dizzy from the hamster-wheel laps of the brain thinking about an entire lifetime of floating and sitting. It'd been a year of sitting around waiting to die. Rob swore it was only nine months, as if he fucking knew the difference. He spent all his time lost somewhere in his head, and Sestra couldn't be sure of his grip on reality, let alone his basic math skills. She wasn't so sure about herself either. It's not like it mattered much.

Rob, however despondent, was never short of criticisms of her performance. "Get your hands out of the water if you ain't even gonna try."

Sestra draped her right arm over the boat platform. She said she was catching fish, but her arm had fallen asleep ages ago. All she'd done to pass the time was flip-flop between numbness and a painful pins-and-needles sensation. Since she passed most of her days in similar fashion, her arms from the elbows down were the only parts of her not turned to jerky from the sun and an overabundance of sea salt.

"That water's not safe," Rob said.

"Jesus, is it noon already?"

"Ain't nothing saving you when a shark grabs those fingers."

"What a pity," she said, keeping her arm exactly where it was.

Her stomach lurched. By now she thought she'd have gotten used to being starved all the time, but it never got easier. Rob seemed to handle it better than her. He'd close his eyes and lean back as if to nap, looking so damn peaceful while Sestra's organs tore her apart from the inside out. Before the flood, she'd heard stories of people who'd slipped into euphoric comas, their brains leaching sedating hormones as their bodies ate themselves alive. Sestra counted the hours until that moment came, but it hadn't yet. She was miserable every second that passed, angry at everything, feeling herself ripped apart as her cells died bit by bit.

She couldn't understand how Rob just closed his eyes. The times she tried to copy him, the agony of her insides just roared louder, as if silencing one of her senses just made the rest of them more aggressive. She'd chuck water at Rob's face sometimes, just to shock him out of it, afraid he might never open his eyes again. Sometimes she'd just start talking and talking so that she had something to do, forming coherent sentences being its own sort of chore nowadays.

Rob threw the tarp at her. "Cover yourself, at least." Sunburn had eroded her skin over the months. The welts were the worst—something about the excessive salt clogging the pores, at least according to Rob—but luckily, she managed to get those under control with some light rinsing with fresh water. This, of course, was a contentious use of their limited supply, as evident by Rob screaming at her to stop using all their clean water to rinse her stinkin' vagina. Those thigh creases, though—they were the worst.

Sestra scratched at her thighs in remembrance. No doubt the welts would return when the rain dried up. Luckily for her, that hadn't been an issue for the past few weeks. The sky clotted with prepubescent clouds still considering what they wanted to be when they grew up, and it had rained every day for the past week.

There may not be any food, but they had clean water. For now.

Sestra scanned the water's surface in either direction. Smooth as glass. A bad sign. There were no crabs to pick out of clumps of seaweed, no fish to needle out of islands of trash, nothing to rummage or drag her attention out of the gutter. She'd stab her own eyeball out for a turtle right now, but there hadn't been a sighting in ages.

"Everything is dying," Rob said.

"Just now getting that, are you?"

"One day I'm just going to toss you overboard."

Sestra righted herself. "Then who would you yell at every fucking minute of the day?"

"I'd finally save my breath."

"Your head would pop off your shoulders like a cork with all the pressurized judgment. Your slow leak of annoyance is all that's kept you going."

His mouth didn't move, yet his lips turned to stone.

Sensing the overstep, she redirected. "Give me the hook."

"What for?"

"Just give it to me."

The hook wasn't so much a proper hook as it was a bent piece of metal from the boat's engine. Rob had taken it apart after the propeller had warped in some rough seas. They had no gas, but he'd refused to touch it prior to that. You know, just in case they happened upon a fuel pump.

Hook in hand, Sestra punctured her forearm and flung it back into the water before Rob could protest. It stung like crazy.

"You'll pass out before you catch anything with that."

"Calm down." It wasn't like her personal well-being was what concerned him.

"Only the big ones like blood."

She shrugged. He was probably right. So what if he was? "I could go for some shark fin right about now."

"You know what I meant."

"I know what you meant." She just didn't care.

"You're obsessed."

"I'm obsessed? Shit."

Sestra was wandering into dangerous territory. Posies were always dangerous. Just bringing them up was like a call to arms between the two of them. Sestra instinctively clutched the hook, while Rob cloaked himself in his own sense of righteousness. All the man had left was his unshakable faith in a purpose. There was a reason for all this horror, even if he didn't understand it. There was a reason his wife and son were dead and he was not, even if he didn't like it. There was a reason he was stuck on this boat with Sestra, even if he was miserable. Who was he to challenge the will of God? He'd rather die a prolonged, offensive, unhappy death, all on the risky bet of divine reward for his dogmatic perseverance.

As for Sestra, she was more inclined to spit in the face of any god who would do this just to make a fucking point.

After about ten minutes, Sestra drew up her arm and clamped her hand over the shallow wound. It wasn't even bleeding anymore. The saltwater had licked it clean until all that remained was a jagged pink cut. A waste of her time. She could slit her throat and nothing would come in an ocean this vast. It didn't help that their long line had snapped in the mouth of a whitetip a few weeks ago. The thing swam off with it in a frenzy, taking with it all the plastic jugs used to keep the line afloat. After that happened, they were left with just their hook and hands.

She gnawed on the tip of her pinky, consoling her hunger with the sensation of something meaty in her mouth. Even if it was her meat.

"Stop that," Rob said.

"I'm hungry."

"You're the last thing I'd ever eat."

"I got a few good steaks left in me, I think." She bit her

finger hard enough to bruise.

"I wouldn't eat you," Rob said.

"Why not?"

"Food poisoning."

Sestra snorted, letting her finger drop.

The two each fell into their own starvation stupor, staring at things, making irritating noises with their mouths, chewing on their fingers. Sestra clicked her tongue. It stuck to the roof of her mouth like tacky sandpaper.

Rob closed his eyes, but his brow scrunched every time she clicked her tongue, so she kept doing it, and he eventually opened them again.

Sestra quieted every time he did and listened to the stillness. It was quiet, as if all the sound had been sucked away with a straw. Quiet not because she couldn't hear anything else, but because nothing else was there.

Rob looked toward the sky and grimaced.

The air was heavier, though Sestra didn't know the scientific reason for it—barometer dropping, humidity rising, things that an experienced seaman would notice with one good sniff to the air. Sestra's nose and eyes were shriveled and useless now. All that worked anymore were her ears.

Storms brought with them everything a person expected a sea storm to bring—violent winds and waves, water, sinking, drowning, death. They were terrifying every time, yet somehow, she and Rob had managed through each without dying and, magically, without being separated either. Somewhere up there, Rob's God was laughing his ass off.

Destruction was only one of the appetizers a sea storm brought to the table. With it also came whatever had been dredged up from the sea floor. All sorts of shit bobbed to the surface in the hours following a typhoon, all mixed up as if with a soup ladle. Anything alive rushed to the spot the storms had just left.

They might even catch enough of something to keep them alive another few weeks.

But fish and dead turtles weren't all the creatures a storm stirred. The larger monsters always followed the littler ones.

Rob ran a finger over the edge of the gunwale. This beauty had suffered through a lot and kept floating. Sestra rubbed the fiberglass of the platform lovingly—this stupid boat was as stubborn as she was.

"She can't handle much more," Rob said.

"Beauty will be fine. She always is." She had to be.

"If you say so."

"Besides, there will be fish."

"Storms always bring something, and it ain't always fish."

Sestra snapped. God, he was annoying. "Well, you could just die now if your patience is waning," she said, knowing that pesky faith of his would always get in the way of her good ideas.

Hours passed, and the air became thick, smelling of home, as if the only part of earth not totally sunk was the little bits clinging to the clouds. It reminded her of that first day, before she'd known exactly what was happening, back when rain was just rain. The wet-dirt smell made her long for a park bench and grass and stoplights. It made her hungry. It'd been so damn easy to get food then, even if she'd been strung out and poor. All the convenience stores to steal from, garbage cans—shit, she could get arrested and they would feed her. All that food she'd pushed away—now she got a cluster migraine behind her eyes just thinking about.

She'd been so stupid. Everybody had been stupid. Now everybody was dead.

"What are you doing now?" she asked, before her memories drove her crazy.

"Camping," he said.

Sometimes he was camping, sometimes hunting. One time he was watching the Super Bowl. The point was that, whatever he was doing, what he wasn't doing was floating on a boat in the middle of a ruined world.

"The mountains?"

"No, but lots of trees. I'd make a fire and stay up all night until it burned itself out. We'd eat beans, and David would complain until I sent him to the tent without dinner. But he'd find the jerky. Nose like a bloodhound, that one. I wouldn't care, though."

"You made that jerky yourself, didn't you, Rob?"

A scoff was his response. "Elk."

"Like reindeer?"

"Like elk."

"I always thought they were the same thing."

"Elk are bigger. Reddish. Reindeer are brown and live farther north."

"Like the North Pole?"

He nodded. "What are you doing?"

"Sleeping in an abandoned car behind the Food 4 Less."

Rob pursed his lips. He disapproved of such talk, even if that *was* what she'd likely be doing right now, under more favorable circumstances. She'd be so high, and it would be glorious.

"I used to walk this road near the house I grew up in. It was next to the dump, so there were these huge walls of dirt and there'd be tractors and bulldozers and shit driving along the top of it. The dump was closed, so I always wondered what they were doing there. Rearranging old garbage? It was just like every other street, really. It didn't even smell like a dump, except sometimes early in the mornings. The road was lined with palo verdes, and every spring they would bloom yellow. It took just a little bit of wind at just the right time, and the blooms would fly off."

She wasn't sure what made her even think about it. She'd never paid much attention to it all those times she'd paced that sidewalk. It was the first thing to pop into her head that wasn't inside a needle.

"I'd be eating a cheeseburger," Rob said.

"Tacos."

"I used to brew my own beer."

"You did?" He had told her before. Many times. But he either forgot or didn't care.

"None of that IPA bullshit. A good, stout beer. Bottled it in my garage."

"I'd slit my wrists for a good beer," she said. And she meant it.

Rob tried to smile. It was more a seizure of the lips over dry teeth. "The best."

———

Sestra fell asleep hungry, if what she did could be called sleeping. It was like staying awake all night and suddenly it was morning, but instead of morning, her boat was flooding, and Rob was screaming at her to wake up. One of those types of sleeps.

The storm she'd predicted heaved them into the sky and down again, their boat sloshing around like the last ice cube in a glass of lemonade. Water attacked from every angle—up, down, east, west, from inside her and above her. It poured down, the atmosphere split like a waterfall, and they were trapped in the crash. Every breath was a choke and a gasp to keep it out. Eyes closed, she bailed water out with her hands, unable to think straight and come up with any better ideas.

Nothing she did could keep up. The water rose from her toes to her ankles to her knees, and then it was everywhere, nothing below her feet but emptiness. Thrashing and kicking, she sank anyway. Down, down, down, suffocated by darkness.

Then the boat was fine. The sky was clear. She had been dreaming.

The boat teetered as she startled awake, the sloshing of the water against the hull the only noise in a soundless night.

She'd been certain of a storm, so certain that it had haunted her sleep. Was she sure she was even awake? Had she finally just drowned and gone to another, blacker layer of this swampy hell?

Rob remained where she'd left him, leaning against the side of the boat with a hand over the edge.

The moon shone like oil over the water, shimmering as it gently swayed. Sestra stuck her hand overboard, grazing the surface just enough to get her fingers wet. Ripples ricocheted like delicate lace, fading into the ocean's girth.

So calm. Too calm.

If you're there, she thought, *come on out.* She knew they couldn't hear her, but sometimes she thought she could feel them, the posies. Rob had pinned her down and called her a demon the last time she'd made the mistake of mentioning it. Posies terrified Rob. He hated them. As much as she tried, she couldn't bring herself to hate them, even though she should. As if the flood wasn't enough, these beasts came along and picked at the survivors. Dragged them to the depths with their merciless grip.

The bodies always disappeared. Of all the dead bodies that popped back up because of gasses and decomposition, none seemed to have been taken by the posies. Sestra would turn them over, searching for suction marks or bruised choke marks around their necks, but never found evidence of such an act. Every other flavor of death might show on the surfaced corpses—shark bites, decay, disease, starvation, even some that looked utterly beat to death by human hands, but never a mark of the posies. Those victims were wrenched below into a murk Sestra could only imagine.

She herself had never seen more than a glimpse of a posy— an electric flash of tentacle. They'd drift in the current like gobs of kelp or coast just below the surface only to zip away like a frightened school of fish. Every shadow made Sestra clamp her mouth shut just to keep her insides from spilling out in alarm. Then they'd be gone.

Those sea monsters invaded the last refuge of the survivor—

their minds, their hope, their willpower. They took those last few things people assumed to be their biological and philosophical rights and left them barren.

Now, in all this silence, Sestra was sure there was a posy close by, but it concealed itself well. It was always the things she couldn't see that scared Sestra the most. The water was still warm, which surprised her, even though it shouldn't. The water was always warm, despite the weather or the time of day or location. Sestra always figured that the end of the world would be cold. But expectations had a way of letting a person down. At least hers did. Maybe one day she'd stop making them, but until then, she'd continue to recoil at the heartbeat warmth of the water below her, wondering what inky bastion of bad energy lurked below.

She fully submerged both hands, the ripples of the water tearing her image apart, warping and bending the light through a watery lens. Just call her the Invisible Woman, defying physics and all that shit. People used to say that mutant abilities like that were impossible, but they also might have said that it was impossible for a single storm to wipe out the whole of the world in a single go. Where was the fucking science behind that? It seemed to her that nothing was impossible anymore. Perhaps it never had been, but thinking so was the same as it being so.

The boat rocked. Up, down, up, down, up and down again. She yanked her hands out of the water, tucking them across her chest. Then it stopped. Something out there was moving.

"Do you see it?" Rob asked.

"Not a damn thing."

"It's a posy."

"Maybe." Maybe it was and maybe it wasn't, but doubt didn't stop the hammering in her chest and whooshing noise in her ears.

Up, down, up, down again. It started and stopped in little bursts. A frenzy? The waves slapped at the hull in a panic, as if in a hurry to be anywhere else.

A lumpy bulge materialized in the distance, an uneven mountain in the middle of the sea. The stench hit shortly after, the familiar scent of rot.

"Whatever it is, it's dead," Sestra said.

Smaller shadows bobbed up and down, encircling the mound like rats. Sestra grabbed one of their oars. They weren't really oars, but disassembled pieces of the boat propeller. The curvature made them decent emergency paddles. It had taken Rob months to slowly shave them off the main shaft of the propeller, and as such he was particularly protective of them.

"Be careful," he said.

"I'm not going to drop your stupid oar."

"You said that last time."

"Not like we needed more than two anyway."

The carcass turned out to be a whale. Big—a sperm whale or maybe a gray whale. In the dark, it was difficult to tell.

Creatures shot away from the carcass as they approached. Rob slapped at the water with the oar, hoping to stun something. The bigger animals couldn't be bothered by their stupid antics. There were sharks on either side of her, whitetips or blues probably, but it was hard to tell. If anything, Sestra's presence made them nose their way into the whale even harder. Smaller fish pecked about at a safer distance, making little marble-sized whorls in the water as they flurried about.

Sestra took it all in; it was alive. The death of one of Earth's mightiest drew the survivors out of their ghillie suits.

Rob whooped.

"You catch something?"

"No, but I whacked it good. Watch for a floater."

The hook clattered about the floor of the boat in the excitement. Sestra took it and said, "Keep the boat close."

Before Rob could open his mouth, she hopped overboard, launching herself at the whale. Never much for physical fitness, the added stress of not eating and muscle lethargy guaranteed the two-foot leap was a miss, and she landed farther away from the damn thing than when she'd jumped. Despite the temperature, the water shocked her. The sharks, burrowed into the side of the whale, paid her no mind as she squeezed her way in between them.

"Oh God, where's the hook?" Rob said.

Spitting water between her teeth to answer, she held it over her head. "I still have it, asshole."

"Watch out for the sharks."

"Yeah, thanks."

The energy of the frenzy seeped into her. She was one of them, crazed with hunger, fueled by a testosterone spike and animal carnality. The tearing of flesh from the dead animal reminded her of the sound of zippers on a long jacket. It wasn't quite the same noise, but it had a rhythmic quality and her mind couldn't help the comparison.

Using the hook, Sestra rappelled up the whale's flank and just started stabbing it. Though not edible, it was perfect chum. Rob thwapped at the water, hoping to hit something they could eat.

She jammed the hook down and down until it couldn't go anymore. The whale must have been floating for a day at least. Its belly was loose and beginning to slough away. *Zip zip*, she followed the lines of the underbelly, cutting through it rather easily. Healthy skin was taut, elastic, had a meaty density to it, but this felt more like a banana peel. It cut too easily and stank like death.

Freeing a one-foot section, she heaved it in Rob's direction. He'd maneuvered himself right behind her and caught it with a disdainful glare.

"This don't look great, Ses."

"Want me to check the cellar for the prime rib? Fuck—ow—I got bit." Her foot slipped in the water without realizing.

Not a shark. Smaller. A barracuda or some other pointy fish.

"Get out of there before you get eaten."

"I'm okay. It wasn't the sharks."

"No. Ses, get out of the water."

"Just a little more. This is primo chum, Rob."

Rob didn't protest any further, but he also didn't catch the next piece of whale rot when she chucked it to him. Luckily, it still made it onto the boat.

"Damn it, Rob, what are you doing?"

He stared past her, beyond the sharks and the whale. Then she felt it.

Her toes chilled suddenly, pierced with a blast of cold. The kind of cold that arose from a deep place where nothing could possibly be warm. Sharks untangled themselves and fled, and everything else darted away like shrapnel, leaving Sestra alone with a stinking heap of decomposing whale.

"Get on the boat. Get on the boat right now."

Rob was already grabbing for her, and the panic between them made her clumsy. It took twice as long to get her into the boat than if she'd done it by herself. It was one of those moments where the brain clicked off and all she could see was *RUN* scrolling across her eyelids. Get the fuck out of the water. Get out of there, get away. The primitive feelers she'd cast out without thinking had sensed danger.

A goose egg formed from her headfirst collision into the floor of the boat. Rob stabbed the oar into the water, paddling as fast as his arms could work, but it was a big boat for such small oars.

The silence and emptiness returned. Frenetic tearing and splashing funneled into the singular, frantic thwap of oars hitting the water and heavy breathing. Her terror was almost soothing. Fear was a comfortable, familiar place.

Sestra watched the whale carcass slowly recede into the shadows again. If anything else was there, she never saw it.

"What did you see?" she asked.

"A wave."

Her stomach leapt and sank.

A wave. One. She'd felt the cold, and she was still here. Rob was still here.

"It's out there," she said, because it was.

Neither of them would sleep that night, each taking turns paddling, cleaning meat, paddling, staring aimlessly, paddling again. They continued that way until sunrise, staring at each other and not speaking, observing the other's slightest twitch, blink, the slightest shift of position making the other jerk in alarm. By morning they had returned to their regularly scheduled indignation of one another.

"It might not have been a posy," Sestra said, hours later.

"Does it matter?"

"Probably not."

The smell of rotting whale meat turned her stomach, and hugging her knees, she clenched her jaw and prayed not to vomit. Rob refused to chum with it, still fearing what it might attract.

They passed the time sunning strips of the one fish they'd managed to catch and fighting over the parts that couldn't be jerkied, like the liver, which was surprisingly sweet and dessert-like.

They napped. Rob snored softly, never more than a hard blink away from total alertness. Sestra focused on her elbows, the only part of her not in pain. The bite on her calf stung as it dried, cruising full throttle toward infection. It was deep, but not particularly large, and so perfectly circular that it made her anxious to look at it.

Nightfall didn't bring much relief, but she was tired of laying like a useless lump. Grunting, Rob stirred at her fidgeting. He kicked the oar toward her.

"You need something to do."

She did, so she took it and plunged it into the water. She rowed and rowed, trying to ignore the sting of her wound throbbing through her ankle. She rowed because she had nothing else to do.

She rowed because, no matter where she was, she was never far enough away.

CHAPTER FIVE
THE AFTER

IT SOUNDED LIKE teeth and bone. The jolt of the collision made Sestra forget what she'd been doing just seconds before. It was night and storming and raining and Rob was barking at her to hold the water jug up higher. *No, higher!* Then they crashed into something big.

Ever since they'd run across that whale, Sestra had felt off. That sensation of being watched crawled all over her, so when the boat crashed into something large enough to stop them dead in their tracks, she felt certain they were about to die.

"Oh Jesus," Rob said, lurching onto his feet too fast. Sestra yanked him down again by the tails of his shirt, or else he might have thrown his dumb self overboard.

Despite the roaring in her head and espresso shot of adrenaline, Sestra calmed herself enough to trace the silhouette of what had struck them.

"It's a boat," she said. "It's a fucking boat, Rob."

Their shitty skiff rubbed along the long, boxy gunwale of the shadow boat, their prow hooking against the exposed anchor of the new invader. The sea was calm despite the rain, and the two vessels floated alongside one another. Sestra and Rob stared and waited for an explosion or a machete-wielding pirate to attack them. They stared and stared until it hurt to keep at it.

Minutes passed. Maybe an hour. Sestra finally stretched out her legs. Her hands ached as she pried them away from the oar handle. They used to meet a lot of people in the beginning. Some of them were scared, meek and pleading, and then they died and were eaten by the desperate few who remained. People weren't people anymore; they were bags of precious meat.

"I think it's empty," she said.

"They could be doing the same thing we are."

"Or it could be empty."

It looked like a tugboat, something out of one of the Little Golden Books she'd read as a child. It was cartoonish in its exaggerated, patchwork construction. This thing had been beaten, taped, nailed, zippered and prayed together, probably with only recycled pieces of itself. It could collapse at any minute.

Her knees popped as she stood, and Rob glared at her with shiny eyes, refusing to move.

"I'm going to go check it," she said.

"No, you ain't. Not yet."

"You want to stare at it all night then?" she asked, with complete understanding that this was exactly what he intended to do.

"Wait until daylight. Make them come to us."

"If you're so fucking terrified, then pry us loose and let's be done with it."

But he wouldn't do that. He wouldn't dare cast away any boardable vessel when theirs was such a heap of shit. Pontoon boats weren't made for long seafaring voyages, and they'd been swept into the ocean more than once as waves pounded at them in all directions.

The portholes oozed black, hiding everything behind them. There were a lot of places a person could hide on a boat like this. In the old days, it had probably housed six to eight adults comfortably, which translated to fifteen-plus people post-flood. Something like this was either crammed with survivors or a floating morgue for their corpses. Neither of which she was particularly eager to find, but the dead kind had the built-in benefit of not being quite as stabby.

"Look at those," Sestra said, pointing to a porthole. "They'd have to peek through those to see us. You think we wouldn't have heard someone tiptoeing around by now?"

Rob closed his mouth and passed her his hook.

The tugboat sat about a foot higher than their boat, and Rob raised a knee for her to launch herself. The movements felt foreign, like she wasn't the one making them, and she flopped onto the deck in a heavy tangle of limbs. The *thwomp* of her sack-of-sticks body reverberated in a seismic ripple across the wooden deck.

Behind her, Rob cursed at her. "God damn it."

"Language, Rob."

"Shut your mouth, woman."

Pointless. "Why? If anyone's there, they already know I'm here. Hello?"

Smoothing her rags, she squeezed the hook and called out a second time. "Hello?" The *o* dragged on, uncertain.

This was a lifeless vessel—she felt it in her bones—but dark was dark, and her mind was more deranged than ever. She remembered watching a neighbor kid play a video game when she was eight years old, and in it, the good guys had to fight a giant squid that snaked its tentacles around a sunken ship, beckoning the characters through portholes just like the ones on this boat. She imagined that now, but instead of happy primary colors, this tentacle was gray and slimy and moved like suffocating smoke. Anything could exist in the dark. It was the only region logic had yet to map.

She stomped, heavy-footed in part because she was clumsy on a good day, but also because she'd rather not surprise anything.

The helm appeared abandoned. A ladder, glistening with

grime, clung to the wall like algae. Climbing it was like learning to walk again, but she managed, peeking her head up just enough to see that it was unmanned, then sliding down again.

Rob said nothing as she shook her head at him. *Down I go*, she thought. *Down we go.*

"Hello?" she said again, hoping that someone might just respond and save her the trouble of having to appear braver than she was.

It was quiet. Moonlight poured like spotlights onto the defunct two-way radio and a foam ring buoy. The stairs at her feet sunk into a deeper, hotter dark. The mouth of it sweltered, thick and humid and dank, like the smell of clothes left to sit in the washing machine a day too long.

For all she could tell, not even the tiniest sliver of light seeped into the boat's depths, and that boded anything but well for her.

Her heart thudded voraciously, it not having to work this hard in months. Then again, the pressure felt good. This was different than the usual panic—this was an adventure as rare as discovering the ruins of some famed, lost city. Fuck, it might as well have been a lost city. How long had it been since they'd run across a functional boat? Four months? Probably more. It was amazing to realize just how little they were in such a big world. It had never appeared that way to Sestra before the flood, her world comprised of nothing but the pavement under her feet and familial disapproval. With no family of which to disapprove and no lonely roads to stalk, she now spent most of her time staring down the barrel of an incomprehensible vastness. An unending, terrible emptiness that wrecked her so thoroughly that even a haunted vessel such as this was a greater find than she could ever dare to hope for.

Plus, this she actually signed up for. It was nice to have a bit of agency for once, which made her all the more eager to continue on.

Her eyes adjusted after a few moments, but only enough to make out the depth of the space. It was sparse, yet contained.

Beyond the tugboat was wilderness and depths far darker than this windowless room. People had lived here; someone had slept on that dinette made into a bed, another on the floor. Her feet snagged on fabric bunched on the floor, as if left in a hurry. Left where? Gone where? The space from wall to wall was hardly larger than the span of her arms. It smelled like animals, like people. But there didn't seem to be anyone here.

"Fuck," she said, because she knew.

Feeling her way along the walls, she found a window, found nails driven into the sill holding up a piece of wood. It wouldn't come up.

A cursory inspection of the remainder uncovered a small kitchenette space, all the cabinet doors missing aside from one, and when she opened it, hundreds of little things tumbled out at her. In the dark she couldn't discern what, but it was a Chex Mix assortment of textures and sizes, popping out at her like an overstuffed confetti gun.

Debris clattering to the floor around her, she called up to Rob. "There's no one here," she said. There wouldn't be. Sestra knew exactly where they'd gone but didn't have the heart to say so. Not to Rob at least. As if he needed her to remind him.

"They're gone," she said again, feeling the sway of the boat as Rob stepped aboard. His girth, impressive for a starving man, blocked out the light she didn't know she had until it was gone. The total blackness was better. She couldn't bear to look at it for too long and didn't need Rob to see it like this. Lived in, as it appeared to her. Just missing them was almost worse than having never found them.

"Just barely."

"Yeah."

The ripeness of people still lingered.

"I can't see shit down here," she said.

"The deck, then."

"I think I'll stay down here for the night." The dark concealed more than just enemies and spies. It concealed her, too, and she took a modicum of comfort knowing that nothing could see her, just as she could see nothing. Being in the dark was bad, but having it below her was worse. She had enough darkness wiggling around under her back while she slept.

And she did sleep. The last sounds she heard were those of Rob hefting himself in and out of the engine room, searching for anything salvageable, usable. Nails, bolts, and the like were excellent fishing and stabbing tools, and there were never enough to help keep the fishing line attached to the hull. She knew he was looking for gasoline, but secretly, because he knew it was a fruitless venture. They each had their own impossible search. It gave them something to do.

A trickle of light and the sound of sparrows in the trees woke her, until she opened her eyes and remembered that there were no more trees and no more sparrows, and the sound was just a poisonous memory. She missed the birds. In the beginning, before all the birds died, she would lure them to their boat with pieces of fish, if even that. The birds were as desperate as she was to find a place to rest, and they'd often land on the deck out of exhaustion and lack of options. Once there, she'd catch and kill them, stabbing them with the hook and drinking their blood. It sounded grotesque, but grotesque survived where dignity did not. Rob, however repulsed, never complained when he got his share.

The light crawled down the stairs and into the cabin, just enough to blanket her lower half. The two round windows were nailed shut. Not even a pinhole of light from outside penetrated beyond the barriers.

Rob's tinkering dragged her out of her sleep fully. She wondered if he'd ever stopped from the night before. It must have been at least two or three hours. There couldn't have been so much left to sift through to keep him occupied that long.

Her body ached as she pushed it up off the floor. The wood was softer than the fiberglass of their own vessel, and she hadn't slept in anything but the fetal position for nearly a year. Her limbs stung as she moved, punishing her for not keeping them tight and protected against her body. Awakening from her slumber stabbed like needles as the blood rushed back to her.

Rob was sitting cross-legged on the deck, engine parts strewn around him like a nest. His back to her, she watched as his blackened fingers fiddled with a new kind of treasure.

"No shit," she said. "How much?"

"Half a spool, at least."

He'd found more fishing line.

"There's hooks on the back of the boat that they used to tie off. If they had a line going, though, it's gone now."

"Anything else?"

He kicked a hollowed-out motor. Leathery strips of fish rolled out of a bundle of loose, dirty grey fabric.

"It's where I found the fishing line, too," Rob said.

"Is this it?"

"So far as I can tell."

It wasn't much—a few strips of half-dried fish that smelled slightly rancid. Whoever had lived on this boat before them had been seriously close to starving to death unless they put that fresh line to use.

"You think they were boarded?"

Rob didn't look at her. "Who knows?"

"What do you think?"

"If I had to wager a bet, I'd say no. There isn't a speck of blood anywhere. No signs of a struggle up top."

"Or they were taken under." Sestra had to say it. She preferred to avoid the indigestion of ignoring the elephant in the room.

Rob's head dropped a notch. An ever-so-slight affirmation.

Fuck. Somehow it was worse with Rob's acknowledgment.

A single splash and *bloop*—another person was gone forever. As if the flood hadn't taken enough.

"I'll check the cabin again."

Rob ran his fingers over scattered pipes, ignoring her.

The cabin glowed from the light of the stairwell, contoured by the purple shadows of dawn. There wasn't much. She ran her hands across the wooden walls, smelling cedar but knowing it wasn't actual cedar wood. The barren walls ran parallel to a low-hanging ceiling just tall enough for Sestra, yet too short for Rob, who stood just a few inches taller. The dinette to her right was missing three of the four cushions, and the Formica tabletop had veiny knife gouges running its length, doubling as a cutting board. The back wall housed a slim counter and four small cabinets, all empty aside from the one she'd dumped last night in her hasty search. To the left of her was nothing but empty screw holes where some sort of furniture used to be secured.

The blanket tangled around her ankle as she meandered across the boxy cabin, then caught on something, catching her feet like a tripwire.

From atop the deck, Rob sniffed at the clatter of her body smacking against the floor.

"Shit. I'm fine, by the way."

She tried to kick the blanket away from her, but it caught again. This time she noticed the corner of it tucked underneath the wood, then following the slightly lifted plank, saw the small divot where a handle used to be. Nearing it, nose to the wood, was the unmistakable odor of ammonia and sweat.

"Oh, fuck. Rob, come here."

She'd been sleeping right on top of it.

"Rob!"

Attuned to the white noise around her voice, it took another yell or two to get him to his feet. But by then she had already lifted the small trap door and dropped it again. By the time he reached the stairs, she was pointing at it, open-mouthed.

"What?"

"There's a fucking person in there."

"A body?"

"A kid. It was a kid, and he looked right at me."

"What do you mean a kid?"

But Rob didn't wait for an explanation. The two crowded together as Sestra raised the hatch door again. Crumpled, fetal, and shivering was a boy with terrified round eyes gaping at them in a soundless scream. He couldn't have been more than ten or eleven years old, and with him he brought an overpowering stench of urine and anxiety. He had been there the entire time, locked inside while Sestra tossed and turned and snored on top of him, while Rob tinkered and tore apart his home.

"Jesus." Sestra stared at him for a moment before regaining enough civility to extend a hand to him. The boy refused the gesture, moving only to dart his gaze between the two looming adults.

"Are you alone?" Rob asked.

Then Sestra: "Are you hurt?"

"Where's your parents, kid?"

"What happened?"

"Can't you talk?"

"Will you talk?"

Rob clawed at his forehead. "This ain't good, Ses. This ain't good at all."

"Shut up, Rob. You're scaring him."

"Good."

"Just go away, damn it. Fucking hell."

Rob retreated, but only to the top of the stairs, perched like a vulture.

Sestra knelt low next to the floor compartment, just looking at the boy. Deep cracks puckered his dry lips, sweat clung to his hairline and armpits, and his rags slumped over his pointy shoulders, consuming him, having been stagnant too long.

She didn't know what to do with him. He was terrified of her, and taking care of scared kids had never been a talent of hers. So she did the only thing she could think might be useful.

They had one full water jug left—an old milk jug they'd found floating among a family of bodies. It had a crack at the top and no lid, but it still managed to hold water. She fetched it and tried handing it to the kid.

"Drink," she said, a command the boy flatly ignored. He contorted his way into that confined space with his limbs hugging his body. From the jaundiced look of him, he'd been this way for days.

Sestra rested back onto her elbows, ignoring the child in return but refusing to leave him alone.

Rob weaved in and out of the room, oscillating between curiosity and a panic attack.

"Just another mouth. Has he said anything? It smells of shit in here. Are you prepared to dip another mouth into the water rations? Has he drunk anything yet? Is he still alive?"

The boy didn't move, blinking hard at her as if just waking from a dream. Sestra wanted to yank him up by the collar and shake him out of it. Child or not, he was going to die if he didn't snap out of this comatose terror.

Wake up, kid. Wake the fuck up and get to work. Surviving is work, so work.

How had he made it this long anyway?

Hunger stabbed at her gut, intolerable knowing that there was food on board, but Sestra couldn't bring herself to eat it while this kid lay in his own piss, staring at her. She wanted to. Rob had already shredded one of the jerky strips, and just thinking about the brittle, toffee-like texture spraying like glass shards in her mouth—something of substance, not gooey and rotten—was more than she could bear. She wanted that fucking food. Oh God, did she want that food.

"Fuck it," she said, and launched her hands at the boy, who promptly began to scream with a power that made Rob drop something metal on the deck above them.

"¡Mijo! ¡Mijo mijo mijo!" the boy said. "Mamá vengan por mí!"

Rob blundered down the steps. "What did you do to him?"

He kept screaming over and over. Sestra tried to shout over him with little success. "I didn't do anything to him! I didn't touch him!"

"What is he saying?"

His words had blurred into gibberish by then, just a shrill, trilling noise.

"I don't speak Spanish," Sestra said. She had taken a few classes in high school but had been hungover through most of them, reduced now to understanding a few words here and there—one of which she thought she recognized now.

"He said something about 'my son.' Mijo means son or something. I think. I don't know. Maybe it's his name."

"Why would he be talking about a son?"

"Not his son, jackass," she said, wondering to herself if the boy was repeating his own mother's last words to him.

When she knelt next to him this time, he turned up his chin to her, shiny eyes loosing a flurry of tears down his cheeks. The slight tremble from before exploded into a tremor.

"Fuck, kid. You're a wreck." Again, Sestra lowered a hand to him. This time, he reached back, grabbing her arm and almost pulling her into the compartment with him.

The boy clung to her. Sestra didn't need to hold him back—he gripped her chest and sobbed into her, a wet, sticky spot oozing between them.

Rob winced, pulling back lest it be contagious.

She didn't know what to do. Her arms hovered inches away, as if embracing him would make him disappear. The kid burrowed further into her, refusing to let go, and though Sestra didn't know it then, this was where the boy would stay forever, somewhere nestled into her chest cavity like an impending heart attack, always seconds away from igniting. Not that this was a difficult task. Her heart had been a barren place for some time. It had ached for warmth, for someone to graze against it, for ages—she suspected long before the flood. This child need not more than glance in her direction for her heart to open wide and swallow him whole.

But that's how everyone was now. Or, at least she suspected that's how everyone would be if they were alive—full of love with no one left to give it to. As far as she knew, she, Rob, and this boy were the only three people left on earth.

The boy hugged her, and it would be a long time before he stopped.

CHAPTER SIX
THE FLOOD

THE BOXES HADN'T been enough. Water crept up unfailingly. The attic floorboards swelled with it like a disease, angry and swollen, fighting it. Doris kept her palms to the wood as if to soothe it.

Thea stomped on the pile of wreckage from her perch on the roof, checking its stability before attempting a third run at hauling Doris up it. The first two attempts had ended before they'd began with Thea putting a foot through a box or cutting herself on an exposed beam as her legs wobbled on the unsteady surface. This was as good as it was going to get.

"It's good," Thea said. Or Doris thought she said. It was hard to hear over the roar. "I think it's good."

Doris studied the mound of things she'd forgotten she owned—a striped ironing board, porcelain dolls that she hated that everyone thought she loved, a floor lamp with a broken shade that she'd sworn to fix someday, soggy boxes full of dull gray things doomed to the dusty, cobwebbed nook of her house, things she feared for one reason or another to throw in the trash where they belonged. Things she'd wanted to forget about, things she couldn't forget about. All of it was useless trash now. It always had been, she understood only now.

Thea lowered herself back into the attic. The pile held. She stared down at Doris, studying her.

"What?" Doris said.

"I'm thinking."

"About what?" But Doris knew at once what needed thinking.

"I don't think I can carry you."

"I wouldn't expect so."

"You go first. I'll help your legs up."

"That's not going to work." She wouldn't be able to keep steady—one misplaced hand or shift of a box would send her crashing to floor, and one more fall like that, and she might not be able to get up again.

Unless she took the ketamine. She didn't know how much it would even help, and then where would they be? Both doped to hell and in pain. They might as well dive into the water now and save the flood the trouble of chasing them.

"Why won't it work?" Thea's already sunken cheeks sucked in further as she furiously attacked the remnants of drugs inside her mouth.

"I can't climb."

"Then why'd we bother building this fucking mountain, Doris?"

Doris looked to the roof, then to Thea.

"God damn it, Doris. You are coming up, one way or another. I'll pull you up by your hair if I have to."

"You keep saying that as if it's a noble gesture."

"To want my sister not to die?"

Doris clawed her fingers into the softening floorboards. "Who are you doing it for? For me or despite me? Because you couldn't live with yourself otherwise?"

"Oh, *fuck*, Doris. Of course I couldn't live with myself. How am I the bad guy for that again?"

Because then you'll have stolen my drugs and left me here to rot.

Because then you'll have no choice but to admit what you've done.

But she shouldn't say that. She shouldn't.

She had to get up, but everything was wet and slippery, and the thought of moving made her insides howl. She had to get to the roof but didn't even have the energy to pull herself to a stand, let alone climb an unsteady trash heap.

Her insides went stiff and heavy, the dread of knowing what she would have to do settling over her.

Thea peered down at her from the hole, expectant. Doris could feel her anxious energy without even looking at her.

She squeezed her hand over the gelled square Thea had given her, trying to douse the rage in her gut—rage at Thea for finding them, rage at Thea for abusing them, rage at James for filling the script, rage at the people who made the fucking drugs her sister loved so much, rage at the money it made them, rage at herself for watching it happen, for not being there, for not grabbing her sister and shaking her out of it, for not even noticing until it was too late. There was rage and rage and more rage, because fury was easy. It was an encompassing emotion that was simple to understand and blotted out the rest. The fuel that lit the blaze—the guilt and shame and everything else—well, that was much trickier stuff.

"Stop looking at me," she said. "I don't need your pity."

Where she expected a fight, she instead was met with nothing. Thea backed away from the hole, swallowed by the storm. It unnerved Doris anytime her sister did what she asked without complaint. It usually meant she was up to something much more sinister.

She had an entire pack of troches burning a hole in her pocket.

"Thea!"

Thea popped back into view. "You just told me to stop looking at you."

Doris exposed her one troche, squished from anxiety. "I need you to promise me something."

Thea narrowed her gaze, listening intently. "What?"

"If I take this, you need to promise me that . . ." She wasn't sure where she was going with this. *Promise me that if I do drugs with you now, you'll stop doing drugs later.* It was nonsense, and part of her wondered if Thea had been right as she placed the ketamine in her hand. The water crept higher still in a barrage from every direction, her injured body neared collapse with every breath, and here she was debating the opioid crisis and lecturing her sister instead of doing whatever she could to survive. It was nonsense.

She was nonsense.

"Never mind."

Before she could think any more on the matter, she dropped the troche into her mouth.

———

Arms wrapped around her knees, Thea absorbed the destruction. Muddy rapids coursed throughout the neighborhood. The road she'd walked to get here had disappeared under six feet of water. It was angry, with rain like little hands pulling her down. Bracing herself, she wedged the heels of her shoes into the roof shingles. Every direction was brown and gray and pieces of things meant for another world.

She scanned the rooftops for more people while Doris grappled with her conscience or whatever the fuck she was doing down there. Whatever it was, she knew by now that her presence would only complicate matters. Doris would give the word when she was ready, and it wasn't like she had anything else to do besides feel like shit and wait for the ketamine to kick in.

Every other roof in the cul-de-sac was empty. What were the odds that every one of them had been away when the water hit? She could smell the bloat of corpses—all in her head, of course, but closer than she'd like. It wasn't as though this was her first encounter with death, but the thought of a drowned grandma sticking to the panes of her front window like a dead fish in an aquarium was not an image she relished.

A family of four huddled atop their roof one street up. The mother wrapped her arms around the necks of her children—not *little* little, but small enough to not leave home alone. Two sisters? A boy and girl? It was impossible to tell from this far away. The dad army-crawled from one end of the roof to the other, then back again, searching for an escape that wasn't there. Caged and helpless, his hyper-masculinized need to protect would be the last bit of him to succumb to the flood. Thea almost felt bad for him.

The flood slammed against the side of the house, making sucking noises as an undertow pulled debris underneath the surface.

"This water is angry." Thea looked at the sky as she spoke.

"Water is always angry." Doris's voice was far away, and Thea tried not to let that scare her.

"It's dumb and strong, like a bad cop."

"You'd know."

At this, she turned to peer into the hole. Doris remained just where she'd left her, huddled at the base of the mound. The sky spat at her toes. Get a fucking grip, woman. It wasn't just the water that was angry.

"It's not going to stop," Thea said.

"Yes, it will."

"You don't know that."

"It's a scientific fact. It cannot rain forever."

"It could for our forever."

"Maybe."

Thea marveled at her sister. Still, to this day, so sure of everything that she felt certain enough to boss around the sky. Thea wished, for even just a moment, to know what that kind of immutable confidence felt like.

As if reading her mind, Doris locked eyes with her. "We are not going to die." It was not a question.

But she wasn't up here yet. She hadn't seen.

"Ready to join me on the roof, Your Majesty?"

And to Thea's relief, Doris nodded and stood up.

———

Doris wanted to laugh. She wanted to scream. Thea liked to think it was Doris who looked down upon society from her regal throne, but she was too deluded and drugged out of her mind to recognize her own pedestal. It couldn't get any worse for Thea, because someone would always be there to catch her when her Grecian column wobbled. Someone was always there to prop her back up, whether it be mom's wallet or dad's ostrich head burying, or Doris herself opening doors she swore to seal shut. Thea didn't know a thing about the mire and muck and stagnation of real life; she'd done nothing but run from it from its very first knock. Thea was nothing but a cloud of dust.

Not knowing how to respond to Thea's dig, Doris decided to stay quiet. Her sister might be delusional, but she wasn't stupid. She just hoped the water didn't catch up to them before she realized it.

Doris gave her house one last look, landing on a broken snowman Christmas decoration shoved in a corner. Some kids had thrown rocks at it on New Year's Eve last year, denting the mold in a dozen places. James insisted on keeping all the Christmas decorations out past January first, but she'd wanted them taken down the day after Christmas. They'd argued, and just as Doris had been about to launch herself into the yard and start yanking multicolored lights from the trunk of their mesquite tree, he'd set a hand on her shoulder and said, "Please?"

It was a multilayered "please" that could've meant anything, but it had been enough to get her back into the house. He'd been furious, near tears, when he'd discovered it vandalized. Doris thought he'd thrown it away. She should have known better.

She was steeling herself for the climb, back rigid in anticipation, when Thea turned away from the hole. In a fit of frustration, she began to scream.

"Hey! Hey, you fuckers! HEY!"

There were people out there. Other people close enough to talk to—or yell at, anyway.

Doris braced herself against the heap, so very close, yet leagues away. An urgency bloomed—she needed to get up there *now*, but her upper body strength wasn't enough. She wanted to know who they were. Did they have a boat? Was it the army or the police? Somebody had finally found them, and Doris had nothing to do but guess and listen to her sister scream at them.

"Hey! Over here! We're here over here! Where are you going?"

Thea stomped across the roof. She sounded like a monstrous roof rat, like the one that invaded this attic a few years back.

"Motherfucker!"

The water had reached the second-to-top step. It was coming. The attic walls swelled, threatening to fill the entire space. Tighter and tighter. It was harder to breathe. There were people out there, and they had no idea she was there. Thea was acting insane. No one would pick her up. No one would ever know that Doris was down here.

"You fucking pussies, fuck you!"

Screaming and screaming. *Just shut up, Thea.* If you want anyone to listen, you must shut up first.

All the while, the walls closed in and the roof grew taller and taller. She'd drunk the wrong ribbon-tied bottle and physics didn't matter anymore. All that mattered was that she was stuck in the attic and the water rose anyway.

Thea's heavy feet stomped above her, and Doris expected one of them to come through at any moment. Her sister had become incoherent and manic. Jesus fuck. Doris had to calm her down before she tore the whole house down.

"There will be more, Thea!" Doris tried to shout, but lacked the willpower, partly out of fright, partly because she didn't believe it. "There will be others."

Whether Thea heard her or not, she wasn't sure, but she had quieted a few decibels. When she finally peeked through the hole in the roof, her eyes were hard and calculating. She stared at Doris like a predatory bird deciding whether it was hungry.

"You're coming up," Thea said. "It's just us. They left. They looked right at me and they left anyway. Fuck 'em. You're coming up here now."

"I can't climb on my own. I need you to help lift me."

Rain poured over the back of Thea's head. The room smelled increasingly of mud and mildew. The wetness of the air was enough to suffocate her. She wanted nothing more than to be free of this coffin.

"I got it."

Thea braced herself as best she could, hanging her body through the hole, arms stretched down to meet her. Blood from the cut on her arm dripped down, pooling around Doris like mildew. The water had reached her. There weren't any stairs left to see, just a gleaming topcoat of the flood. Every ounce of her screamed to remember this. It felt like a test—the pop quiz could arrive any time. What color was the scarf of her snowman? Had her wedding dress been white or ivory? What did pressboard feel like? What was dust? What was mud? The questions pressed against her temples rapid-fire. *Remember this. Remember this.* It scared her, because her instincts knew something she did not, because they told her memories like this would someday be precious.

"This is fine," Doris said aloud. "I'm coming up." But she was scared. She didn't want to be scared, but she was.

Blood splashed like fireworks into the unsettled water

surround her. Each drop sank, and then was gone.

"You ready?" Thea said.

Of course not. "Sure."

Ignoring every opposing instinct, Doris sprang toward her sister. Their hands met, threatening to slip away from each other, but they caught. Thank God, they caught. Thea grasped her with a steady and surprising strength, holding tight despite her injury. Holding tighter still as Doris scrambled, reeling and out of breath and threatening to black out again. The ketamine wasn't working. It wasn't enough.

But it had to be. She refused to die in her horrible attic. She would not die here. She would not be loose skin sloughing off bloated bodies. She and Thea would not be statistics. Not this time, at least.

Together, they got her up. Doris broke through the hole, spilling onto the roof with a splat. Thea lunged on top of her to stop her from tumbling down it, right back into the water. It was the closest the two had been in ages.

There they stayed, heaving against each other and trying to regain some sort of composure. Doris couldn't stop trembling. She was sobbing and didn't know why.

It was the rain that finally raised her from her stupor. Aggressive liquid pellets slammed against every inch of her. Thea had unknitted herself from Doris. Neither sister faced the other. The rush of water crackled closer now, more immediate, angrier.

Her stomach felt like a brick. Doris noticed the way the rain cascaded against Thea's cheeks, pummeling her eyelids and running down her nose.

"You made it," Thea said. "You did it. You made it."

"I did." Her response was almost blotted out by a loud crack of thunder. "Have you seen anyone else?"

"No one that isn't stuck like us."

"No more boats?"

"None," Thea repeated.

"Where are all the people?" It was a rhetorical question, one she didn't expect an answer to.

But she got one anyway.

"It's just us," Thea said. "It's just us, sis."

It was both everything she'd ever wanted and everything she'd always feared.

They might survive the flood—surviving each other was a different story.

———

The water rose. Doris dragged herself to the edge of the roof, draping a hand over the side while Thea relaxed as if nothing was wrong, gazing into the sky while cloaked in a distant glaze. The ketamine must be taking hold. Doris didn't feel much of anything herself aside from a slight dulling to her body. This was enough to grant her a bit more mobility, just enough to shift around without wanting to die. This, she supposed, was something.

She tried to avoid thinking of Thea's pocked face and tracked-up arms. She didn't want to think about how, even in a catastrophic flood, she was able to get high. She just wanted to shake her as hard as she could. It didn't matter that they might drown at any moment.

The surrounding air felt wet. The water neared her fingertips. Only minutes more and she'd be able to lean over the lip of the roof and touch it.

"We've got to get in," Doris said.

"Get in what?" Thea's words shot away from her.

"The water. What else?"

"You'd better be fucking with me."

"It's coming now, Thea, no matter how relaxed you feel."

Thea rolled onto her side. "Oh, fuck off." Dragging herself to her knees, she shivered and cast spotlight stares from behind her eyes.

"You really do look terrible."

"Weird. I feel great."

Thea's cargo pants sank in the pockets, clinging wet to her spindly legs.

"Jesus, Thea," Doris said.

Her jaw stiffened. "Stop it."

For once, Doris truly didn't know what to say. *I didn't want this for you. I fucked up. This isn't your fault.* All bullshit, stupid genialities to make herself feel better when all that was needed were two words. Two words Doris just couldn't bring herself to say right now. She owed her sister more than a deathbed apology, a last-ditch, frightened, pathetic excuse to clear her own dirty conscience.

It wasn't all her fault either, though.

Her little sister loomed over her. Doris reached up to her. "Help me up."

Pausing a moment, Thea extended a hand, yanking Doris upright in a single motion.

"We have to get in," she said again.

"And do what?"

"Swim, I guess."

The sisters sat on the roof, one kneeling beside the other, both searching for a way out. They looked up, listening for manmade noise. The *wuhwuhwuhwuhwuh* of helicopter blades or the dull thrum of passing planes—anything at all to indicate that people were out there surviving. Even if they were left behind in the process, to know people were there and trying was a comfort. The isolation of their predicament was almost more unbearable than the prospect of failure.

Doris kept her head down. The water moved in strange ways, hypnotizing in its way. Her body was numbed from cold and exertion, her head a burnt bulb, but the water and its top-slick of old life was entrancing, almost inviting. Looking at it from above, it appeared pained and strangled, an angry flood like any other. But just below, it flowed unfiltered. It knew exactly what it was doing.

The water followed its own current, sucking debris below the surface with its riptide, but some of the bigger stuff kept afloat—mainly uprooted trees and splintered bark, a mattress made for a toddler, the top of a neighbor's patio table, corrugated aluminum siding from a house or a shed. It all whipped by, up and over the block fences the water had now consumed, but the siding stuck under the lip of the neighbor's house.

Doris slapped her sister's arm. "Look."

"What?"

Pointing, Doris said, "That metal siding there."

Thea glared at it. "I don't think that'll work."

"It floats, doesn't it?"

"How you expect to get to it? How do we get on top of it without tipping it over?"

"It's better than nothing."

"Better than a house?"

"Look at the water," Doris said. "Anything that floats is better than a house that doesn't."

Thea bit her bottom lip until it bled. "You're insane."

"We don't have many options!"

"Fuck! I know, Doris! You don't need to keep pointing this shit out to me." Thea screamed over the rain, now louder, more immediate, as if sky and earth were trying to pinch to a close, one end meeting the other.

Thea watched the flood, scowling. "I need a minute. I just need one fucking minute to figure this out."

They both knew she didn't have a minute. One minute could be the difference between the metal raft being within reach or miles down the road. One minute meant more water, more distance. It meant more everything. There wasn't anything to figure out.

Doris dragged her fingers over the rippling spray of rain pelting the shingles. The flood was nearly within reach now.

"What are you doing?" Thea asked.

"Nothing."

"Get away from the edge. You're making me nervous. Jesus, I need a cigarette."

Doris ignored her. Thea needed to get it all out already, and Doris hadn't the patience for entertaining another of her sister's hysteria attacks.

Thea paced, stomping in circles behind her. "Can you just— will you move?"

"I'm fine."

"I know you're fine, but just move."

"I don't need to move, Thea."

"But will you? Goddamn, even here you're disagreeable."

That familiar rage sparked again, just when she'd thought the water had snuffed it out for the moment. "Your discomfort isn't my problem."

"Oh, I know, Doris. I fucking know that you don't give a fuck about anyone's discomfort but your own."

"Why the hell should I? You're a goddamn adult, are you not? Act like one. I'm not going to wipe your ass like Ma does."

If Thea had had anything in her hands, Doris was sure she'd have thrown it at her. Instead, she stood there picking at her scabs. "I never asked you to. It would be nice if you cared, though, even a fucking little bit, about things."

"I care about things."

"About me."

"Jesus." Doris pushed the words through clenched teeth. "We do not have time for this right now."

"If not now, when?"

"There'll be plenty of time while trapped on that." She pointed at the metal siding twitching precariously against the neighbor's house.

"I'd rather not, thanks."

"Oh, that's great. Just like always, Thea stomps her feet and gets her way. You run amok, vomiting your bullshit everywhere and letting the rest of us clean it up, and then complain that we don't care about you. As if my life isn't already all about you."

Thea slapped her thighs, almost jubilant in the irony. "Oh my God. Oh, fuck, isn't this just rich. Queen Doris thinks it's all about me. That's pure slapstick."

"Fuck you, Thea."

"Please," she said, flopping cross-legged onto the roof. "I can't even start with this right now."

Anger turned over and over and over in her gut. Doris could have hit her. She wanted to throttle her and slap her across her face, but she couldn't get there quick enough. So she did the next best thing. The only thing she could think of.

"Have you seen James's wallet?"

Thea drew her jaw in close.

"Do you remember what you did with it?"

Rolling up from her crouch, Thea towered over Doris, expression torn in a hundred directions. She didn't have to speak; Doris didn't want her to. Whatever she might have to say was totally irrelevant now.

"Where the hell is my husband's wallet, *sis*?" Where the hell was her husband while she was trapped here on her broken roof with her broken sister and her broken body and everything was broken? Where was he the one time she'd truly needed him in years?

But she knew—she didn't have to guess. Her chest buckled as she avoided the thought of it. She cried. She was tired. She was angry, but that's not why she'd said what she said.

It took Thea a minute to compose herself. Doris didn't care.

"I don't have his wallet," she said finally.

"Anymore."

Thea nodded once. "Anymore."

More silence. Some thunder. Some lightning. Nothing louder than the rift between them.

"I didn't know that you knew."

Doris returned her sister's earlier sentiment. "Please."

"Did he tell you?"

Doris dipped her fingertips into the oncoming water. It was none of Thea's business what James might or might not have said. What did she care if he'd come home that same day and bled his heart out to her or remained distant until Doris had finally asked where his wallet was, where he had been? Who cared if she'd known the moment he'd walked through the door, carefully crafting her next move over the course of the following weeks? It was just words—stupid, impotent words dissolving in the rain like everything else.

Thea started to speak, stopped, started, and stopped two more times before abandoning the idea.

To her credit, she didn't try to apologize.

"I can't do anything about it now," she said instead.

Doris acknowledged her again. "You literally could do anything. Anything at all. For once."

———

Thea searched the space over the top of her sister's head. *For once,* she said. Loaded words, always loaded with Doris. Every word a tamped-down musket. She probably deserved it, but right now Thea didn't feel like granting her sister the satisfaction of hitting her mark. As if Doris ever missed.

The metal siding Doris kept going on about still clung to the side of the next house. Not far, maybe twenty feet. Thea could get it if she jumped now, but she was pissed. Leave it to her sister to ruin a perfectly good high. God damn her.

Doris remained near the edge of the roof, a relic of her former self. Thea had always gone to such great lengths to avoid thinking of her this way—everything was fine, Doris was still her sister, her accident didn't define her. But all the family's efforts to prove that nothing had changed had done nothing to sway the fact that everything had.

She wasn't sure what to do now. She felt like shit. How long had Doris known about her and James's shady dealings? How *much* did she know? How much was really Thea's fault? Was everything her fault? Part of it, of course, was her fault. Fuck.

This wasn't supposed to happen today. It was supposed to be like any other day, scouring the streets for a place to rest and something to steal, and not having her insides revolt while the sky tried to kill her. Her eyes were dry as hell despite all the water. There was water everywhere except where she needed it.

Lacking the compunction to do anything but lace her fingers across her stomach, she dropped again to her knees and thought about sleep. Just a good nap. That's what she would do when this was over—sleep and sleep until she couldn't sleep any longer.

A splash in front of her. Brown water sprayed onto her face from the direction that Doris had just been laying, now conspicuously missing.

Thea arched like a cat and scrambled to the edge of the roof. A body thrashed in the swirl, flapping, uncoordinated, and then sank.

Doris was in the water.

Hearing white noise, Thea dove in after her. She reached, spread her limbs and fingers out like feelers in hopes of catching a glimpse of Doris's collar or skirt or hair. But the water was strong, and it ripped at her. Bobbing to the surface, she screamed for her sister, choked on water, and screamed again. She swam, felt, swam, dove, feeling and feeling, getting bombarded with twigs and sharp things and oozing slicks of detritus that made her jump. It was foreign and difficult to breathe, and Doris wasn't anywhere.

She called her name over and over, but she could barely hear herself over the din. "Doris! Doris? Doris! Where are you, Doris?"

Then she felt it. She was surprised that she did through all the trauma of the moment. For a second, she thought it was her sister grabbing her ankle—whatever touched her leg had the unmistakable air of cognizance. But it was too slippery and long and smooth to be Doris, too jointless to be human, and just as quickly as it touched her, it released her. Doris surfaced about twenty feet away, forcing her way toward the metal stuck against the house.

Thea took off after her, less agile and totally without focus, punching the water out of her way more than swimming. Doris bobbed up and over the water, down again, up and down, up and down. Her legs flailed loose, catching her back in the tumult, but she always realigned herself, two steps forward, one step back. She'd always been a swimmer.

Reaching the siding, Doris lunged for it, slipped off, lunged again, and held. Thea chased her, behind by a mile. By the time she caught up, Doris was pinned between the metal and the house, gripping the sharp edges with one hand and the house with the other. Blood poured from fresh gashes in her hands. Thea landed next to her, back to the house, hitting her head against the roof's edge as she gripped it with her life.

The current was stronger than she expected. She coughed up water and wondered what the hell to do next.

Yelling at Doris was the best idea she could come up with. "Are you trying to fucking drown yourself?"

"Get on!" Doris pointed toward the roof.

Where were the neighbors? Was this part of their shed? Their house? Water covered the windows. There wasn't any escape now. The neighbors were either gone or dead. So few people on roofs. All of them gone or dead. Was it flooding everywhere?

"Thea!"

Doris's weak grasp of the metal and the roof waned. Water sloshed over her chin.

Thea took off swimming to where the roof dipped lower, an easier lurch for her tired body, but even the smaller gap proved difficult. Just a few inches from the top of the water to the bottom of the roof, and Thea scrambled to even get her hands above her head. There just wasn't anything left.

"I can't," she said, unsure if Doris could hear her. Thea's voice cracked. "I can't make it."

Doris wouldn't know that her sister couldn't make it. She'd just drown and then Thea would drown and then someone in a too-late rescue boat would pull their bodies from the water in a few days. Or they wouldn't, and they'd wilt underneath the water to be picked apart by fish and turtles and time, feeding the flowers their poison once the water receded. God help them. Or maybe He already was, but she and Doris were part of the problem.

And then whatever was in that water touched her again, this time drifting casually against her lower back, a nudge, a warning. *I hear you*, it said.

"Jesus Jesus shit!" The fire returned, and Thea clawed at the peeling shingles. There was something in the water. There was something in that fucking water, and it kept touching her. On purpose. The bone in her pinky snapped and bent back as she hurled herself up, but her entire body was sparking like firecrackers and she didn't feel it.

Her sister clung to the house. Thea could see her fingers grabbing at the edge a few feet away. Then she couldn't see them anymore and Doris's hand was gone.

Nonononono. Thea made it in time, caught her hand as it slipped below the water, pulled her up again.

Doris took a breath and hung her head to the side. She was

fading. Thea was, too. There wasn't much fight left.

"There's something in the water!" Even though Thea screamed, she wasn't sure Doris heard. Her sister's hand felt limp in her grip. She pulled, lacking strength, lacking sanity.

"There's something in the fucking water, Doris. Come on, come on. Let's go. There's something in it! Doris—"

A splash.

How she even heard it—a splash like that amongst the chaos and rain—but Thea was certain she had. Something big, like a dolphin, sleek and silver, leaping up and crashing down. Thea had been staring down at the top of her sister's head, so she hadn't seen it straight on. Big and silver, and it was out there in the water with them. Doris hung limp and dazed, gaping ahead with her mouth open.

"Come on!" She was shivering and cold, and Doris was out of it. If it weren't for the warmth of her skin and slow pulse beating in her wrist, Thea would swear Doris was gone. She shook her. Doris's hand bled from grasping the edge of the metal. She'd let go of the house, but not that metal. Thea couldn't haul them both up—metal and sister. It was one or the other or neither, but not both.

"Doris, let go," she said. *You will not drown, sis. You will not.*

Another splash. This time Thea caught the silvery glint of it just under the water's surface. No more than twenty feet away. Whatever it was, it was moving closer, coming toward them like a taunt. No hurry—this thing had all the time in the world.

Doris stared, transfixed. Thea couldn't bear her to be in the water one more second. That *thing* was coming. It was here.

So Thea jumped. Releasing her sister's hand, she sprang on top of the sheet metal, knees slamming hard on the corrugated side. She almost lost it, tipping it too much to one side and slipping, but righted it in just enough time to get steady and center herself. All the while Doris remained lost, hand clinging deeper into the siding's razor edge.

Reaching out to Doris, she pounded on the metal. *Thwaang.* The water rippled around them. Doris blinked.

"Grab my hands," she said.

The noise or the jump or Thea's crazed face inches from her own or a combination of them all finally broke her sister's trance, and she winced as she uncurled her hand from the metal. The blood from her wound oozed against Thea's palm. Doris hissed and reached up with her other hand.

Together, the sisters pulled, all the while waiting for another splash, a closer one. Instead, the siding ripped apart Doris's blouse and tore into her skin as they muscled her aboard. Doris screamed. It shredded her, but anything was better than being in the water. Alive and bleeding was better than dead and drowned or stuck in the gut of some flood beast.

She hauled Doris up. They crumpled on top of one another in the center of the sheet metal as they bled, and it spun away from the house in the torrent.

Thea couldn't look. Head down, she wished it all away and tried not to hurl. The pressure of Doris's body on top of hers was a small comfort. Her sister's heartbeat was so slow, as if it had already stopped working, but every time she began to get worried, it'd pick up again, just enough to keep Thea calm. Her eyes felt filled with sand, and they stung like hell. Her throat was shredded, and it pained her chest to breathe. Sound oozed over her in echoey thumps, her ears clogged with water. But she was alive.

Doris melted on top of her sister for ages, hours, probably only a few minutes because that's all they had before their metal raft crashed into something, threatening to knock them both overboard again. Thea jerked up—another house, nothing more than a roof now. Not a monster. Not that thing, whatever it was.

Ricocheting off the house, they spun into the flood surf again, this time with little else to stop them for a long while. Rain crushed the horizon in black and lightning. Whatever might be out there would be underwater before they reached it, unless it stopped soon. Thea looked toward the sky, an unbroken blanket of overfilled clouds. It was not stopping.

She shivered. She was cold and sick and thirsty and tired. She needed rest, some sleep. Doris needed it, too, but neither would get it.

Casting wary eyes at the water, the sisters floated and waited. Thea looked for anything familiar but saw nothing but the tops of streetlights and highway signs and shadows of other tops of things she couldn't quite discern.

Doris looked up, seeking help she knew would never come.

Water lapped over the edges of the metal, lashing at the long wound down her torso and legs from the edge of the siding. Warm blood and cool water pooled around her hands, funneling down her and Thea's bodies. They floated. They waited some more.

Thea turned after some time, releasing herself from her sister's weight. "This is bad."

This, as in the flood, or this, as in their aches and wounds—it didn't matter.

Thea spoke again, croaking out a hoarse whimper. "We have to stay out of the water."

"We can try," said Doris.

"There's something in it."

Doris tried to resituate her body but lacked the strength. She sagged deeper into Thea's sharp corners. "There's a lot of stuff in the water. It could have been anything. A dish towel. A hose. A body."

"It could have been, but it wasn't. I know what I felt."

"Just tricks. The drugs are making you see things."

Thea squirreled out from underneath her. Doris rolled onto her side. The metal pulled up, but Thea slammed it down again with her weight. Water sprayed up, then settled again.

"It touched me. I saw it."

"I was there, Thea. I didn't see anything."

"You were looking right at it!"

Doris didn't say anything else but drifted in a way that told Thea she wasn't being exactly honest, that she was trying to convince herself that Thea was wrong.

"So what if there is something there? What are we supposed to do about it?" she finally asked.

Thea lay cheek-down on the metal, arms at her sides. "Stay away from it and hope it doesn't catch us."

"Why do you assume it's bad?"

Clenching her hands, her sister spoke slowly and quietly. "Do you really enjoy arguing with me this much?"

"Who are you to decide, Thea?"

"This argument is stupid. They're huge fucking monsters. Are my labels offending their slimy monster sensibilities?"

Doris slammed an open palm against the makeshift raft. "Just stop!"

Thea stopped her mouth, but nothing else. Her body was limp, but her eyes were sharp and angry.

Night approached. Every gurgle, every swish, was a threat. Doris lay ragged at her side, fury lining her lungs. Thea wasn't even sure what she was most mad about—the destruction, or Thea herself, or both, or everything.

But Thea couldn't bother with it now. A haze dragged over her. Exhaustion. Maybe the drugs, she wasn't sure. She wanted to sleep, to uncoil her muscles and let her body do whatever it was going to do, but then she'd hear something or feel something, or their shitty raft would dip or bob and her heart would catapult to her throat. She expected more noise, distant cries for help, the sound of crunching metal, but all was dulled by the roar of water. Sometimes she'd see other people clinging to floating pieces of their lives, scrambling to keep their chins above water, but just as quickly as they arrived, they were whisked away again. It was just like before, people drifting in and out of her life and leaving just as quickly.

Everyone except Doris, even if it was only spite that kept her there.

Thea listened to the water, and she waited.

CHAPTER SEVEN

THE FLOOD

IT WAS BECOMING more difficult to see, which was a comfort for Doris. She could imagine then, in the dark. It covered her up. Life was easier when all of her was in the dark.

Thea breathed raggedly, laboring like a pneumonic wheeze. Doris listened to her for a long time, grateful for the noise.

They were quiet for a while before Thea couldn't tolerate it any longer. She never could handle silence, stuffing the void with her noise whenever it got too quiet. Always a bark, a gnaw, a stab at Doris's senses. Always sharp—Thea would never let Doris fade out. She took it as more of a personal slight that she had to remedy, another break she had to try and fix, until she finally began spewing explosives like, "I stole his wallet."

Doris didn't respond.

"After he gave me money," Thea clarified, as if that made it better.

Every nerve in her body quietly fired off. All the emotions involved in an exchange that Doris had known about, though never explicitly named. The undeniability of Thea's confession socked her in the chest harder than she expected. *He gave me money*. And here Doris was stuck on a piece of metal, sliced up the gizzard and shivering, and Thea said what she said and laid that ickiness in her lap with nowhere for Doris to throw it, like a child's tantrum. *Here, you deal with this.*

"You knew," she said.

Doris didn't respond.

"He told you."

James hadn't said anything—never confirmed, never denied. Doris had only asked him once, and it was the only time she'd seen his face so empty. So, she'd known. And yes, he'd been the one to tell her. He'd been giving Thea money for months, possibly years. He'd gone behind Doris's back, lied to her for ages, even after they'd both decided to cut off all contact with her. He might as well have stuck the needle in her arm himself.

"What did you do with his wallet?" Doris asked.

Thea shrank, trying to disappear. "What is with the wallet? Jesus."

"What did you do with it?"

"I took his fucking wallet. I took his money and then I stole his wallet and then I bought heroin and threw the wallet in the dumpster behind Walgreens." Her pointed words dropped like needles, loud and painful and splattering everywhere as they hit Doris's surface. "Is that really what you wanted to hear?"

"Yes, it is. It's exactly what I wanted to hear."

Thea rocketed upright. "Why? Why, Doris? You just want to get out of me the one thing I don't want to say? You think I ever forget, even for a second, that I'm just another degenerate addict? You gotta drive the nail deeper and deeper so that I hate myself as much as you hate me? If I kill myself, will you finally be happy? Or will you hover over my grave and *tsk* that I didn't do it sooner?"

But Doris was too tired for this. Some of it was right, some of it was bullshit, all of it was . . . she didn't know. She didn't care. Why did she want to know about the wallet? Thea didn't tell her anything Doris hadn't already guessed. She'd been spitting nails at Thea for years. Maybe she did just want to be sure that one had stuck. Probably because she was just as rotten at the core as Thea, just as messed up, and it fucking sucked to see her anemic reflection getting everything Doris had ever wanted. Like James.

"And now you're ignoring me. That's great, Doris. Just fucking great." Thea's teeth chattered as she shouted.

"I have nothing to say, is all."

"Bullshit you don't."

"I don't know what to tell you," Doris said.

Thea was quiet, then asked, "Do you even care?"

Did she? "I can't tell," she said.

Doris turned away as her sister glared at her, indignant. Eventually she lay back down without saying anything.

The mixture of shock and exhaustion and old news rendered Doris emotionless, which was like an incendiary for Thea. Doris just didn't have the capacity to feel anything now, so Thea fidgeted, unsatisfied, bracing for an attack that wasn't coming. Her adrenaline suddenly had nowhere to go.

Lightning whipped across the sky, the resulting thunder shaking the water from the ground up. Every flash revealed a new shadow under the water—willowy, distorted lines that could be anything and everything. Doris cringed at each of them but refused to look away. Thea had no idea what she was dealing with. These were different monsters than she was used to— these were Doris's monsters, the liminal and unclassifiable kind. The monsters of old stories that shouldn't exist, but do.

Which was of course when Doris spotted it, as if waiting for her silent acknowledgement. Lightning scored the sky, casting a bright glare against the flood, and a black, tangled shape below. It was gigantic, far more immense than Doris thought possible under the circumstances. She stifled a yelp, praying Thea didn't see it.

It was right underneath them—its limbs spiraling out like the whiskers of some massive virus. A dread deeper than death sank into her. It found her. It found them both. That sneaky fucking monster of her childhood now bloomed into a fully-grown terror, and she was helpless against it.

"Thea," she started. She wasn't sure what she was going to say. She wasn't even sure if her sister had heard her.

"What?"

The words caught in Doris's chest. She wanted to scream, to lunge for her sister and wrap her arms around her, to hold her and tell her that she would never let anything bad happen to her ever, ever again. She wanted to say that she was sorry. Doris wasn't sure what to say she was sorry for, exactly. There was too much. No apology could ever be worthy, but it would be something.

She wanted to tell that she had failed—the monsters she tried so hard to keep away had found them anyway. She wanted to beg Thea not to hate her for everything she didn't do. She wanted to scream at Thea in turn. There was so much, but just when the emotion felt too huge to bear, just as it threatened to spill into coherent sentences, the lightening would come to reveal the nightmare looming just below. It moved, limbs swishing with power and strength. Did Thea see it? How could she not?

Her thoughts branched in a dozen directions, writhing not unlike the tentacles of the monster beneath the water's surface. She feared that if she opened her mouth Thea would finally see her for what she was, so she stayed quiet.

Below them, the monster responded in kind—quiet and looming.

For now.

———

The waters faded, taking a familiar shape.

Doris was home again. Her old home. Her mother's home. The home where Thea lived. A fog blotted out everything but the living room and kitchen. Normal. Fine. There was always a fog here. She tried remembering the room without the fog, but couldn't.

She sat across from her mother, who hadn't removed her hands from their white-knuckle grip of her mug. Thea had been missing for thirty-six hours. The kitchen smelled of smoke from the frozen pizza Dad had burned in his effort to do something other than "sitting around being pissed off." As with most of his help, it failed in spectacular fashion. He'd left the house to purchase more scented candles to cover up the smell. She didn't expect him back for another few hours. Maybe he would go and search for his youngest daughter, but she doubted it.

Each of them was four cups of coffee into the evening, and Doris got up to make another pot. Ma didn't budge.

"You want Folgers again or the vanilla macadamia nut?" Neither of them gave a shit, but she asked anyway. She made the Folgers.

The police left two hours ago, asking the family to call if they heard anything. They wouldn't hear anything, and the cops weren't going to bother looking too hard. Everyone knew what she was doing—she'd just never stayed away this long before. Ma didn't even want to file a report.

"She's out. Just out. Working. She has a new job. She's probably fine."

Doris called 911 herself, knowing none of those things were true. She spoke to the cops in code so that Ma wouldn't have a coronary once they left, furious about spreading filthy lies about her sister. Because it was easier to believe that her oldest was a liar than that her youngest was an addict.

Still, despite her thriving denial, there was a stillness about Ma that suggested how deeply uprooted she was at the moment. It was unnerving to know that her mother was experiencing emotions other than frustration and savageness, and Doris wondered how hard they all would pay for it on the back end.

Providing Thea ever returned. But the alternative wasn't an option. She knuckled the worn buttons on the coffee maker, trying not to think about what new ring of hell she'd descended to where Thea was the one to run away, while she was stuck here, in this suffocating house, alone with their mother.

The coffee machine gurgled, settling into a steady drip whose sound ricocheted off the walls. Doris watched Ma through the reflection in the glass, catching her flinch at some invisible offense.

She should be out looking for her. That's what she should have done as soon as she found out. Ma probably wouldn't even move, just sit here until her mug shattered in her grip. Yet, knowing that, Doris was still here, pouring coffee into her mother's mug and waiting patiently for her to spiral.

Doris's hands were shaking. *Too much caffeine*, she thought, knowing full well that wasn't it.

"She's fine," Ma said.

Doris stared at her but said nothing.

Ma caught the omission. "What? Say it."

"Say what, Ma?"

"She is fine!" She slammed her mug onto the table, exploding scalding coffee all over the table. Little molten rivers ran across the tabletop, dropping over the sides and onto the rug.

Mother and daughter stared at the mess, then at each other. Doris's phone started to ring from inside her jeans pocket.

"Aren't you going to answer it?"

"No." She knew who it was, and he was the last person she wanted to speak to now. James always caught the distress in her voice, even when she didn't notice it herself. He'd catch it and then he'd get in the car and come here, thinking himself a prize for his charity, unconcerned that his presence only tightened the noose a little further around their relationship.

"It could be her."

"It's not."

"Answer it."

Digging the phone out of her pocket, she tossed it onto the table without looking. It splattered into the spilled coffee.

Ma glanced at it and sniffed.

"It's not," Doris repeated.

The front door opened. Ma's eyes darted toward the noise, sparking full of fire so instantly that there was no doubt as to who had just arrived.

Doris didn't want to look and was immediately sorry when she did. Her mouth failed her, veins icing over as she saw her sister waltz through the door. No one seemed to see it—no one said a thing—but Thea wasn't alone.

It was here. The monster of her childhood, slithering around Thea's face and neck and torso, all its hands, all those fingers, denting Thea's pale skin. A pattern of bruises bloomed under its touch, and no one said a thing about it.

Ma lunged out of her seat. "Where were you? What do you think you're doing? Good God, *what did you do?*"

Thea smiled in the doorway, possessed. Her hair clung to her sweaty scalp, her shirt and pants askew.

Ma stopped short, as if afraid to touch her. "What have you done?"

"Hi, Ma," Thea said. The door rattled the photos on the wall as she slammed it shut. "I see you've brought in reinforcements."

The monster squeezed. Thea's voice choked under the strain as she wobbled in place, unable to keep herself upright without swaying.

The phone again began to ring. Thea moved toward it like a snake. "For fuck's sake, what the hell happened here?"

She tossed the soaked and slippery phone toward Doris. "Your husband needs you."

It clattered to the floor, Doris refusing to catch it. That thing coiled around her arm. Doris imagined its hot breath against the nape of Thea's neck.

Thea shrugged, gliding past her mother and sister, heading toward her room. "I'm going to bed."

This time, Ma didn't hesitate, slapping her across the face with every ounce of strength she could muster. "How *dare* you?"

Thea sneered, but before she could drag her fists out of her sluggish stupor to retaliate, Doris was in front of her, accepting the blow. It struck her in the shoulder. Thea was so high, she couldn't land a punch if her fist was the size of a bowling ball.

Ma screeched like a parakeet in Doris's ear, while Thea recoiled at the sight of her sister.

"Oh, of course," she said. "Here comes the fucking queen."

Doris wanted to shake her. "Don't you see it? Don't you feel it?" she asked.

Ma swatted a hand over Doris's shoulder, aiming her claws at Thea's face. "You ingrate. Look what you've done!"

Both were screaming, passing insults through the open cracks of Doris's barrier. Ma lunged again, but Doris swung around to face her, catching her by the shoulders to hold her at bay. But it was too late—the woman had ignited and refused to be stopped. Without hesitating Ma landed a palm on Doris's cheek in the same fashion as she'd done with her youngest. The contact stung, jostling Doris out of her dissociated calm.

"*Don't*," she said, and shoved her mother until she flew backward, crashing into one of the dining room chairs. She didn't even push her that hard, but the shock of it must have disoriented her more than the contact itself.

She felt it then—the monster's slither around her waist, the way its touch ignited her nerves into a frenzy. It was going to get her, just like it got Thea.

Doris shook it off and leaned over her mother, taller than her by a good three inches. She spoke quietly so that Ma had to really focus on what she said, because, for once, she was listening.

"You won't ever do that again, Mother."

Ma drew her chin tight, saying everything that needed to be said with a repugnant stare. Doris had to look away.

Her equilibrium was off as blood thrummed through her temples at high speed, rocketing from her heart after the new surge of adrenaline. She felt ill, off balance. She might have been sick if not for the slow clap that startled her out of her own head.

"Two peas in a pod, you are," Thea said. She leaned against the railing, perched halfway up the stairs, smirking.

"Quite a show, but as I said before, I am quite tired."

Doris had to pick the words out of her inebriated slurring, but the message was there all the same.

Doris shouted at her in a voice she hadn't known she possessed. "Where are you going?"

But Thea didn't miss a beat. "To my room, *Mother*." She said it with intention, fully aware that Ma hadn't opened her mouth. The monster clung to her back, cloaking Thea's body completely as she retreated to her room.

From upstairs, a second door slammed, silence resuming after the chaotic intermission.

Ma hadn't moved, and Doris grabbed her things and left before she could. The front door swung outward as she fled, a thousand needle-like thoughts stabbing at her. She knew she couldn't leave Thea there, but Doris couldn't stay either. Honestly, she wasn't sure which of them was more dangerous at the moment. What she did know was that all of them being together would get someone hurt.

Or at least that's what she told herself.

This is what's best. She unlocked her car.

I'll figure out how to stop it. I won't let that thing touch her again. She started the ignition.

What could I do, anyway? She drove away.

Ma won't dare touch her now. She pulled over a few blocks

away. Everything was fog again. She'd driven into nothing. Water sloshed along the brake pedal.

I hate both of them. She dropped her forehead to the steering wheel as the fog seeped into her car.

What have I done?

She cried.

———

Doris awoke with a cough, a sob catching in her throat. How the hell had she managed to fall asleep?

She reached a hand toward Thea, who shuddered slightly at her touch and sighed. Also asleep. Doris's head was simultaneously heavy yet light, her pain a subtle throb instead of a scream. They must have been floating for hours, settling into a lazy drift as the waters smoothed over the top of her neighborhood. Street lights poked through the surface. A city-issued garbage can floated just out of reach. Somehow, everywhere, there was noise—the constant roar carried with it needle-pricks of screams, metal on metal, snapping and crumbling and cracking of wood and concrete, and familiar yet out of place sounds like zippers and the clinking of plates in the dishwasher as it was loaded. The associations were close enough to create a layer of nostalgic dread that settled over her. Her pulse thudded inside her head like footsteps trodding up and down some faraway hallway.

It had been a long time since they had been this close to one another, and Doris listened to her sister's wheezing and tried not to cry.

Thea eventually spoke first, having woken up without Doris knowing it. "What's wrong?"

"Where do I start?"

"Did you really not see it?" She spoke if the words pained her.

Doris's hackles rose in defense, anticipating the undercurrent of blame that wormed its way into every conversation, but whether

Thea was just tired, or the flood blotted it out, it wasn't there.

She had no idea how to respond. So much of her character was packaged by resentment that it stained everything. She felt exposed, like a black hood had just been yanked from her head and all the sounds and smells and sights formerly muffled in shadow were now achingly clear.

But she had to say something. Even after all this time, the compulsion to soothe her baby sister hadn't faded. Now, for once, Thea was actually asking for comfort, and Doris hadn't a clue how to provide it anymore.

"I don't know what I saw," she ended up saying, hoping Thea was able to fill in the gaps herself.

She was quiet for a while, but just when Doris was sure Thea was ignoring her, she started up again.

"Do you remember Jay?"

"Jay?"

"That kid down the street. He moved when I was like eight or nine."

"Jesus, what made you think of him?"

"Did I ever tell you how he taught me to ride a bike?"

Doris just went ahead and assumed Thea was playing fast and loose with the word *taught*. It was likely more akin to an interrogation than a lesson, especially considering what she remembered of Jay, and what she knew for certain of Thea.

"How on earth did that even come about?"

"Ma was saying a bunch of shit about not wasting money on things I wouldn't play with, so I decided I was going to show her a thing or two. Jay was the only kid I knew that had a bike, so I waited by the front window for hours one Saturday, watching for him to come outside. He finally did, going to play basketball or whatever, and before he'd even made it to the end of his driveway I'm halfway down the street, yelling at him to let me see his bike. I wasn't sure it would even work. Figured this big kid would tell me to shove off or throw something at me, but he kind of looked at me funny and then goes inside the garage and gets it. Didn't even ask me why or anything. So, he's holding it by the handlebars, just staring at me, and I ask him to show me how to ride. If you could have seen his face, Doris—I've been in some bad shit, but I have never seen fear like I did then. I'll never forget it."

Doris cupped her palm, catching the rain and watching it trickle little rivers across her hand. "Was he afraid you'd break his bike or something?"

"I mean, probably, but that's not what was wrong. He said something like, 'Well, you just get on and peddle.' Which, of course, I knew already, but I want him to show me first. I'm doubting myself; maybe Ma knows something I don't about bikes? Maybe that's why she doesn't want to get me one—"

"She's just a bitch."

"I didn't know that then."

"Yes, you did."

She was quiet, and Doris wondered if Thea was reliving the same memories that she was. "So, what happened?"

"He got on the bike, wobbled a bit, and crashed it right into his dad's truck. I start yelling at him, because even I know that this isn't how you're supposed to ride a bike. He got on again, crashed again. He does it a few times until he gets a few houses down before crashing in someone's yard. The whole time I'm asking him if he knows what he's doing, and he's getting redder and redder until he finally throws the bike down in the street, tells me to go ahead and try it if I think I can do better. So I do, and promptly wreck face first into his dad's truck. Again. That truck was like a magnet for dumb kids."

"Wait." Doris peeled herself from her sister and faced her. "Is that why you and Jay were helping plant those trees in their front yard? Ma refused to tell me what that was all about. Tried saying that you were being a conscientious neighbor or something stupid."

Thea tilted her chin back in a cackle. "She told me that she'd get me a bike once I finished paying off my debt."

"Did she?"

"What do you think?"

The storm picked up. Rain slammed against the metal like artillery. "Must have been a nice truck."

"It was."

The conversation ended as abruptly as it started, dragging with a lingering sense of incompletion. A mist billowed up from the water's surface, the storm slamming down on them thrusting water particles into the air. Doris grabbed for her sister's hand—she knew Thea was still there, but the air started to gray, and it was harder to see, and Thea had slipped between her fingers so many times before that just knowing wasn't enough.

Tracing Thea's trembling arm, she found her hand and squeezed.

"Do you know how I met James?" Water filled her ears so that her voice thrummed and snarled inside her head. She hadn't expected Thea to hear her.

"No," she said.

Doris struggled with where to start. She wasn't sure why she even brought it up. Thea was the last person with whom she wanted to discuss her marriage. Though Doris never wanted to discuss her marriage with anyone, not even her husband.

"Coffee."

"What?"

"So fucking cliché." She screamed the words, fighting all the barriers she spent years creating to hold it all in. "I hate that we met in a coffee shop. I don't know why. Maybe I just hate telling the story."

Thea flexed her fingers to stall her shaking, pulling them in and out of her sister's grip whenever it seemed to crescendo. They both needed a distraction.

"It was a donut place. Cheap iced coffee for a buck. I went there every Thursday—it was when I was still working at Aetna. Staff meetings every Thursday morning. Then one time, James was there. He told me later that it wasn't me that initially attracted him, but the barista that saw me coming and called out my order before I was even inside the building. She nodded at me as I got in line, and I paid for my coffee—the same large Americano as always—without even speaking. He said that the rest of the room buzzed on like usual, but the exchange was the most fascinating thing he'd seen all year. His words. He said that he just had to 'know the woman that commanded the room.'"

She sneered at having to repeat it. It was a sentiment that rubbed her raw as soon as he confessed it. Like she was something to tame. Like she existed for his domestication pleasure. He'd sworn up and down that he hadn't meant it that way.

Had he told her that prior to their rehearsal dinner, she might not have ever married him.

"The next Thursday my coffee was already paid for by the time I got to the register. I handed him a few bucks on my way out and told him that I'd rather he not bother. To his credit, he took my money and folded it into his wallet. He also never bought my coffee again. Not even after we were married. He just . . . was always there. He waited. He was so patient. I suppose he fascinated me the way I fascinated him. We were so different—I thought, at least. Turns out we were cut from the same black cloth. We each had our experiments. So determined to expose each other. Both so certain that there was something hidden within the other one, something we would be rewarded with once we found it. I'm not even sure what I was looking for in him. I think . . ."

She trailed away, petrified even on the brink of destruction to admit the truth. "I think I wanted him to attack me. I could handle that. I *deserved* that. Because if someone like him could snap, then it meant that I wasn't alone in my shittiness."

Thea laughed, the sharpness of it slicing clean through the rumble. "You definitely weren't alone in the shitty person department."

Doris felt her skin heat up against Thea's palm. "I hate heroin."

"So do I. Mostly."

Something big bumped against the side of their raft, and Thea bolted upright. "What the fuck was that?"

They'd hit something, dragged over the top of it as they skimmed the surface of a drowning city. "A pole. A tree or a car. I don't know."

"It was that thing."

"I don't think so." Whatever it was felt hard, rooted in place. "There's a lot of stuff in the water."

"I know there is. I've seen it."

Thea flipped onto her haunches, wobbling the raft in uncomfortable ways. Her fingers gripped the edge of the metal. They floated along, trailing blood for whatever monsters lurked underneath.

She stayed that way for a while, until her eyes disappeared into thought. "Why did you marry him?" Thea released the edge, pulling her palms close to her chest. "I never thought you'd marry anyone."

"It made sense."

"That's bullshit. You know that's bullshit."

"What does it matter?" She didn't mean to snap—she wasn't even angry, just annoyed. The question threw her off guard, partly because she thought she'd already answered it, partly because when Thea asked, she couldn't come up with any sort of response.

"I know why," Thea said.

"Yeah?" She probably thought it was because of her, because everything was always about her.

"To escape."

"Escape what?"

Thea looked away.

Bingo. "I've done a lousy job of it, if that's the case." She had it wrong, though. Close, but wrong. Doris didn't want to escape— she wanted to disappear. What Thea could never understand was that Doris could never escape *her*. It wasn't Thea's fault or her doing—Doris did it to herself. The tether that tied them was too strong—they could light each end ablaze and still not sever it in a lifetime.

Sometimes Doris hated Thea for it, but mostly she hated herself more.

Their raft dipped suddenly, tossing them down a rapid that nearly capsized them. The unbroken parts of her weren't quick enough or strong enough to keep her body steady, and she'd have flown off if not for Thea throwing all her weight on top of her. She didn't budge even after the water settled.

"You can get off now," Doris said.

"What was that?"

Doris tried to push her off. "The water is crazy. That's all."

"Did you not see what I saw? You were there."

"I saw *something*, but it doesn't mean that everything is *something*. You've got to calm down."

"Jesus, whatever." Thea waved her sister away, as if there were anywhere to go.

Doris dropped her fingers into the water. It was so cold. An ache ran up her body. Scanning the water, she searched for any indication of the *thing*. She tried to pretend that she wasn't even sure what it was; everything she'd ever known had congealed into a brown wall of water anyway. God only knows what it dragged with it.

"Is this fun to you or something?" Thea spat dart-like accusations with precision.

Doris waved Thea away in kind. "I'm just loving life, sister."

"I'm not crazy."

"I never said you were."

"You always do this. Shit on anything I say, just because I'm the one saying it."

Doris was tired and all the way done with this nonsense. "You caught me. I've just been rubbing my hands together in the dark. Just waiting for you to fall so I could be the first one to stomp on you while you're down."

"Fuck—," Thea said, whatever she really meant to say catching in her throat. Thankfully, she didn't finish the thought.

Clothes clinging to her skin, Doris could see every ripple of Thea's spine. Her oversized sweatshirt circled her body like loose skin—she was too thin, probably starved. Closer to death than any flood could bring her.

Thea spoke under her breath, her chest shuddering as she did.

"I can't hear you," Doris said.

"Why do you always have to be so fucking mean?"

The questions were nothing but a fuse, and Doris was fit to explode. Years of damming up everything that made her human had taken its toll. To Thea, she was mean. To herself, she'd been screaming into an empty room for years.

And still, the one person she'd hoped and prayed and expected to understand, didn't. What was there to do about it now?

So she covered her eyes with her arm and said nothing. Thea kept to her side. They no longer touched.

———

Thea stared into the distance. A wall of water surrounded them. It bellowed from the sky and bubbled from the ground. The city spun into itself, consumed and ravaged, the sisters clanging against it on their metal raft. It all happened so quickly—Thea assumed by now they'd have been upended by something. Perhaps smashed into building, knocked off by thrashing debris, capsized and done for. Yet they carried on in a surreal drift. Or maybe it just seemed like they did. Her head was slow, seeming to react a beat or two behind her brain. She stared at the water for what seemed like days but could not have been more than minutes. Or maybe it was hours? Or days? She really couldn't tell outside of the incoming dark.

It was growing darker by the moment. It couldn't have been days. The first night had yet to begin.

The sheet metal wobbled as she jerked. Doris lay motionless next to her, a hand dangling over the edge. The flow of fresh blood had slowed, and what remained had coagulated underneath their bodies.

How the fuck had she managed to fall asleep again in all this rain? She was worse off than when she'd gone under.

Where were they? How far had they floated? The storm hadn't stopped, still seething and hurling atmosphere at them, but it was dark—so dark that she'd forgotten what the word meant. Dark before had still meant streetlights and televisions, glowing glass doors of the Circle K, the bright fluorescents of the gas station at the Union Avenue intersection. It had meant voices and people and whirring noises, electricity and static, but this dark was absolute. Nothing but occasional lightning and her sister's breathing to keep her centered.

Every whistle and swish and plinking patter of rain against water was magnified. The flood world smelled like wet wood, obliterating the comforting sheen of gasoline and car exhaust familiar to her. This space had now been reclaimed.

So when something bobbed up and down in the water a short distance behind her, Thea wheeled around to greet it, popping bones lethargic from rest and exhaustion.

"Doris," she whispered.

Bloop. The sound of *something* plunking itself under the water. It was here.

"Wake up, Doris."

Her lungs were fit to shout, but she thought better of it. She didn't want it to hear her fear, whatever it was. She wanted to shake her sister awake, but then again, what good would that do? Doris wasn't afraid of it. In fact, she seemed downright entranced by it, so she was safer asleep than awake. Conscious, she might just dive in after it.

Thea didn't hear much else for a while, just the normal noise of wreckage floating about in the flood. Their thin raft collided with some of it—mostly sticks and splinters of larger things, then something even larger upended one end of their raft, speared on the corner. It was a body, a man, bloated and snagged by the collar of his shirt. Thea kicked at it until it dislodged, wanting to get up and run to get away from it. An older man, probably just reading the paper and eating a sandwich or watching basketball, maybe thinking about retiring, and whoosh, out he goes into the water, filled up from the inside out with brown mud. Only to be kicked in the jaw by an itchy tweaker who'd managed to survive against all logic and sense of propriety.

Loosed, she watched him flutter away in a tailspin, up and down, under the water, then back up again, until he was a vague lump almost out of sight. He went down again, and this time never returned to the surface.

Thea searched for him, panicking, dread threatening to sink her entirely. It was out there, and it had taken that man's body and stolen it and it was out there waiting to take them too, and then—*bloop*—behind her. There the body was, simply moved a bit.

But it wasn't a bit. It was at least twenty or thirty feet in a matter of seconds. There, then gone, then back again, and it wouldn't leave them alone.

"Fuck you," she said, her voice torn and struggling. "Fuck off. Go away. Fuck you!"

Each word built off the one before it. Before she could stop herself, she was screaming at the water, everything spilling out. "Fuck off! Just go away! Fuck you fuck you fuck you!"

Only once Thea started pounding at the water did Doris jolt awake. Thea saw her pull her hands to her chest as if bitten, but still Thea smacked and screamed and thrashed at the water.

"GO THE FUCK AWAY!"

Doris craned her head to see her sister, just watching it all pour out. Thea thought she might puke but didn't. As if she didn't have enough shit, enough everything, just her luck—there were monsters here, too. As if the water wasn't dangerous enough on its own.

Screaming curses, screaming commands, screaming for the sake of screaming until she felt a clammy hand on her exposed shoulder and knew it was time to stop.

"There is something out there, Doris. I'm telling you. And it's big."

Doris tightened against her sister. "And if it wants us, it wants us."

"No." Thea shrugged her off. "Fuck that noise. That's not how this happens. I'll be damned if I let that disgusting thing so much as look at me."

Doris placed her hands over her stomach. "How do you plan to avoid that? It's probably looking at you as we speak." Fingers entwined, she rolled her argument around as if no more than a generic pleasantry. *Oh, you must try the shortbread crackers. I've got a new tea blend that's so relaxing. How is the family? The kids? Oh, and exactly how do you expect to slay the gigantic sea monster?*

"I'm not going to roll over and take it up the ass. It can fucking try me."

"You with all your prideful might. It'll sink you before you get a toe in the water."

"How do you know? You some kind of monster expert?" Her eyes darted away immediately after saying it.

Doris clenched her jaw, but otherwise let the slight pass without comment.

"If it's as big as you say it is, and it's stalking us, for Christ's sake, what the hell are you going to do about it stuck on a piece of sheet metal with me?"

"I don't know, but I'm not gonna jump into its mouth."

Doris stared sideways at her. "And I will?"

"You ever stop to think that my many acts of rebellion aren't always about you?"

"That's not what I meant."

Thea shrugged. "It's what you said. *And I will?* Just jump in, for all I fucking care."

Hefting herself onto her elbows, Doris sniffed the air, hoping to seem indifferent. "Do we have to do this now?"

"All I said was that I wasn't going to die without a fight. You seem to think that's just a *crazy* idea. I don't know what to tell you." Thea's hands jazzed out as she spoke.

"That's not what I said. That's not what I meant." She turned up toward the sky again, closing her eyes to the steady pound of rain.

"Oh, I know what you meant just fine."

"Oh, yeah? What's that?" Her sentence drawled on an extra syllable.

Thea pulled her shin close and tied her loose shoelaces. "You don't think I can survive. At least, not on my own."

"Bullshit." She laughed because wasn't this some nonsense? But then she turned her cheek.

Silence lay over them. There wasn't much else to say. Doris folded into herself, her feet still dangled in the water. Thea tried to yank them up, but Doris snapped at her to keep her hands off her. Thea hadn't liked that much, bubbling over with the urge to protest—*But that thing, you'll get cold, they'll fall off*—but decided against it. Every word with her sister was like a snake bite anyway.

"What was that?" Thea said.

And that's when the sheet metal lifted—was thrown—at one end, and sister toppled on top of sister as both of them rolled into the water in a tangle of bruised limbs and confusion. Water shot up her nostrils and down her throat, and she choked. The pressure of Doris's body lifted—her sister was gone. Up, down, everything was dark. She couldn't find the surface. Her arms struck at the water as she went down and down.

The noise was the worst, like glass crushed between teeth, like broken whale songs. It was the sound her ears made to fill the silence, but loud as a jet engine. The noise filled her as quick as the water until all she wanted was to be free of it. She'd do anything she had to do to get away from it—rip a hole in her skin, drown, anything.

Just when she thought she was done, just as the last bit of air slunk free of her lungs, she surfaced. Gagging and choking and screaming, she surfaced. She called out to the sister she couldn't see.

Doris was gone.

———

Air. She couldn't breathe. Pressure mounted in her skull, bulging at her sinuses. She just kept sinking. Bodies were buoyant, filled with all sorts of gases. Shouldn't she be floating by now? Was Thea up there calling for her as she sank and sank and kept sinking?

Sinking and sinking . . . This was where she was supposed to be, down here. Down in the dark.

There wasn't any light, but she could breathe again. Could have been an air pocket or the surface or God knew what, but retching and gasping was all she could do. What she could feel of her spine lit up like a zipper up and down her back. If this was dying, it sure as fuck wasn't calm, it wasn't peaceful, and nothing flashed before her eyes. It was dark and wet, and she was scared. She couldn't hear that she'd been screaming. She couldn't tell that she had surfaced. Her sinking had been floating, her head was upside down, her throat felt like fire, and snot spewed out of her nose.

Then she opened her eyes.

The metal was gone. Thea was gone. "Thea!" Her voice cracked. Waves lapped into her mouth until she choked, calling again and again to her sister. She fought the flood to keep herself above water, but her arms and her body were so weary. She wanted to sleep and forget about it. Fuck, she just wanted a real nap.

A call from somewhere. Her name.

"Thea, where are you?" Doris gagged on mud. The wounds on her torso ripped open again. She was losing it. "Thea!"

A garbled shout in return. Panicked. Repeatedly until Doris caught all the words: "It's following me."

Out of ideas—she couldn't swim; she could barely stay above surface—she returned the chatter. "Follow my voice. Follow my voice. Come here, follow my voice." She dipped under the water for a rest, then pushed herself up again. "Follow my voice!"

Each rotation took longer, more labored, her voice softened with fatigue. "Follow my voice!"

Doris couldn't hear her anymore. She screamed, and her frantic paddling got closer, but Thea was quiet now.

Up, down. Up, down. Climbing an invisible ladder. Silent. Eyes flashing. Drowning.

And she felt all right.

CHAPTER EIGHT
THE AFTER

THEA'S GLANCE GLIDED over the puckered metal of the towel rack. Clutching green cotton under her chin, she dried her face. Cold water didn't do much for the purple bags under her eyes or their bloodshot centers, but it was enough to perk her up a bit to fake it. The din of the party downstairs surged and dimmed— hoots and yells to hushed silence. She squatted in the bathtub, not wanting to deal with any of it, wishing she could fall asleep right then and there and be left alone for a single fucking night.

She was dead tired, the kind of tired that infected the bone, but she couldn't pinpoint why. Probably hung over, but she couldn't quite remember. Probably because she was hung over. There was water all over the floor.

This had happened before, and all she needed was a little time to sort herself out. Her brain powered on a bit more slowly after a rough night. By the time she got downstairs, most everything should have clicked into place.

One voice distinguished itself over the rest. It was a man's voice that Thea didn't recognize. Whoever he was, he had captivated the room. Some woman wheezed her emphysema laugh over and over, the pain of the effort crawling up the ceramic steps, snaking under the crack in the door like a gas leak. She could hide in the bathroom all night, and the party would still find her, so she'd better put herself together and get it over with.

Resigned to the task, she pulled herself up and started throwing open the drawers in the vanity. Combs and brushes, mirrors and a hair straightener, lip gloss and all sorts of girly shit clattered together, and she rummaged through them in search of her concealer stick, eventually finding it on the floor behind the toilet. The makeup crumpled against her skin, and she smoothed it with a rough finger. Long past its expiration date, it was the only thing keeping up appearances these days. Every time she used it, she thought, *I'll get a new one tomorrow*. But she always seemed to forget by the time tomorrow arrived.

No amount of cover-up or mouthwash could remove the stench of her hangover, but even a disheveled appearance would raise fewer questions than no appearance at all. Honestly, she wasn't even sure what the party was for. Wait—shouldn't she know? Pausing with her hands palming the marble counter, she mucked through her memories in search of whatever the fuck she was doing here, but it didn't come. She didn't even remember walking into the bathroom, for that matter.

That was probably a very bad sign. Oh well. It'd come to her eventually, whatever it was.

Smoothing her shirt, she sucked in her stomach, rolled back her shoulders, and hoped her queasy gut stayed put. Then she opened the door.

The hallway revealed a disappointed look from the face of her sister, who had been standing outside the bathroom, waiting.

Surprising—Thea would have expected Doris's presence to curl smoke-like under the door. "Hello, sister."

"You're up," Doris said. She couldn't even fake the pleasantries.

"Do my bathroom habits interest you?"

Doris peered over Thea's shoulder, as if to catch her with a secret lover hiding behind the towel rack. "Just waiting my turn."

"Pardon me. Were the other two toilets in the house unacceptable to Her Majesty?" But whatever Thea lobbed at her, it slid off her cold façade with ease. If she'd even heard her at all.

"You done?"

"Help yourself."

Doris provided a wide berth, then separated them once again with a closed door, leaving Thea to her own devices in the hallway.

The air smelled of fire and cheap cologne. Someone laughed again, that same loud man whom she already couldn't stand. There was a tremble in his voice of a man trying too hard. That same shaky faux confidence that marked every one of Doris's man-toys she'd deemed worthy enough to bring around. She might as well pee on them, though Thea doubted that her sister really gave a shit if they wandered, as long as they did whatever it was that she needed them to do first. And for all Thea's pondering, she never could figure out what that was. Doris was the last person she expected to tolerate the emotional neediness of another human. It just wasn't her.

Arriving to the party was like waking up in a strange bed and not remembering how you got there, but instead of a bed it was a party and everyone was staring at you as if your eyeballs were melting and they didn't care about your eyeballs so much as the drippy eyeball stains you were leaving all over the floor.

An urgency crept into her gut, winding up to her chest. She was missing something, forgetting something, but what?

A cluster of neighbors and Ma's friends—so total strangers as far as Thea was concerned—huddled around the loud man, drinking him in like the prized possession he must have been to have been invited in the first place. The few other men in attendance remained congregated in the back, where they could burn shit and pretend their testicles weren't still in the house, lost somewhere in their wives' purses.

A firm hand dropped onto her shoulder. "You look ill."

"Thanks for your concern."

"You were up there for twenty minutes."

Jesus fuck, did she need a smoke. Something was off. The fireplace was roaring but it was so cold inside. She should have smoked with the bathroom fan on. Ma wouldn't have said anything with all these people here. It murdered Ma's sense of propriety to have such a young daughter that smoked those cancer sticks. Just twenty years old, and look at those lines around her mouth, look how brittle and dry her hair was, *just look at her, Helen*.

Thea didn't actually know any of Ma's current friends' names, but Helen was a good moniker for the kind of lady Ma dragged home at the end of her social grappling hook.

Like a breeze that shouldn't exist indoors, Doris slipped down the stairs, head turned toward the crowd. Her presence distracted Ma enough that Thea could slip from her grasp and flee into the kitchen.

Their mother descended on Doris, sweeping her eldest daughter into the crook of her arm with a grin. New Guy— whoever he was—had to reach out and snatch her away. Doris accepted his hand.

Thea filled a tall glass with ice from the fridge ice machine, dumped it out in the sink, and filled it again.

"There's ice in the cooler, dear," Ma said without looking.

"I know."

The drinks were lined up along the kitchen island, and she thumbed through the plastic jugs of soda and punch, until she finally settled on the beer. Nothing but Coors. At least it was better than Bud Light.

She never did end up needing that ice.

Beer in hand, she drifted to the nucleus of the party. Time to observe the fresh meat.

Mid-story, New Guy was spinning a yarn about falling on his ass while skateboarding when he was a teen. Yak yak yak. Same old shit. He was handsome enough, same chiseled jaw and haircut straight out of the Marines that Doris seemed to like so much, but Thea quickly grew bored of his self-deprecating tales. It was never the men that captivated her as much as the way her sister swung them about like jewelry. She wound her arm through his; she smiled; she nodded. She did all the things a good girlfriend should do—an enamored, beautiful, perfect girlfriend. And yet Thea could fit a fucking boot through the space she maintained between their bodies.

She orbited her sister and New Guy—the stars of the party, whatever the fuck it was for. Probably just to celebrate the fact that Doris had graced them all with her presence. Doris showed up, thinking she was just going to introduce this new guy to the folks, and the second her regal feet touched the foyer, their mother rang the entire fucking neighborhood. My God, everybody! She's here! Hark, oh hark, ring the steeple bells.

But Ma was stupid, because all that fanfare did was back Doris into a corner. It made her edgy and sharp and sullen. Thea skirted through the people unnoticed, the same family as Doris—same born-again uncle, same noxious auntie, same neighbors across the street who'd watched her grow up. The neighbors that had hand-painted Christmas ornaments for them every year, but it didn't matter how many ornaments had her name glued onto them. Thea skipped over the top of the family like a rocket. Everyone glared—oh, they looked at her, all right—but their attention fizzled out just as quickly. They darted away from her as if she was about to burst into flames. She might. Maybe she already had, and everyone could see it but her. *Look at that girl, waltzing through the chicken skewer buffet as if she's not shooting sparks everywhere.* Thea's head had been soaked in a fog lately. Perhaps they all knew something she did not.

But her mother didn't seem to notice. The tilt of the room was off, but Thea couldn't quite place it. She wished Doris would just leave. Then the party would collapse, and Thea could escape.

Doris was like gravity—everything spiraled out of control without her around.

Thea was itchy for some nicotine. Water dripped somewhere she couldn't place, and the noise of it agitated her beyond measure.

Dad nodded at her as she escaped to the side yard to smoke. It was a nice place—dark and hidden, and she had a lawnmower and an old garden hose to keep her company. The exterior light had gone out last year, and to his credit, Dad kept it broken despite Ma's nagging. Or Thea liked to think he did.

If not for the treacherous orange end of her cigarette, no one would ever have known she was there. So when she heard the crunch of approaching footsteps in the gravel, she knew it was someone looking for her.

"Mind if I join you?" said the man. Doris's man.

"Are you following me?"

"Forgot my lighter." The shadow of a cigarette bobbed between his lips.

"And you follow strange women in the dark on the off chance they got one?"

Though she couldn't see too well, she could feel the white of his teeth aimed at her.

"Your sister has told me a lot about you."

Thea extended her lighter. "That so?"

"Sure."

Thea laughed. He was a terrible liar, but she wasn't going to tell him that.

"I'm cutting back," he said.

"Why?"

"They say they're bad for you, but I say that no one who's ever been a smoker would say something so stupid."

Even in the dark, she covered her smile, not wanting him to know he created it. "Seems to be going well in there."

"They're easy." New Guy dropped his ash into the rock and coughed. Cigarettes really were awesome.

"Unlike Doris."

"So you say."

This time she laughed for real and not in the kind way. She just loved the "you don't know her like I do" talk from new flings. As if their dick tapped into some top-secret emotional reservoir.

"She's going to eat you alive," she said.

He glared at her, cigarette pinned between his lips. "What fun is an easy life?"

She could have thrown up right there if not for the cigarette keeping her mouth busy. "Your funeral. Don't come crying to me when she spreads your ribs with her fingernails."

Water sloshed around her feet, gathering at a rate that should alarm her, but this guy was fucking bugging her. The water could wait.

"Goddamn, you two really are alike."

Thea crushed her cigarette and immediately lit another. Ash dropped into the sloping rivulets forming on the side yard. "So, she *has* spoken of me."

"You talk like the entire world is nothing but sharp teeth."

"Well, shit." She sucked in half the new cigarette in a single drag. "Maybe we are onto something."

"You're both obsessed with monsters."

"And what would you know about monsters?" The response was immediate and defensive. What did this motherfucker know about anything? What right did he have to even bring it up? He corners her in the dark and starts prying at her mind like he owns real estate there or some shit, and what—is she supposed to just be happy that anybody cared enough to ask?

New Guy snuffed his cigarette underneath his shoe and started to say something but stopped.

"What's your deal anyway?" Thea asked. "It's not like you're marrying her or something." Water now soaked both their feet. They ought to go inside soon, before this really got out of hand.

And finally, he had nothing to say. The party spun into sudden clarity. The punch and the beer and the people—people everywhere—and the fascination with New Guy. The way Doris wound herself around him.

"Well, aren't I dumb? And me without a gift. When's the happy day? Or I suppose that doesn't really matter, does it? Since it's you telling me all this in a dark corner rather than my lovely sister."

"To be fair, there was a party."

Any other time, she might have laughed, but not now. At this moment, indignation overrode her common sense. Was she the last to know? Or had she just not been listening? Not that this was ever important, so long as she showed up and followed the rules. Like Doris. Always like Doris, yet always not.

"I suppose it's appropriate that I know my future brother's name."

"James." Thankfully, he didn't bother to offer a handshake.

James was a fool. He would always be a fool. Frankly, she'd thought better of Doris before having met him. The water was up to his waist now, and he didn't even notice. Just kept smoking his stupid cigarette.

"I believe this is my cue." She had to swim. Time to swim. The flood was coming.

He didn't try to stop her as she escaped through the side gate, though she thought she heard him whisper some dumb shit like, "Nice to meet you, Thea."

Nice to meet you, brother.

Then the water washed him away, cigarette and all.

———

Sestra awoke with her nails pressed into the floor, trying to stave off the flood of her dream. It had been so vivid. So real. She could still smell the smoke from those cigarettes. The memory of James's voice clung to her, blotting out anything else.

Her sister was there. She could have reached out and touched her. She could have grabbed her by the shoulders and screamed at her. *You don't know what's coming. Run! Go somewhere safe. Somewhere far.* But she didn't, and Doris was still dead.

That feeling of wrongness had carried over.

It seemed like nothing at first, just a bad feeling in the back of her head, like the *zing* of a knife being pulled from the knife block. It was dark and it was late. Rob's snoring hummed behind her from where he sat, rested against the wall, sleeping upright as always, despite the extra space.

What was wrong? She knew this feeling, had known it all her life. By now she'd learned to trust it. What was wrong?

The floor hatch lay ajar, propped open on its spring-loaded hinges. The boy was gone.

"Fuck," she said, and sprang to her feet. "Fuck."

Rob stopped snoring but did not open his eyes.

Sestra had tried for a week to get the kid to do anything beyond following her around. A boy-shaped growth had developed on her side, wrapping around her torso where his arms had clamped on and not let go. His constant watching was unnerving—she couldn't tell if he was terrified and looking for comfort or plotting her murder. Either way, one of them was shit out of luck.

But now he was gone, and Sestra found the boy's sudden absence far more upsetting than his clinginess. It took only a moment to understand why.

After a quick scan of the dark cabin, she bolted up the steps and onto the moon-stained deck.

She said, aloud and for herself, "Where are you, boy?"

Water sloshed up the sides of the boat—*thu-thunk swish, thu-thunk swish.* The night was heavy with brine, and it coated her skin like ropy tentacles. It stung her eyes until they watered. What was wrong? What the fuck was wrong here?

"Kid?"

She found him at the back of the boat, balancing on the rail, his top half staring at the black water below. Just a thin, waif-like shadow of a creature that used to be a child.

"Get down from there, kid," she said. Her voice broke like a pubescent boy's as she spoke the words. "Mijo. Vámonos. Now."

The few phrases he'd managed to utter in her presence had been in Spanish, and it was only through the grace of introductory Spanish class in high school that she had any words at all to use on him. Vámonos. Rápido. Me llamo Sestra. ¿Donde está la biblioteca?

But the kid ignored her as he always did, and his trance-like stare at the water unnerved her more than it should have. Logic tried to explain away her fear—he hadn't moved until now, in the dark, alone. Did he do this every night? Had she truly been that oblivious? Did she really have so little grasp on this child, boxed up in the floor, that she'd had no idea he was sneaking out every night?

But that's not what unnerved her.

What was he looking at? That was what propelled tremors down her arms. That was what made her legs refuse to cooperate with her brain.

"What are you looking at, kid?"

Thu-thunk swish. Thu-thunk swish. Thu-thunk thu-thunk thu-thunk thunk thunk thunk.

The water changed, disturbed, because there was something in it.

"Kid!" she said—screamed it, actually. His feet tottered on the rail.

Fury, terror—a slew of confused emotions corralled her senses, and sprinting for the boy, she caught him by a heel as he tipped his weight over the top of the rail.

"Fuck you, fuck you, fuck off, you sonofabitch!" Angry words poured out of her, uncontrolled, not stopping until she had the kid pinned on the deck underneath her knees.

She expected fear out of him—big confused eyes, watery and terrified—but instead, he looked past her as if in a trance. "Conmigo," he said. "Conmigo."

"What are you saying?" she said, gripping him until the flesh of his arms turned white.

His gaze snapped away from the sky and onto hers.

Rob appeared in front of her, splitting his disapproval between her and the boy.

"He was looking at something," she said. "I didn't see what."

Crossing his arms, Rob didn't speak.

"Just . . ." Sestra fought to catch her breath and her nerves. "Just take him downstairs."

"Ses . . ."

"Take him the fuck downstairs!"

Rob kept his attention on her a moment longer before motioning to the kid. Helping him up, he thrust the boy toward Sestra. "You take him."

Then he disappeared again, escaping into the engine room.

Upset water rapped against the boat. "Go," she said. "Go go go vámonos, Mijo. Vámonos."

She was leading the boy by the shoulders across the deck, nearing the stairs, when the boat lunged. It bellowed as if the earth split in half and they were being sucked into its molten center. White, foamy water broke across the deck, and the boy skidded out of reach. His eyes were big now, all white and full of fear. This time he caught himself before being flung overboard.

Sestra toppled forward, splayed on her belly. The water whipped her skin.

Then it was done.

Just the one wave.

A hand thrust its way out of the engine room, followed by

another gripping a long pipe, followed shortly by Rob's face and body. After a militaristic survey of her and the boy's condition, he took off toward the back of the boat.

The bite on her ankle stung from the salt, but otherwise she felt okay. The boy scrambled along the slippery deck on his hands and knees, his spindly limbs like a spider, scrambling toward Sestra, then beyond her into the cabin, not stopping until the floor hatch slammed down with a splintering force.

The boat resumed its usual rhythm, and if not for the wet deck, she might not have guessed anything was wrong.

For all her run-ins with posies, she'd never actually seen one. Just bits of it, a smear just under the surface. But it was big and was always in more than just one place. She and Rob could watch in opposite directions and see it at the same time. That gluttonous marine-blubber skin, iridescent gray—could be a whale. Maybe a dolphin. Fuck, a shark even. A shark was fine. But then it was there and here and there and everywhere, and it was clear that it was no damn shark or whale.

That's what scared her the most. Eyeballs alone bigger than her own head, and yet it eluded her so easily. It was faceless and pervasive, and she didn't know when or why it would come or when or why it would leave.

"Do you see it?" Rob said from somewhere else.

Thu–thunk swish.

"No."

Somehow manifesting just behind her ear, Rob said, "Maybe it left?" The pipe dove pointy end down into the deck. His knuckles were white around the other end.

"It's still there. It could be under the boat."

Under the boat, just a few planks of rotting wood between the boy and the monster he was hiding from.

Grabbing the pipe again, Rob paced the boat. Circles and circles, staring at the water and grunting.

"What are you going to do with that pipe anyway?" she asked.

"I'm going to kill it."

"With that?"

"You got anything better?"

"I'm not trying to kill it."

"What are you planning to do then?"

She didn't honestly know. "Watch it."

"Watch it kill you."

"What if I do?"

"Then why bother at all?" He stomped off toward whatever part of the boat Sestra did not occupy.

Sestra had little plans to move anyway, so his maneuvering was all for naught, though sometimes the act itself was all the catharsis a person needed.

Why bother at all? What he meant was why didn't she just kill herself? She wondered that sometimes. Why keep fighting? Fighting was exhausting, and she was so tired.

And then she'd think about those slimy-skinned monsters waiting for her down there, and she'd rather be anywhere but with them. She'd die alone, sun-scorched and dehydrated on an old tire, before giving those things the satisfaction of taking her.

A slap against the surface of the water just to her left sent her spilling her way toward the sound—a cat on ice, not a sliver of grace left within her. Rob beat her there, but whatever had made the noise had disappeared.

"It's toying with us," Rob said. He dug his palm around the blunt end of the pipe, leaving dark smears of blood behind.

Sestra nodded. "I think it is."

"Filth," he said. "Devil thing."

It wasn't a devil. It was mean, but it wasn't evil. Not even she would dare to venture into that minefield, though, not when Rob was shredding his hand without noticing.

"So, what do we do, Rob?"

His shoulders tightened, ready to explode, then sagged, defeated. "We wait. We watch."

"And if we see it?"

Rob was quiet for a moment. "Promise me, Ses, that you'll let me try to kill it. Even if I can't."

Sestra hunched over the rail. The water looked like paint. "Is that what you've been doing in the engine room?"

"Sometimes."

"Thinking?"

He nodded. "Too much thinking."

"Okay," she said. "Kill it if you want."

Rob stared alongside her, not moving. "One more thing."

Pushing herself off the rail, she instinctively pulled her hands to her chest, arms tucked and crossed.

"Watch yourself around that boy," he said. "He's not a toy."

She stayed awake that night. No reason to check on the boy. If he ever left at all after this, she'd be surprised. It had almost happened again. Almost. This time she'd stopped him before he'd been taken. There'd been too many already, and the only thing they'd all had in common was that look in their eyes right before it happened, so disturbingly calm.

It bothered Sestra because she'd never in her life felt so calm, as if the ones who were taken knew something about the water foreign to her, beyond her. She felt strange emotions like envy. These deranged people leaning overboard, unafraid of the danger or of dying, and she was actually envious of them. Why them and not her? Even in this world where everyone had died or was dying, where she and Rob and a few bloated bodies were all that seemed to exist, there was still something more to which she wasn't privy, that she didn't know.

She stayed awake, thinking about what she might have done had Rob not awoken. Would she have kept the boy under her knees, interrogated him? Would she have thrown him overboard if that's what he wanted so badly? She might have, and this churned her insides to think about. She might have simply beat him until there wasn't anything alive left to beat. *Why you why you why you? Why do I care? If you care so little about living, why are you here? Why now, after all this time? After all this hope? After all this terror and perseverance?*

Why did she care?

And every time that fear of herself welled up to unbearable amounts, she'd focus on the steadying waves and Rob's methodical marching in search of the enemy. Eyes closed, she knew the sound of the impending dawn. The ocean quieted then, almost silent, nothing more than a breeze in the trees. Sestra could hear her old life in the dawn. It was the only time her memories allowed it, only when the waves hushed.

She dozed off sporadically, with eyes-open alertness, laying across the deck and facing the sea. It was one of those sleeps that rolled across her vision like an old film reel. Water evaporated into a thin crystal film of salt left on the wood deck like a Rorschach ink blot. Her stringy strands of hair crunched with more salt, audibly peeling away from the floor as she sat upright. The sun was teasing, invisible but making the black night sky turn purple with its presence.

The posy had left sometime within an hour of its appearance. The waves changed once it finally fled, nothing more to lap against. It was big; she thought it must have been huge. The girth of it had encapsulated their stupid little boat. She'd hadn't seen it all laid out, but she didn't have to. Posies were never small. They were never seen in totality, but certainly never small.

Stomach grumbling, head pounding, and cotton-mouthed, Sestra descended into the cabin, favoring her unbitten leg. The wound still stung from the water, inflamed and angry. Infection would be bad, as if there was anything to do about it now.

She wasn't sure what to expect with the boy, but him sitting cross-legged on top of the floor hatch door wasn't it. His back was erect, shoulders rolled back. He didn't seem at all terrified. Sestra paused at the bottom step.

He'd almost died, and now he sat there watching her like an entirely different person. Maybe he was.

"What are you doing?" she said, speaking English and forgetting for a moment that the boy did not.

Considering her words, the boy bent his head to one side and said, "¿Quién es?"

"Shit, kid. I don't remember Spanish class all that well."

"Shit?" He pointed at her.

"What? No. I'm Th—Sestra. I'm Sestra."

"Thestra?"

"No. Soy Sestra. Llamo a Sestra or something like that."

He smirked; innocence hidden behind his teeth. He thought she was stupid.

"Llamo Sestra," she said, then pointing at him. "You?"

The boy shook his head. "No."

Little fucker. "I just saved your life, you know."

"No."

"Why not? Por qué?"

"No."

She was beginning to think she liked him better under the floor. "Familia?"

"Se han ido."

Sestra had no idea what that meant.

"Madre?"

The boy shrugged, but his gaze receded. "Conmigo, mijo."

That was what he'd been saying last night. The word *mijo* struck a memory—he was talking about a child. Himself maybe? Or a sibling? The boy was clearly remembering something he'd prefer to forget.

What had happened to his parents? It hadn't crossed her

mind that whatever had happened to them might not have been recent. She and Rob could have been the first people he'd met in months—first people since the flood. How long had it been since he'd seen anything besides water and wood laminate and fucking monsters?

There used to be more people. At the time of the flood, she kept thinking, "This is it? This is all that made it?" And every day that followed had been a mix of hope at the prospect of finding civilization again and dread as they'd floated farther and farther between the remaining scraps of humanity. There had to be a secret government base somewhere. Someone had to have seen this coming. Where were the fucking doomsayers when you needed them? Someone had to have survived, bound together, and made an honest go of this garbage life.

But soon the dread had overwhelmed the hope, and then it had shriveled into itself and filled her full of a protective numbness. Eat, sleep, float, shit off the side of the boat, repeat.

"Mijo," she said to the kid. He shook his head. It wasn't his name, but it was something, at least. "I'm gonna call you that from now on."

"Donde está el monstruo?" Mijo asked.

Donde está—where is. Where is the monstruo?

She asked, "Monstruo?"

He locked his fingers together, prying them apart like a mouth. "Monstruo."

"Oh." Monster, he meant. "It's gone."

He copied her. "Monster."

"Posy."

"Poh-zee."

"Yeah."

He nodded. "Sí."

A shadow covered them both. "What's going on down here?" Rob hovered at the top of the steps, still clutching his pipe.

Sestra kept her eyes on Mijo. "He's talking."

Rob relaxed his grip, rubbing the exhaustion from his eyes. He leaned against the door frame. "I can see that."

"Maybe the near-death experience snapped him out of it, whatever it was."

He sniffed and wiped his nose with his fingers. "His whole life has been a near-death experience."

"He's, like, twelve years old. He remembers the before."

"That boy ain't twelve."

"Well, whatever. Ten. He remembers, anyway."

Rob snorted. "You think you've won him, do you? He's not a dog to lick your feet and make you feel good about yourself."

Only then did she strike her gaze away from Mijo, who impassively watched the exchange unfold. "Jesus, Rob, what the fuck you want me to do? Drown him? He's finally talking to me. You'd think that'd be good news."

"He's finally talking to *somebody*, Ses. Don't forget that."

"God damn it, just go kill something, will you?"

He left, but not without a complimentary, dissatisfied grunt.

"So," she said, returning her attention to the boy. "Food?"

Sestra sat cross-legged on the deck, the boy perched next to her. Both stared out at the water as it swelled and lurched over the sides. The sea had been unsettled lately, as if warding away demons or bad takeout, roiling in ever-present pain.

Even after all this time, deep ocean swells like these made Sestra nauseous.

"¿Qué?" she asked, gesturing to the endless ocean.

"Agua. El mar."

It was nature day. They'd already scoured the inside of the cabin, naming and explaining every one of the meager components inside. It passed the time. It kept them both busy learning shit and not thinking about dead family.

Rob had hardly shown himself to them in the past few weeks, preferring to sharpen tools in the cramped engine compartment or pluck at the fishing line at the stern. Food had been scarce in the days since the posy had revealed itself. Starvation loomed over them, beating away any other sensations. It wouldn't be so bad if not for a third mouth. Rob hadn't said it, but he thought it every time he side-eyed Mijo scrambling past him on the deck or peeking his head out of the floor hatch. Rob scrutinized the boy's every move, but still maintained his most critical gaze for Sestra. She wished he'd just say what he was thinking. His sideways looks were like rubbing shark skin the wrong way—they had teeth.

"Agua," Mijo said. "Azul."

"Blue," she said. "Azul."

She thought she heard a bird and looked around for it, but it wasn't a gull or a pelican or any other bird because they'd all died. Or she assumed they had. She hadn't seen one in months.

Looping her thumbs together, she flapped her hands like wings. "Bird."

"Pajaros."

He might have understood her, or he could've been saying *bat* or *butterfly* or *hands*. "Manos," she said, remembering the word for hands.

Mijo fidgeted and went to stand, but Sestra grabbed him by the ragged shirt and pulled him down again. "Where are you going?"

He didn't answer, because he couldn't. Maybe he didn't know, but Sestra was certain he wasn't going near the rails again by himself. She'd make damn sure of that.

"Okay, vámanos," she said. Mijo stood and glared over his shoulder at her as she followed him. Just as he settled on a spot, he'd glance at her, as if waiting for something. Then he'd be off again. They continued like this for minutes, circling, footfalls thudding hollow on the deck, frustrated creaks of the old wood snapping at them. Go, stop. Stop, go. Round and round until Mijo finally stopped for good.

As he stepped to the edge of the deck, Sestra again clawed her fingers into him, gripping his shoulder so hard his pointed bones jabbed into her palm. He yelped, but then fell back, conceding to her will.

Then he dropped his pants and shit right there on the deck.

Finishing, he drew up his pants and shrugged at her. *Now what, lady?*

And she laughed. It pained her abs to do so, but she laughed, more and harder and louder, and it was wonderful. The smell of his shit wrenched at her nostrils and was horrible, but still she couldn't stop.

Peeking topside from his underground lair, Rob piped obscenities from behind. "Oh, sweet hell," he said, then sank below once more.

"Go," Sestra said to the kid, whose expression cracked with confusion. "Go. I'll clean it up."

She listened to the rhythm of Mijo's feet as he plodded out of sight, the heavy *thop thop thop* of his bare feet stepping one after another on the well-worn track to his safe space below the floor.

Just her and a pile of feces and a problem to solve. Sestra couldn't help but feel comfortable, as if she'd been in this kind of predicament before. Hundreds of times, even.

"Are you telling me that kid ain't even potty trained?" Rob said. His voice was muffled by the things between them.

"It's fine," she said, because it was. With one side of her lucky shoe, she swiped the shit across the deck toward the rail, shaking it off the boat and into the sea.

She couldn't help but pause as she did, shit clinging to her like it always had. The sea behaved today. It glittered blue, rippling with the tug and pull of the tides. For a moment she could imagine that this was nothing more than a pleasure cruise. Just her and a few buddies spending an afternoon at sea before heading back to land for a nice meal and comfortable bed. Mijo's parents would be there, and he'd run to them, babbling about his day. He'd have seen some seagulls and maybe a stingray. It would have jumped out of the water as if it were flying. Rob would have told him that they often did that to shake off parasites clinging to their skin. He would have been careful not to mention that they also jumped like that to avoid predators. No one would have mentioned that to a little kid. He didn't need to imagine what sort of horrors lurked just under the surface. He was just a kid. No kid needed to think about stuff like that.

Except that Mijo did need to think about stuff like that. Every minute of every day. It pervaded everything they thought, said, and did.

Everything.

Sestra gazed at the sea, a chill creeping up her body. A posy could be anywhere. It could be here, right now, staring back at her and she'd never know. Not until it threw its tentacle upward and seized her.

There was a splash behind her, on the other side of the boat. Whether it was a confirmation or coincidence, she suddenly lacked the urge to check.

Let the fucker come and get her.

"It's fine," she said again, trying to forget the stench of shit as she returned to Mijo's side.

CHAPTER NINE
THE AFTER

It STARTED AS a cough—a deep rattle in her chest that spasmed into hacks. Sestra got it, and then she got better. Rob got it and recovered in equal measure. Then Mijo caught it, just as she'd expected, and days passed with everyone expecting him to improve, but he didn't. Then he did, and for a day, it seemed he was finally on the mend. He climbed out of the floor hatch even and joined her on the deck, and they watched Rob untangle some kelp out of the fishing line. She'd fallen asleep with ease that night, a knot unwinding as Mijo got stronger. Soon this would all be a bad memory.

Until a fresh coughing fit arose her from her slumber. She held him in her lap as blood from his lungs splattered onto the floor. She held him while Rob watched from above deck, whispering under his breath about things like *pneumonia* and *real sick* and *not good*.

But he would get better. This was bad, sure, but he would get better because he was a kid and kids were resilient. If it hadn't taken out a former addict and an old-boned curmudgeon, it didn't stand a chance against the blinding vitality of youth.

Clouds masked the sunrise. The boat rocked and dipped. Mijo slept through it, limply lolling about in the sway. Sestra braced his little body against every wave. The muscles in her back and thighs were on fire, but she would remain that way as long as necessary. He needed rest more than she needed comfort.

This happened sometimes—large ominous waves that threatened bad weather, then suddenly flatlined into glass. If she could have gone topside, she'd have seen the wall of melting black clouds just to the east. The air smelled of earth. It was the only time it smelled that way besides her dreams. It was as if the clouds were so strong, they sucked the swollen dirt right up from the bottom of the ocean. But still she didn't acknowledge the incoming torrent. Storms still scared her, and she didn't have time to be scared right now.

Unable to ignore the present situation any longer, Rob tramped down the stairs, one heavy foot at a time, and stopped just inside the doorway.

"You need to put him back in the floor."

Mijo's chest rose and fell only slightly, so rapid and shallow it mightn't have moved at all. Sestra sweat through her shirt as she clutched at him. He was warm, and it wasn't just her or the rising day. The heat came from his fever.

"I can't leave him in the floor. He's barely breathing."

"Storm's coming, and it's going to be big. You can't keep yourself safe when he's unconscious like that."

Sestra swatted sweat away from his hairline. "What if he needs help?"

"Your holding him is the worst damn place for him to be now."

"We can't just leave him in the dark. I can't do that."

"Then he can drown in good company."

She wanted to keep quiet, didn't want to wake Mijo or startle him, but just like that, she couldn't. "Why are you such an asshole all the time?"

He cocked his head to the side, about to loosen a year's worth of clogged frustration when the boat kicked to one side.

Rob tumbled forward, landing on his face. Both he and

Sestra stared at the stairs as if they expected something to come crawling down it.

"What the fuck was that?" she asked.

"Storm." His eyes were way too big to believe what he was saying.

Sestra pulled herself up, Mijo in her arms, just as they lurched again. The motion jerked her against the wall. The boat tipped. Mijo slammed on top of her like a sack of bones.

"Grab him!" She waved for Rob's attention, but it had grown dark and it was difficult to see his features. The floor vibrated with motion. Her stomach dropped the way it used to before she'd gotten used to the water.

Grunting, she rolled the boy off her and started snapping. "Rob. Rob! Hello?"

Something blocked the light. Then Rob was there.

"Damn it, I told you to put him in the floor."

"You told me a storm was coming."

Hoisting Mijo over a shoulder, he crawled toward the hatch. Sestra scrambled after him, helping him brace against the rocking. Through all of it, Mijo never once opened his eyes.

Light briefly scored the floor in front of them, then was swallowed up again as something big squirmed in front of it.

"Oh shit."

Mijo's body thumped into the hatch. Rob slammed the door shut. "Let's hope this holds."

Sestra rose, her gait unsteady, like that time she stole a skateboard and crashed into a bench.

She broke into a sprint up the stairs, Rob cursing after her.

"Girl, damn it, what the hell are you doing?"

But he was right after her—still a swift old bird when he wanted to be. He caught her by the ankle, and she slammed her chin on the top step as she fell.

"What the fuck?" She spat a piece of chipped tooth at him.

There wasn't much left of them anyway.

"You can't go up there, Ses."

She kicked at his hand. "Get off me!"

He made no attempt to hide his fear, the façade of unshakable machismo cracking like two-day-old makeup. "It's a posy."

"I know."

It took another kick, but his grip wasn't as tight. He released her, and before she could think twice about what she was doing, she emerged topside into a nest of monsters.

It was enough to make her stop breathing. She might have just up and suffocated if not for the jostle that buckled her knees. Down she went again, supplicant to the god that held her.

It sounded like a shitload of snakes slithering inside her head, except that it wasn't coming from her imagination, but the tentacles wrapping around the bow of the boat. They looped around it like a snake killing a rat. It took a few moments for her to understand that the groaning was coming from the shift of the boat and not the posy. She was afraid to move, yet mesmerized.

Somewhere below her, water slammed viciously against itself, though she couldn't see it from where she stood.

She should be able to see it. Where was the water?

There was movement behind her that instinct told her was Rob, but as it grazed against her back, it was obviously much bigger and stronger than him. Darting forward, she faced a wall of tentacle writhing in front of the door like a barricade. They were everywhere—behind, on top, on all sides of everything. Just heaps of gray rubber, so many that she couldn't even fathom the creature they belonged to.

The cabin was silent.

"Rob?" The words were faint—too dainty and delicate to be heard.

Where was the water?

There wasn't a place anywhere not touched by the posy. She

didn't know what it would do. It could heave her overboard. It could snatch her up. It could snap the boat in two and catch her as she sank.

It could have done any of those things by now, but it hadn't. She took a step. Aiming for a spot along the rail less congested with tentacles, she took another and another step. Nothing flinched. Nothing moved but her and the occasional flex of posy-muscle. If she didn't know better, she'd think the thing was growing tired of holding the boat like this, but she couldn't explain where that idea came from.

Step.

Two more.

Step.

As soon as she reached the rail, she immediately stepped back again, unable to believe what she was seeing.

Where the *fuck* was the water?

The sky opened, dropping itself onto the top of her head. It splattered against the boat. It filled the ocean that now raged a good twenty feet below her. The posy held the boat in the air, presenting them like an offering to something larger and meaner.

In shock, she froze there for she didn't know how long.

The posy slapped here and there against the boat, every movement sounding like a bad cold.

"It's holding us up." She wasn't sure if Rob could hear her, but she said it anyway. "It's holding us above the waves." As if physics itself had had a stroke, this thing held them up.

She didn't know what to do. It was everywhere and it trapped her topside with it, but otherwise ignored her. Like it wanted her to see it, to say to her, "Look, bitch. You see all I do for you?"

As if an affirmation, the boat jostled again, flinging Sestra to one side. Things thumped and crashed inside the cabin. The beast loosened its grip on one side, tilting them threateningly.

"No no no." The boat tipped more, and she slid across the

top. Just when she was sure she would fly overboard, the boat would settle. Each toss got her nearer to touching one of its tentacles, and each time she'd claw at the floor to avoid it. They continued this sparring match until she was sure it would toss her aside and be done with her. It couldn't—it shouldn't—be doing this on purpose, but it sure fucking felt like it was, and she was outmatched in every way.

Wood cracked and bolts rolled across the deck. This crappy vessel couldn't handle much more. The posy could set them down with the care of a new mother and still sink them. And it sure seemed intent to toy with her, in particular.

Thinking of Mijo and Rob, of the flood and soggy attics, she let the posy fling her once more. This time she didn't resist, landing hard in the knot of tentacles blocking the cabin.

It felt like rope and muscle. It felt slippery. It felt strong.

And she felt nothing.

She wasn't sure what she was expecting—some epiphany, a vision. Something to explain all this. She was so sure that it was trying to communicate with her that she was disappointed when it appeared to have nothing else to say. It could at least have the decency to strangle her or some shit.

She reached for it, grazing her fingertips against its smooth skin, which it allowed for a moment before pulling its long tendril away. Not that it seemed to mind much—the posy did not flinch, simply removed itself from her reach. Each time she picked a new spot, the posy would readjust itself, until she set about her curiosity with more purpose, picking and choosing which to touch and which to leave.

Well folks, this one's a structural tentacle, so it can't be removed. But we can fancy it up with some real nice sconces.

She didn't understand the game but felt sure they were in the middle of playing one. Somewhere beneath her, a man began to curse.

"What the fuck are you doing, woman?"

Sestra had never been more relieved to hear his shitty, condescending voice. "It's fucking with me."

"We're going down," he said.

"It's still holding us. It hasn't let go."

"I see water through the window."

Now that she thought about it, they *were* moving. She assumed her stomach lurching stemmed from the close proximity to a faceless creature that could crush her in a single flick. The frothy peaks of waves darted around her like a game of whack-a-mole.

"What do I do?"

Rob was quiet, then offered all that he had. "I don't know."

"Great. Thanks."

They couldn't have been in the air that long. Minutes maybe. Now it was just going to set them down as if nothing had happened. For what? Just to sink now instead of a few minutes ago.

Tentacles whipped themselves away from her back as the boat lowered closer to the water. Their swiftness threw her up, backside crashing down again in uncomfortable places.

The boat landing on the choppy surface stole her breath away like a punch to her sternum, and she flew feet-over-head into the cabin.

Rob appeared over her as she moaned in pain. "Foolish girl," would be all he'd say regarding the matter.

Caught in the ocean again, the boat throbbed in the waves, occasionally jerking in the crash. Rob went up to watch, to look for the posy probably, to be the first person to announce their inevitable death like a bitter Paul Revere. Sestra scooted toward the floor hatch. Shivering yet alert, Mijo whimpered as she lifted it up.

"Hey hey hey. *Shhh.* It's fine. You're okay." The heat of his fever penetrated to the bone, but he was awake. He was scared. He was listening.

"Kid," she said, too shaken to think in another language. "It's okay. It's okay."

Up and down again, she lost her grip and the hatch slammed shut. From inside, Mijo began to scream.

"Shit, kid, I'm sorry. Sorry sorry sorry." The moment she lifted it again, his hands darted toward her. She helped him out, bracing against the sway using the metal holes in the floor that used to support a table. Mijo curled into her lap and she held him, rubbing her fingers through his sticky hair.

The posy was still out there. She watched the windows, waiting for it to yank them down. Rob's heavy thumping reassured her that he was not only still alive but pissed off and confused as well. She was better suited for down here anyway.

It bothered her that she couldn't contain Mijo's trembling. She could hold him and whisper at him all sorts of shit about it being okay, and neither one of them would believe it. He had his ear pressed against her chest— he could hear how fast her heart was beating. Fear coursed between them like a parasite. They breathed it on each other. Inhaled it.

Fear was all any of them had in common anymore.

"My sister told me story once," she said. "Mi hermana, she told me about monsters when I was a lot littler than you. I don't even know if this is true or not—maybe I dreamed it—but I'm remembering it now and I'm fucking terrified so I'm going to tell it to you just so we have something to do. Okay?"

And to her surprise, Mijo nodded.

"Good. Okay." Sestra took a breath, suddenly afraid to continue. She hadn't spoken of her sister in a long time. It fucking killed her that she wished more than anything that she was still here.

"She used to read me stories. Every night I'd go into her room and she'd pull the same storybook out—I can't remember the title of it now—but they were fucked up. I remember them being scary as hell. But I liked them. Something perverse about the both of us, I guess. We read each of them so many times that sometimes I can still remember little bits of them, or, more the cadence of them. The words don't stick, but the rhythm of a story stuck somewhere in my brain like a song that sounds familiar, but you know you've never heard it before. One night, she didn't bring out the book like usual. Said she was going to tell me a new story. Shit, I had to have been a toddler—three or four years old—and I remember thinking that she was about to drop some heavy shit on me, and I'd better pay attention. Funny how it comes to you, decades later. She probably thought I forgot about it, and to be honest I *did* for a while, but . . ."

They rocked violently. Water dripped onto her head from a leak somewhere above them.

"Anyway, she starts on about this little girl that had run away. She was barefoot and cold and in her jammies and stuff, but she kept running. She made it down a couple streets and then it got really dark. It was cold and things were watching her and growling. The girl tried to hide but the things—the *thing*—found her anyway. My sister said that a monster came after the girl. She said it watched her. That it was always watching. She tried to run, and it followed her. She said it had a dozen hands and sharp teeth. That didn't scare me, though. Most of the shit she read to me was about nasty, evil things, and they always described the bad guys in detail. Trolls and witches and evil men, all with bad teeth and long fingernails and beards and shit. But my sister refused to tell me any more about this monster. Could have been one of those insert-personal-demons-here kind of thing, but I think it really scared her. And I'll tell you, seeing her so damn scared was the most frightening thing to ever happen to little me. I was a stupid kid."

She reasoned she was an even stupider adult.

"So, she tells me this, then tells me that the girl ran back home because she could hear her little sister crying. She made sure to run for a long time, to hide for a long time, just to make sure that the monster didn't see her. When she was as sure as she could be, she came home. The cops were there. They asked the girl where she'd been, but she refused to tell them. They wouldn't believe her anyway. They asked and asked until they became angry with her, but still she didn't tell. What the girl did do was keep quiet, move carefully, and plot. The girl learned what was really important and what wasn't. She learned that no matter how hard you try, your monsters always follow, so you'd better get that vagina good and tough and ready to fight. Well, she didn't exactly say that, but you know. That's when we started playing the monster game. Wow, I forgot all about that."

Sestra trailed off despite herself. While the sea around them raged and Rob marched, shit knocking against the hull like missiles, she'd forgotten that she'd been speaking aloud and retreated seamlessly into thought.

The bad memories and the good ones must have gotten all tangled up—she'd repressed them all. It frightened her now how easy it had been to forget herself.

Knotted together, they stayed below in silence. Even when the water leaked in, forming a film on the floor. Even as the storm smothered itself and the sky cracked a purple dawn. She held him, listening to his breathing.

She'd have thought the calm and Mijo's sleepy whimpers would have set her at ease, but something else pressurized within her chest. It felt sticky and thick like mucus. Like the time she got a bad chimichanga from a food truck. Indigestion ate at her from the inside out. Rage, but not really rage.

Closing her eyes, she saw black. With blinking, the black became clearer. Uneven and full of holes. Pebbles vibrated across the surface. It was split in two by broken white lines. It was asphalt and she was speeding across the top of it in her car. Her brain was a flat tire, just slapping at the road. Sparks flying all over the damn place while she tried to reach inside and pluck out a coherent thought, but there wasn't anything there to grab onto—

just a melted soup. It dripped out of her ears, out of her eyes. Her face was wet, and she couldn't see.

The hunk-of-shit car rattled as she floored it. Wherever she was going, she was going to get there fast. Going somewhere fast. Anywhere.

Sestra tried to put it all together. When did she get in the car? Why? What had she been doing just before? Why was she so upset? Nothing made sense except the road underneath her and pain her chest, sharp as glass.

She didn't feel the rumble at first. Fuck, she thought it was just her—damn nerves were shot to hell. But it grew. The car popped all over the place until she was pretty sure she wasn't even on the ground anymore.

There's a hole in your roof.

Road and road and road, and then instead of it being below her, it lurched upright.

Monster! Monster!

Rocks rained onto the hood of the car. The road rose like a titan shaking away a long slumber, pieces of it cracking with age and disuse. It pulled itself up, flipping her puny little car onto its back. Turning and flipping and rolling—she smelled smoke, a penny taste soaking into her tongue.

A cry emerged—one she didn't know she possessed. A wail so full of knives that the sound of it slashed at her body. The car was gone and face down on the asphalt. She screamed until exhaustion stole the breath from her.

Everything hurt, and something moved below her. It wriggled like worms in the dirt, but it was bigger than worms. The asphalt wasn't asphalt anymore. She was floating, and below her the monster ballooned in size, limbs lashing toward her.

She was sure it would get her—it moved like it wanted to, but every time one of its pieces got close, it slithered somewhere else. By the looks of it, the thing was holding on to something else, something bigger than her. Ropy monster tendrils lurched out as if grabbing something she couldn't see. And just when she thought she'd seen every part of the thing, another limb snuck out of its middle. One more and one more. It snaked around her, at home in the darkness like she never could be.

Then she was home again.

Ma's oak table was strewn with cards and matching silver envelopes. Thea sat across from her mother and Doris, stuffing, sealing, and stacking wedding invitations. Her fingers stung from the mixture of paper cuts and envelope glue. It'd been two damn hours of this. Water pooled underneath the table, soaking through her shoes.

Doris stretched her arms above her head.

"Yes," Ma said. "We should all take a quick break."

Thea slumped in her chair, the first time she'd been allowed to do so since her nine-in-the-morning, door-pounding wake-up. *Get up. You can't sleep all day.* Every word was laced with another. *You live here rent free. You don't have a job. You're not drunk, are you?* Fun things Ma loved to imply but loathed to say.

When Thea had tried to take a piss earlier, Ma had followed her, so she'd just decided to not move at all until given the official decree. While Doris surgeon-scrubbed her hands at the kitchen sink, their mother circled the table, stacking and restacking piles of completed invitations. Reaching Thea's pile, she paused, grabbed the topmost card, and pulled it to her nose.

"What's this?" she said, thumbing the corner of the envelope.

Thea pushed the chair away from the table. "An invitation, I presume."

"It's dirty."

"So?"

"You can't send this out."

Thea patted the cigarettes in her pocket. "It's just the envelope."

Ma's lips curled around her top teeth. "It's a wedding invitation, not a cable bill."

"Better inform the mailman to fetch his wedding tongs, then, for safe handling. Look—it comes off." Thea wiped the smudge away with her finger, dulling the pearlescent luster of the envelope. "It's just dust."

Letting out a disapproving sigh, Ma tore the tainted envelope in half—invitation and all.

"How is that productive?" Thea smashed a cigarette between her fingers within her pocket.

"Stop," Doris said, back against the sink basin. "Both of you."

"Why can't either of you take anything seriously? Just once. This is your wedding, Doris. Don't you care?"

"It is my wedding. And no, I don't care about a smudge on one of the envelopes."

"Then why are we even doing this?" Ma gesticulated above the mountain of paper, careful to avoid touching them.

Rolling her shoulders back, Doris leveled knives at their mother as she spoke. "If it were up to me, we'd have gone down to the courthouse long ago and been done with it."

Ma, incensed, waved the notion away like a foul odor. "You can't do that. James wouldn't have liked that. He's a proper groom, knows how to honor family."

Thea laughed at this, couldn't help herself. She instantly regretted it.

"What is so funny?" Ma said.

Peeling herself out of the chair, Thea shrugged. "Nothing."

Ma glared at her. Doris had yet to steal her gaze away from Ma. And Thea darted eyes between them both.

"Nothing," she said again, with less emphasis. "I have to pee again."

"You haven't had anything to drink all morning." Mother was swift as ever to pull the imaginary notepad off her breast.

9 a.m. – needed to be woken up. 9:30 a.m. – attempted to go to the bathroom. 11 a.m. – farted and pretended she hadn't. No drinks, no food. 11:30 a.m. – took a second, pungent, hungover piss.

"Would you like to come and watch?"

Ma sucked in her lips in the way she used to when the girls were younger, but the effect had waned over the years.

"I have to pee, Ma."

The women watched her go. The silence in the room felt like lead, and Thea had had enough of the scrutiny of both. Doris made sure to keep her eyes away, but that was worse. It was an effort to keep those fangs-for-eyes off her, and Thea felt every pang of pain as she forced them somewhere else.

Water splashed under her feet as she retreated to the bathroom.

She shouldn't have laughed, although she wasn't so much laughing at James as she was at her mother. Or was she? Thea wasn't sure. She hated them both. Couldn't escape them. The gavel drop of Doris's approval was final and total. James was here to stay. Why did she hate the idea of this so much?

Peeing was difficult because she didn't really have to, but after a show of flushing and running the water as if to wash her hands, she finally decided she couldn't waste any more time in there and had to leave.

The entire bottom floor was covered in water. Neither woman seemed to notice.

"It's fine, I guess," Ma said.

Thea turned the corner just in time to see her mother dusting an envelope in between her fingers. One from Doris's pile.

"It's just a little dust," their mother said, continuing.

Wrenching herself from the counter, Doris paced her way back to the table. "See?"

Both women sat with their backs lifted from the chair backs, erect as startled deer.

"I'll dust them before they go out, if it's so important."

Doris flipped the embossed squares of paper between her fingers, beginning again as if they'd never stopped.

Ma followed suit. "I suppose it isn't, considering."

The feet of the chair sloshed against the slick of flood as Thea yanked it away from the table with one hand. Ma glared at her as she made a show of sitting down, hitting her tailbone against the wood harder than she intended, but she didn't flinch. Doris swam among the invitations, not looking up at the noise, as if focused on not drowning.

Thea laid her clasped hands on the table. "I'll dust them."

Ma's hands worked robotically through the envelopes. While one pile grew, the other dwindled. Thank fucking God, this was almost over.

"It's fine, Thea," Ma said.

"No, Ma, you are so right. It's an important day. They should look *perfect*."

"Let's just finish." Head down, Ma worked as if Thea was a stray television in the background.

"Why not start now? Then it'll be done." Thea lurched her hands out toward the piles of completed envelopes and shuttled as many as she could toward her side of the table. Doris glanced at her over the top of the white piles, fingers never so much as pausing.

Ma dropped the card she was working on. "Stop. Look at this, they're all spilled."

"I'll stack them again after I clean them off."

"They were in nice piles. I had them all organized."

"Your piles are irrelevant once they go in the mail."

"Just stop."

"It's fine."

"Thea!"

"*What?*" Things were about to spiral out of control, but she didn't fucking care. "What, Ma? Is the mess bothering you? How about the floor? Don't you see this floor? Water everywhere!"

Ma did not see the floor. Instead, she was on her feet, glaring over the ruined piles of fancy paper and iridescent envelopes, the sheen of them reflecting her anger. "You need to stop. This isn't about you!"

"It never is." Her head felt unsettled—every move an aching premonition of something worse to come.

Finally deeming it fit for her to bother in the drama, Doris leaned back rigid in her chair. "Who cares about the damn cards? They'll all end up in the garbage anyway."

"And yet I'm still not fit to touch them, it seems." Thea was already stomping up the stairs before her mother could respond or Doris could issue a command to stay put.

The family couldn't help but be strangled by her sister—Thea worst of all. The golden child, the pedestal for all others to be judged against. She wanted to hate Doris; she wanted so badly to tell her off, to blame Doris for her own emotional paralysis. Most times, Thea felt like burying her sister, as if the universe would right itself if she was gone, like cutting off the head of the villain in a fairy tale. But then she'd catch that look from Doris, that watery marble gaze of a drowning person, and Thea knew that her sister hated it all as much as she did. It was a fleeting thing, though, like those floating globs of cells in her vision—it could only be seen when she wasn't looking directly at it. Sometimes Thea thought their mutual hatred was the only sisterly thing they shared. Maybe it would be different if Thea wasn't such a fuckup or if Doris wasn't so insulated. Or if—

She was struck by a memory of arms around her. Every time she got close to truly hating her sister, something floated up out of the repression that made her shudder. It hadn't always been like this. But that was so long ago now, it might as well have been a dream.

She often thought that one of them would be better off without the other. It didn't matter which; the pair of them were like stones on a balancing scale—neither could rise until the other sank. Treading water was all either of them did now.

Turning out her dirty jeans on the floor, she finally found a five-dollar bill and some quarters. Tips from bartending a few nights ago. There should have been more—she'd thought there was more—but ten pockets and a run through her nightstand later, that was all she'd found.

The sky was a groggy gray, so she looped her red hoodie over her arm and headed back downstairs.

"Where are you going?" Ma asked, voice pinched and curt.

"Work."

"You don't have work today."

"How would you know? Going through my stuff again?"

"Thea, please."

"Please what?" Her keys dangled like ominous wind chimes in her hand.

Ma glared at her, and Thea knew whatever she was about to say was a lie. "Please don't go."

She turned her back, preparing to leave, when Doris finally spoke. "Thea," she said. "Be safe."

Thea kept her back to them. The doorknob blurred because she was furious and crying and sucking it all in, so she didn't hurl a chair at them both.

Be safe. Good riddance. Be safe. Doris cares. She wants you to be fucking safe. Go. Get out of here, but try not to die or something, because that'd be a real fucking bummer.

She didn't say anything as she left, and neither did anyone else. Her adrenaline wanted to explode all over the door in a wall-shaking slam, but she wouldn't give them the satisfaction. They wanted the quiet, so she'd grant them that. She waded towards the door as invitations eddied all around her.

Her ears felt like the ocean, blood rushing through them and blotting out all sound. She wondered, briefly, if Doris heard it too.

Then the door shut, and she remembered.

She remembered everything. The flood, the water. It had already started. She whipped around, trying to open the door, to warn them, but it wouldn't open. Her fists ripped apart as she pounded, screaming.

Run.

Get out. It's coming. The monsters are real and they're coming!

Before Sestra knew what was happening, a sweaty hand placed itself on her chest. A loud voice started screaming. Something—someone—stronger than her pinned her down to her back.

It was Rob, and the loud screaming voice belonged to her.

She'd have screamed forever until she died from dehydration if not for Mijo. His small gesture was what she needed. She'd been dreaming, and now Rob was suffocating her with his knee to snuff out the throes of her panic.

No matter how viciously she thrashed, he pressed his palm against her, refusing to let up.

Dread faded to relief. He was alive. He was making it.

That relief quickly dissolved. "Get the fuck off me, Rob!"

"Then stop screaming."

"I have stopped screaming," she screamed.

He lifted himself off her anyway. She was okay. She was still on the boat. Mijo was alive and Rob was annoying the shit out of her already. Maybe it would be okay for once. Just one moment of okayness would be nice.

"What time is it?" she asked. Mijo kept his hand on her chest, and she let him.

Rob had planted himself on the bottom step and studied her. "Dawn."

"How long have I been asleep?"

"I heard you screaming like you was being murdered. That's all I know."

She started her next question, then stopped, telling herself that it was for Mijo's sake.

Is the posy still there?

She couldn't bring herself to speak it aloud. Instead, lumbering upright, she decided to go see for herself. She didn't want to stay in the cabin anyway—that dream clung to the small space like a bad smell. She needed fresh air, which is what she said as she stepped over Rob and ascended the cabin stairs.

It was dawn, just like Rob had said. The sky was subdued and slightly bruised. Sestra groped for the railing and tried not to fall, which was when she saw it—millions and millions of lights in the water. They spread into a vast, hazy ring around the boat, circling them in ominous fashion.

Rob appeared next to her. He must have seen her staring. "Bioluminescence," he said.

"I've heard of it before. Some kind of plankton. Too small for us to catch, but it bodes well for fishing."

"Don't those only come out at night?"

"I wouldn't know."

Sestra slowly circled the boat. Rob matched her, step for step. The lights spread out in all directions, surrounding them.

"How long?" she asked.

"Hours."

"Just sitting there. Following us?"

He spit words at her across folded arms. He was trying really hard not to think about this. "We ain't exactly moving much."

She'd never seen anything like it, not just since the flood, but ever. Lights oozed across the surface of the water like neon vomit. It was so bright. It couldn't come from a single animal.

Unless the fucking thing was just that big.

Rob placed a hand on her shoulder. "I've been watching."

And she knew he had, but that didn't make her feel any better.

"What . . ." Her brain was a pile of old spark plugs. Nothing worked. "What about Mijo?"

"You saw him. He's improving."

She did see him, and he did seem better, but she couldn't shake the sense of wrongness in everything. As if she'd died and woken up here. Like it was going to get worse.

Even the water was wrong. Besides the glowing, it moved differently. If the past year or so taught her anything, it was to respect the water—unpredictable and violent and so deceptive. It killed an entire world, for fuck's sake, but now she felt inclined to whisper as if it was listening. As if it was actively searching for just her.

Lost in thought, she hadn't noticed that Rob had stopped following her until she circled back around to him in her restless pacing. He watched the sea like a man igniting a bomb. It took a moment for her to understand what he was staring at—the lights had disappeared. All of them. Just like that.

Offering nothing, Sestra continued her pacing, leaving Rob alone to ponder whatever he was pondering.

Returning to the stern, she gripped the rails as if they were the only thing keeping her tethered to this world. The dream had her shaken and ill, a twitchy feeling she thought she'd left at the bottom of the sea. She could jump in the water right now just to get away from it—a spine-seizing pain ricocheted inside her body. It was enough to make her scream, and she might have, if it hadn't been for a cough against her back.

Mijo stood just inches from her, trembling with an illness he still hadn't kicked.

"Oh fuck. What are you doing, Mijo?"

He glared at her.

"¿Que es tu problema?"

He extended a hand and she took it, their skin sticking together from sweat and God knows what else. "Ahora no," he said.

"Now no? What is that supposed to mean?" But she wasn't

really asking, and he showed no inclination to explain, instead guiding her back into the depth of the cabin and pointing to the floor. When she didn't move, he grabbed her by the sides of her arms and pushed her down. The two of them rattled together, combining their independent trembles into a unified, mutant super-tremor.

"You need to rest," she said. Mijo knelt next to her and again placed a hand on her chest.

"Rest," he repeated.

There was a confidence in his voice that wasn't there before, or maybe she never noticed it until then. "You understand English."

His gaze flicked toward her, then away. "Some."

Little shit. But still she smiled. It was comforting to think that he was smarter than her. He needed to be, if he was going to survive.

"Did my Spanish ever make sense?"

Now he smiled. "Some."

"You're still sick."

"Mejoraré."

"What does that mean?"

But he just shrugged. Maybe he didn't know how to translate it properly, but more likely he was simply finished talking to her. She was rather experienced in that sentiment.

The kid intended to sit over her, but soon his own exhaustion took over, and he laid down at her side, never once removing his hand from her chest. The constant pressure irritated her, and her skin itched at the contact, but she never moved. It was a protective gesture, and frankly, it comforted them both.

Still exhausted, she tried to sleep but couldn't. Every time she closed her eyes, all she saw was lights. Thousands, millions of neon lights surrounding her, suffocating her. Her dream lit up new places of her brain and all sorts of shit she'd forgotten about swooped back to the forefront.

Doris was everywhere, lurking in shadows and corners. Sestra swore her sister was even in the cabin with her now, and every now and again she'd see a feminine outline when she blinked, as if that was the only time she could be seen.

Sestra grabbed her cheek out of reflex, careful not to disturb Mijo, who snored next to her. Memories were dangerous, which was why she'd locked them up tight in a part of her that was easy to ignore. But whatever mental dams she'd erected had collapsed, and images and emotions and pasts she'd attempted to keep quiet were now screaming at her.

At the center of them all was the monster game, the one she and Doris had played when they were girls.

You need to be ready. You need to hide.

But there wasn't anywhere to hide anymore.

She thought Doris was lying. Fuck, she never believed her. No wonder Doris ended up hating her. No one ever believed her.

Lying on the floor, she began to sob. It started so insidiously that she hadn't realized she'd entered into full-blown panic attack. It felt like being buried alive, and for all that escaped her, nothing else could get in. Not air, not comfort, not sense. *Poof.* Her façade shattered into wails, long overdue by many, many years.

I never believed her. She told me about the monsters. She told me and told me and told me.

They watch you. They hide and watch. Look for them, always.

Mijo backed away from her, observing from a few feet away, his hand tucked against his body. The light of the cabin door split in two as Rob cut through the doorway. Everything blurred, but she was aware, afraid to miss something.

Rob replaced Mijo at her side, cautious to touch her.

Shaking and shaking and shaking. The boat shook and she shook and when Rob circled his palm around her arm, he shook too.

They're always watching. Look for them.

"She told me."

Rob grabbed her other arm.

"She told me about the monsters. She told me and I didn't believe her. Did she tell you too? She did, didn't she? She told you about the monsters."

The words tumbled out, all the things she'd sworn never to repeat. Her face stung, but when she tried to cover it, she found her arms pinned to her sides by Rob.

"She told me about the monsters! She told all of us and now look where we are!" It was funny. So funny. Fucking hilarious, really. Her body seized in a fit of cackles. Lookee here! Look at all this mess! Look at her. Look at them.

A violent shaking erupted below her, as if they were skimming the top of a boiling pot of water.

Look for them. They're here.

She was mad. She was perfectly aware that she was losing it. None of this was normal—she wasn't normal, the posies weren't normal, the water wasn't normal, the flood wasn't normal. Nothing was right and she was suddenly bereft at the idea that nothing, ever, had gone according to plan. Maybe if it had, none of this would have happened. Doris would be alive. James would be alive. Ma, hopefully, would still be dead.

And she would be floating somewhere—between men, drugs, jobs, but always floating.

The shaking worsened, pulling the world apart with a roar. Unrestrained, she clutched her ears. Light leaked away; down the drain it went.

They're coming.
They're here.

She screamed, calling for Mijo and Rob. Calling for her sister.

So loud was the noise that it soon became an entity of its own. It couldn't be heard, because she couldn't hear anything— the screaming had just always been, like a tinnitus she'd learned to ignore.

There was a yank, something massive anchoring itself to the molecules that made up her body. It didn't feel like a rope or a restraint, more like a state of being, and her current state was drowning.

Swell.

Just fucking great.

They're coming . . .

. . . they're here.

And then it was black, aside from a voice she was certain did not belong here.

Although the dead didn't belong anywhere.

It was James. What was he doing here? He was talking to her. What was he saying? Why was he here? What the fuck was going on?

Why was this happening again? James was dead.

I'll drive you.

Thea had laughed in his face. Where was James planning to drive her? To his house? But it wasn't shame that ultimately made her refuse. She reached into her front pocket and rubbed the torn leather just to make sure it was still there. His wallet had been so easy to swipe. She could have dangled it right in front of his face, and he'd have let her take it. He was so damn ashamed. Guilty. But something about him walking through the front door, reaching for it, that gut-punch when he couldn't find it . . . Or maybe the next morning, while getting ready for work, he'd ask Doris if she'd seen it. The thought was thrilling to Thea. So fucking satisfying.

She supposed she should feel guilty too. The memory was a blur, an aftershock to her high. She'd just shot up in the bathroom of Café Lex, snaking her way down the hall back to her corner booth to her order of ice water and toast, when a chirpy little voice had called her name. She hadn't seen either James or her sister in months, having been tossed out by Doris after going through her kitchen drawers. Thea had been looking for scissors to snip the scratchy tag of her shirt, but Doris hadn't bought that. Thea wasn't sure she did either, honestly.

Words were said—*misses you* this, *call me* that, *are you okay*, and other such addiction pleasantries. *We care*. Well, thank God for that. Thea fully admitted she was an addict—not all addicts would say as much—but the problem was she didn't fucking care. She wasn't responsible for their fucking feelings anyway.

He'd slid into her booth, looking terrible. Thea knew the symptoms of sleep loss, and he had them. She might have asked if he'd been sleeping on the couch, and he might have laughed a little and then gone quiet. She might—*might*—have felt a pang of sympathy for the guy. Because she knew exactly what it was like to feel that way. Perhaps they'd talked for a long while, because she hadn't spoken too much to anyone in weeks, until the waitress asked them to leave. Or they could have just walked to his car together after he'd paid for a plate of pancakes and some coffee and then offered her a ride to wherever she was staying.

He'd probably tried to give her money, and she probably took it if he did—to get on her feet, of course. The details had melted away in a haze of desperation and sadness and the comforting lull of heroin dropping a curtain over her inhibitions. Whatever the steps, the fact remained that she'd stolen his wallet without shame or sympathy, reveling at the ease of it, of how stupid he was, and then she was sitting behind a dumpster feeling the foam innards of his old leather wallet bursting from use.

He'd asked where she was staying.

"A friend."

"I'll drive you."

He'd drive her to rehab, he meant. As if transportation was the only thing holding her back.

The cracks in the concrete etched at her skin as she rifled through the wallet. Her jeans were weathered to almost nothing.

A few dollar bills spilled to the ground. The air smelled different—like monsoons. The sky flickered in her peripheral vision, dust billowing up around it. A haboob, people were calling it. A shitload of dirt with just enough rain to make it a muddy brown paste that stuck to fucking everything. She needed to get high.

Visa, MasterCard, voter registration—shit, brother-in-law Boy Scout was an organ donor too. Thea turned the wallet inside out. She could use the cards for today. He wouldn't know it was missing for at least an hour, not until he came to senses, and it wasn't like he was going to dispute the charges.

Yeah, I need to speak to someone about my cracked-out sister-in-law who stole my wallet after I swore I wouldn't have contact with her. Don't tell my wife.

It was funny, and she laughed. A wedding picture tumbled out, and she kicked it out of sight. Thea remembered the wedding fine enough without the photo sentiment. James, perhaps, could use a reminder.

Snatching up the credit cards, she dumped the wallet over her shoulder, and something metal clinked against the cement. Thinking it was some loose change, she scrambled for each precious cent, only to find James's wedding ring. White gold, she figured by the dents in it. White fucking gold. Who the fuck was this guy? She was almost disappointed he was this stupid.

Gold.

Boy, things were really starting to look up.

From the bottom of the sea, *up* was the only place left to gaze.

CHAPTER TEN

THE WAY, WAY BEFORE

DORIS STOOD IN the middle of the road. Her bare feet stamped the asphalt in blood from a cut on her heel. She couldn't feel her toes anymore. It was cold—heavy breaths issued from her mouth, steam rising like clouds before her eyes.

This was what it must be like to smoke. That's what her friends would say, and though that couldn't possibly be true, she liked to pretend along with them—two fingers to her pursed lips, blowing clouds behind the monkey bars.

Look at me! I'm a grown-up.

It was fun because she wanted to be a grown-up. She wanted to have responsibilities and a job and her own house. She wanted to go far away. She wanted to be able to decide whether she could smoke. Instead, she was still a stupid kid without any shoes wandering the streets in the dark, thinking about things that were too far beyond her to be a comfort.

The street tumbled forward through a severe dark that looked like a wall of rock, something she just didn't have the tools to penetrate.

She'd been running a few blocks, but a noise had made her stop. Or she thought she'd heard a noise. A car, a person walking a dog. She should be home in bed with the baby monitor tucked under her ear. Most girls don't sleep with baby monitors, and she wasn't supposed to either, but every night after Ma fell asleep, she snuck into her room and stole it. There was something about her sister's cries that kept her up at night—they were wild and unmanageable. Ma called it colic. Doris called it fear. Even her baby sister, just months old, understood what came to cradle her in the night. Even a baby knew that Ma was worse than any bellyache when she got in a good fit. So Doris took the monitor, and when Thea cried, she made sure she was the first to reach her.

It was then that she realized she'd left the monitor on her bed. Ma wouldn't hear her if she cried tonight. No one would, but Doris had to keep that thought stuffed deep down. She couldn't worry about her sister now, not when those *things* were out there. Those monsters.

Lights reared behind her as a car turned the corner and cruised toward her. Without thinking she sprinted forward, slipping unnoticed into the dark space under the broken streetlamp.

Not a rock after all, just an absence. From the shadows, she watched the sedan crawl by and disappear around another curve. She hadn't been spotted—not by the people in the car, at least.

A crunch made her turn. There was nothing up or down the street to have made the noise. It sounded like tires on gravel—a pressed and heavy sound. The tears came, and she hated herself for it. She couldn't cry. She had to stop crying. Crying was for the guilty and the uncomposed. Crying is what attracted *them*.

She only saw them when she cried. Only when she was terribly upset. She'd been six or so the first time. Ma had taken her candy away for smarting off, and she had gone wild. Much of the moment washed away in a blur, but what had stuck was the brightness of the sun as Ma pulled away from the window, the rattle of her candy down the sides of the metal trash bin, and the thing—the monster—watching her through the window while Ma's back was turned. It was made of teeth and arms, iridescent and angry and smiling, its dozens of hands pressing against the glass as it leaned in to watch her.

She screamed when she saw it then, cried as she remembered it now. Ma had sent her to her room without dinner that night, telling her that she could eat when she stopped making up stories to garner sympathy. At the time, Doris didn't even understand what that meant, but she quickly learned to keep quiet about it. Though that didn't seem to stop them from coming—to her school, to her dreams, to her bedroom window at night. Then, like tonight, outside Thea's window.

Doris flung herself through the front door in search of it, but her adrenaline quickly evaporated into terror. What started as the noble protection of her sister morphed into a flight for her life. She ran at them and from them at the same time, and now she was blocks away, bare-legged in nothing but a nightgown, hiding in the shadows and waiting for a monster.

What she would do when she found it remained a mystery.

She looked around for her mother, expecting her to pop up from behind a bush or climb down from her perch on a street sign. Ma was like liquid—she could be anywhere and everywhere. Every noise out here made Doris jump, just like at home. Because she knew she was doing something bad, just like at home.

The middle school ahead buzzed in a spray of yellow light, shadows of streetlights and trees crosshatching its boxy profile. This was the school she would go to one day, when she was bigger. She shouldn't be here at nighttime—she shouldn't be here at all, being only ten, but that had never stopped her before. The storage shed facing the racquetball courts was usually unlocked. There might be extra shoes and shorts in there. Maybe a hockey stick or something to swing with.

Avoiding the front parking lot, she snuck along the perimeter of the school until she reached the chain-link fence surrounding the field. The track looped through the center of it like a bullseye, the shed she aimed for just beyond the track. Fingers clasped around the metal links, she hopped over easily, just like all the other times she'd tried to run away. There were sand pits for long jump and tennis courts on the other side, but no playground. No swings or monkey bars or any of the good stuff. It always made her sad to think about the kids sitting around with nothing to do. They must be so bored.

Another pair of headlights rounded the street, landing on her like searchlights. Panic hit with a suddenness, and her body reacted in kind. As the car approached, she scrambled up the fence, flopping on the other side. She didn't look back to see if the driver stopped, imagining an angry adult shaking a fist at her as she ran.

Darn kids!

There were fancy words for what she'd just done, words she didn't know yet, but that didn't erase the gravity of it—fear was reliably inarticulate. Her feet hit grass, then the bouncy rubber of the track, alternating again as she crossed the second half of it. She didn't stop until she hit the racquetball courts. Cement shocked her shins into submission, and she slumped next to a water fountain to catch her breath.

There weren't any trees here, not like at her school. The entire field, in all its vastness, sat exposed and unprotected. The storage room was just around the corner.

Allowing her small body a moment to calm, she was just about to get up when that noise came again. That crunching sound, but this time there weren't any cars to blame it on. Every molecule froze, sweat sticking her back to the metal fountain despite the chill.

It was just her imagination. That's what Ma would say. Just her silly little brain creating silly little nightmares for no good reason. Just her imagination. All she had to do was get to the shed and then she could go.

Crack.

Like the snap of a twig, but there weren't any twigs on the racquetball court. Her heart pumped all other sound out of existence, and her mouth was dry. It was there, watching her, that monster with its dozen hands and terrible grin. That thing that loved to watch her. The thing she chased away from Thea's window. And she was alone with it, exposed in the night, with nothing to keep them apart but a rickety water fountain.

She imagined it squirming on the other side, felt the displacement of air as it shifted. It was there; she knew it was there.

Without looking, she flung herself upright and broke into a wild sprint. The slap of her bare feet against the pavement echoed through the empty courts. She didn't stop until she reached the storage room, swinging the door open and slamming it shut in one swift motion. This, as it turned out, was a huge mistake.

There were no lights and no windows in this tiny room. It was dark as pitch. She couldn't see a thing.

Back against the cool metal door, she patted herself down, making sure she was alone more than anything. Legs and arms, fingers and toes, everything was there. Something clattered to the floor a few feet away and she screamed. Probably a bunch of stacked equipment, maybe a rake or a broom by the sound of it. Still, her mind ran amok with the possibilities.

Her vision tried desperately to adjust, but there just wasn't enough light to see anything. It was just her and the dark and that thing out there somewhere.

She spent minutes listening for movement. A bird chirped oddly somewhere in the distance, rotating different calls as if on a loop. It was probably the same bird that would keep her awake some nights. Her dad had said it was mockingbird. They liked to call at night for some reason, which she knew because it was dad out in the night bum-rushing the tree in the front yard in his underwear as Ma yelled about that damn bird keeping the baby awake.

"That's what mockingbirds do," he'd say. "What do you want me to do? Shoot it?"

Now, all its hollering was comforting. Birds were usually the first to take off when danger was afoot. If the bird was yelling, maybe it meant the monster had gotten bored and left.

Feeling a little bit bold and a lot blind, Doris risked cracking the storage door just a tiny bit just to allow some light inside. Spying the field through the sliver of an opening, it appeared that she was alone, and so began rifling through the mess of basketballs and orange cones for anything she might be able to use. There wasn't much—there was one pair of old cleats that looked and smelled as if they hadn't been used in years and a chest plate like the one they used when playing kickball at school. The hockey sticks were gone, and the rest she could see were maintenance items like trash bags and a yellow mop cart with a broken wheel. Unless she planned to pelt the monster with a few deflated dodgeballs, she didn't have many options.

Somewhere in the time she'd been tossing equipment about, the mockingbird had fallen silent. She wouldn't have realized it if not for it starting up again, loudly and suddenly just outside the shed. She was considering the broken handle of a broom when its screech bounced through the room. It could have been just outside the door.

This time she didn't scream, not even when she clattered backward, landing hard on her butt, resulting in a severely bruised tailbone. Keeping the broom handle close to her chest, she was beginning to lose sensation in her fingers as she gripped the splintering wood with all her strength.

Birds don't do what this bird was doing. They don't follow little girls in the dark. They don't leave their comfy trees for empty fields.

She thought about just staying here all night and waiting for someone to find her. Slam the door shut and wait it out. Someone would find her. They'd find her and keep her safe. They'd take her home.

And then she'd be home. Ma would be so angry. What would Doris say then? *I saw the monster? I was running away? I was sleepwalking?* Nothing would work. There wasn't any excuse that would make Ma not be furious.

She had to get out of here. She was cold and scared, and at least if she was running for her life, she'd have something to do besides think about how much trouble she was going to be in later. Who knew how far away she might get if she took off now and never stopped?

But making the decision didn't make opening the door and facing it any easier. Peeking through the opening, she searched for anything—a bird or a monster or her mom, anything.

Nothing moved.

Using the end of the broom handle, she knocked the door open just wide enough for her small body to slide through. The creak of the door was deafening, but as it whined to a stop, she was more relieved than anything. Nothing else was there. The mockingbird was gone.

Her breath puffed from her mouth and disappeared as she stalked through the empty field. *Look, I'm smoking!* She was big and grown and she could handle this, just like adults did that were old enough to smoke. They wouldn't be afraid of some stupid school.

Which was when she saw it. At first it seemed like nothing but a shadow shifting under a distant streetlight across the street, nothing to worry about, until two long gray arms broke away from the shadow. Doris saw just enough of them as they knuckled at the ground like a runner at a starting block, gearing up to charge her, before she launched into a full run in the opposite direction.

Dropping the broom, she ran as hard and as fast as she could until the school was out of sight.

It wasn't until the next day that she returned home. Police cars spun their lights in her driveway, and her mother sprinted across the lawn to snatch her up. Missing, they said. Fourteen hours. Her mother dug her nails into her shoulders so hard she drew blood, shaking her.

"Where were you?"

But every time she tried to answer, her mother barked over her.

"What happened?"

"Are you okay?"

"Where were you?"

"I thought you'd left me again."

"I thought you left."

Thea wailed in the other room. No one seemed to hear it. Police oozed around her, shining lights on her and asking fast questions that Doris didn't feel like answering. And Thea cried and cried.

She escaped her mother's grasp and sought out her baby sister with a parade of adults behind her. She was in her crib. Where her head lay was a wet stain. Doris yanked the baby free and tucked her against her chest. Thea didn't stop crying right away, but her shrieks mellowed enough that she could stop gasping.

As if feeding from the same hysterical teat, just as Thea calmed, her mother ramped up. Such serenity would not do when mother was just so upset. First her father, then the cops had to physically restrain her as she tried to claw her way toward Doris.

"Where were you? What happened to my baby?"

She didn't see her mother for the rest of that day. Maybe they sedated her or cuffed her to the fence in the backyard—Doris never asked. Eventually, the fear would fade. The hair color of the policewoman who had softly pulled her aside would be forgotten, the screeches of her mother would sound like all the rest, and all that would stick to her till adulthood would be the slither of monsters and the smell of her baby sister's head as Thea fell asleep in her arms.

———

Doris gripped the edges of the ladder. Three-year-old Thea sat at the top of the slide.

"Ready?"

Thea nodded.

"Hold on." Doris shook the ladder, softly at first, and her sister giggled.

"More. Sissy, more!"

So she shook harder. Thea had a high tolerance for danger, and it was Doris's job to make sure she knew the line and when not to cross it. It didn't matter that Thea was only three. It didn't matter that she herself was only thirteen. As Thea's laughs turned to whimpers, Doris considered stopping. She hated scaring her, but this was the game. She had to scare her so that Thea understood what it meant to be scared.

"Sissy!"

She shook harder. Thea's hand lost its grip, and she wobbled to one side.

"Sissy, stop!"

Doris stopped just as Thea was about to topple headfirst over the side. "That's what it feels like."

Thea released herself and squeaked down the slide. "Earf-quake," she said.

"Yes, earthquake." Her baby sister had been terrified of earthquakes since last year, when one struck in the middle of the night. No amount of consoling or treats could stop her wailing.

Thea paused, keen eyes watching. Doris folded her arms, observing the sequence of signs that preceded an explosion of compressed toddler. Blink. Rub the nose. Sniff sniff.

But then she grinned and screamed, "Monster! Monster!" The little girl sprinted off, head turned over a shoulder, expecting a chase.

Doris launched after her. It was almost dinnertime. Thea screamed like fireworks, and if Ma figured out what they were up to, she'd separate them again.

"Monster!"

This was the game, and like all good games, it was meant to teach. Late at night when both were meant to be sleeping, they'd climb under the covers of Doris's bed and talk about what scared them. For Thea it was nearly always earthquakes, and for Doris it was monsters. Thea needed to know what was out there and how to be prepared if she met it—or it met her.

It'd been years since her last monster sighting, but that didn't mean they weren't still out there, watching and waiting.

Doris tried to keep Thea quiet, but couldn't shush her if she tried. Instead she chased after her, hoping to corral her near the back of the yard, farther away from prying eyes.

They had to be stealthy about it, though. Ma didn't approve of such uncouth talk like that of monsters and earthquakes, and sometimes would peek a head in Doris's room as they read, pinching her lips together as she listened. It bothered Ma that even though Thea's room glittered her blind with princess sequins and frilly pink, it was the matte dark of Doris's brooding teenagerhood that appealed to the little girl. Though that could have been simply for the fact that Doris herself was there. Things like darkness and sadness never penetrated little Thea. Perhaps she was too young, or maybe she was just too thrilled to have ten fingers and ten toes that she didn't even realize they were there.

Doris refused to allow her sister to be caught off guard like she herself had been that day. She would never let that fear get ahold of Thea. And since Ma had forbidden talk of anything but frills and perfect teeth and dinner parties, she had to be covert in her training, or Ma would employ the most tactical weapon in her arsenal: keeping the sisters apart.

"You need to keep quiet, Thea. Or Ma will hear." Doris said.

The yard was a big square of yellowing bluegrass with a shed near the back wall that had nothing in it but a lawn mower and a nest of black widows. Did spiders live in nests? There were a lot of them, anyway, and along with the shed being dangerous, it was also Thea's favorite place to play. It was where she was heading now.

Doris overtook her, putting herself between Thea and the shed. It'd been plopped in the yard as if a tornado had spun it over the fence and her parents had just decided to keep it there. As such, there was a two-foot space between the back of the shed and the wood fence. A perfect burrow for tiny humans with zero sense of personal safety.

"You'll get stuck," she said.

Thea giggled and tried to pry her sister's legs apart so she could crawl through them.

"There's spiders."

"Spiders," she repeated, but didn't stop.

Very few things scared Thea, and that infuriated and terrified Doris. Thea was small and didn't know any better, but Doris didn't think that really mattered. Nothing seemed to faze the kid. She pushed through mud and bugs and heights and falling, shouts and screams and fights and breaking plates when Ma got particularly ornery. She sat through the stories that Doris read at night with lessons about monsters in the woods and witches that ate children. Nothing settled beyond that innocent glitter perception that was childhood. Thea was smart. She didn't question the truth; she just didn't think it would ever get to her. Unless it was an earthquake.

And then there was Doris, looking over her shoulder enough for them both. She grabbed her little sister by the wrist. "Did you find anything good?"

Thea perked. "Maybe over there?" She pointed toward the house.

The faucet turned on at the kitchen sink. The plumbing was bad, and it clunked like a bowl of rocks every time it was used. Ma was at the window.

"No. Not that way. Let's go sit by the tree."

"No, sissy. Over there!" Thea exploded down the center of the yard. Doris was about to thunder after her when the girl's foot caught in a hole, and she tripped, chin hitting ground before anything else. It was a slight not even tough three-year-olds could forgive, and she burst into a wail.

Doris was the first to reach her, though Ma wasn't far behind. "What happened?"

"She tripped."

Ma leveled a deadly stare at her firstborn. "What were you doing?"

Ma's eyes turned to the crying Thea, expecting validation, but Thea said nothing and continued to cry in Doris's arms. Ma sized the pair of them up with a huff.

"Why don't you come inside, and I'll give you a cookie?" Their mother lurched a hand toward her crying child and Thea accepted. No allegiance could defy a cookie, and Doris released her so that she could hobble away toward the kitchen. She'd forgotten about her limp before she even reached the door.

Doris thought she'd snuck under the radar until her mother craned her chin over a shoulder and called to her, "Clean yourself up. You look homeless."

Thea skipped inside the house, shouting, "Homeless! Homeless!" Her toddler lisp made it sound more like *home-wess*. Doris grinned despite herself, following her family back inside the house.

Ma and Thea had their backs to her as she entered through the sliding door. Thea was pulling boxes out from the bottom shelf of the pantry in a frenzied hunt for snacks while Ma pecked around her like an agitated crow. "Put that back. Not those. Thea, stop—no candy! Where did you even find that?"

Their dad plunked himself into his blue velvet recliner, acknowledging Doris's presence with a curt sigh as he reached for the remote. She fled to her room, shut the door, locked it, then immediately unlocked it.

Ma wasn't totally wrong—her shirt and hands were covered in gray from the metal ladder of the slide. It was an old and dirty thing purchased when Doris was little. It'd just sat in the yard being consumed by weeds until Thea had grown old enough to use it. To this day, Doris had to trim back the plant life with Ma's kitchen shears (though she never told her mother this) to keep the earth from claiming it entirely.

She changed. She washed up. She pulled her hair into a smooth ponytail. The click of her father's recliner signaled the start of dinner, and Doris followed the noise like a farm bell. If Ma was lacking anywhere, it wasn't as a cook. She made some damn fine food.

Tonight was roast with potatoes. Just by smelling it, Doris could pick out the individual spices her mother had used—garlic, onion powder, black pepper, cumin, and some bay leaf. Nothing fancy, but good food didn't need to be.

Thea poked the plate with her fork, and Ma rapped her hand. She didn't speak, just folded her hands in silent prayer and waited for the rest to follow. Dad didn't bother, just lifted the paper to his nose until it was done, but the girls didn't possess such luxury.

Since this started six months ago, Doris had learned not to make a noise until her mother spoke. Ma said they needed some spirit in their lives, whatever the hell that meant.

"What have you two been up to today?" Ma asked, scraping a broccoli floret from her plate with a fork. Apparently, the prayer was over.

"Just playing."

Thea scooped up some rice. She wasn't listening.

"Playing what?"

"I don't know. Games. Tag. Hide and seek."

Ma crushed her vegetables between her teeth. The constant gnashing filled the small void between sentences.

"That's all?"

Dad folded his paper and started shoveling food down his throat. Thea missed her mouth, raining potato bits onto the floor.

"Do you know what they were playing?" Ma asked her husband. He groaned.

"Games, so I hear."

"Not just games. I was watching." Ma ignored her food while leveling a vicious stare at Doris.

"We were just playing, Ma."

"You were doing that damn *monster* game again. I saw it. I heard your sister while I was slicing potatoes."

Running her finger along the tines of her fork, Doris stared at the plate of food in front of her that she wasn't sure she was going to be able to eat. "It's not a monster game."

"No," Ma said. "It's a hideous taunt."

The usual retorts spun circles in her head, but she said nothing.

"Do you really want to be known as the girl that talks endlessly about these things? A girl that speaks of *monsters*? People talk. Kids talk."

"I don't really care." She said it even though she knew she shouldn't. It was the truth, but it wasn't her feelings they were talking about.

Thea crunched her food happily.

Ma's eyes scorched the top of Doris's bowed head.

"It's *unbecoming*!" Her mother spoke as if she was about to spit a broken tooth at the table.

"What do you know?" Doris stared at her now. The

conversation lit the room like a match every time it was brought up. A part of Doris couldn't wait to snuff out her mother's flame with a bare fist, just to prove herself.

Ma talked about monsters like she knew them. She didn't know shit, because if she did, she'd have noticed the one sitting at the table with them.

Dad pushed his chair away from the table, picking up his plate. He left the room in a squeak of wood to linoleum. It was his loudest acknowledgment of the nonsense. Or, at least, that was how he'd have put it if he'd bothered to speak.

"You need to stop this."

The TV kicked on in the living room, volume just loud enough to make them shout.

"Why can't you just leave us alone?" It couldn't have been heard over the television, but it was cathartic to speak the words aloud instead of just thinking them.

"What did you say?"

She wanted to tell Ma to go away. She wanted to run away, but for real this time. She wanted to take Thea with her. She wanted her mother to hug her. She wanted a thousand things that she knew she'd never get.

"You speak up when you're talking to me, girl."

"I didn't say anything."

"Stop lying."

"I'm not."

Ma pounded on the table. "Don't you dare lie to me! And you don't fill your three-year-old sister's head with monsters. There's just things you don't do, and you're old enough to know the difference."

Taking an aggressive bite of food, her mother dropped her fork on her plate before she realized what she was doing. It was rude to drop a fork like that. Doris absorbed the sound of it without reaction, but Thea giggled, then dropped her own silverware onto the floor.

Her laughter was like an echo of hiccups until Ma reared back and slapped it right out of her. The sound of her open palm striking Thea would never leave Doris's mind. It was irradiated, like toxic waste. The kind of thing a person kept with them forever.

It wasn't until Doris jolted upright and snatched her close that Thea began to cry. Ma white-knuckled the edge of the table and screamed, "You see what you've done?"

Clutching her sister close, Doris clamped her teeth together and stared at the Mr. Coffee pot drying on the rack by the kitchen sink. She stared into it like a portal to another place—seeing herself grabbing it and hurling it at her mother's face; smashing it on the floor in a froth of shattered glass; or rubbing it like the magic lamp in the stories she read to Thea, wishing for the genie to give her wings.

In the time it took for her mother to pry Thea away from her, Doris saw all these things, and her teeth were just beginning to peek through her lips in a smile when a rough shake yanked her back into the kitchen—the real kitchen. The kitchen where Thea was howling, and her mother was shrilling, and Doris was praying she could melt into the floor.

Ma had slapped Doris more than once, but for some reason, it never hurt like this.

"Go!" Ma said and pointed toward the hall. "Just go."

She meant to her room, but Doris went to the front door instead.

"Don't you dare— Larry, stop her!"

Larry—Dad—kicked his recliner into place as if constipated, forcing a too-slow lurch that missed his lithe daughter by a mile. Doris was three houses down and could still hear her mother shrieking, but that was fine. Ma wouldn't dare chase her now, not in public like that.

Twilight made it dark and fuzzy outside, with just enough

light to keep the shadows away, but not enough to see well. She marched down the street to the sound of her pulse throbbing in her ears like a battle drum, wondering what she was going to do now. She couldn't go home for a while—probably not until she was sure Ma had gone to bed, or else there'd be hell to pay—and she was already exhausted. The fight was gone. She thought of Thea's scarlet cheek and pulled her arms against her chest.

Ma would dote on her; Doris was sure of that. Ma would make her forget, at least for tonight. Knowing that just made Doris feel worse and walk faster.

Toward that corner. Toward that bush and that broken streetlamp that had never gotten repaired, even after Ma complained about it at the HOA meeting.

The neighborhood still buzzed with people—cars up and down the street, headlights into driveways, kids playing, and other kids being called inside as the streetlights popped on. Outside smelled like exhaust and the sour stench of the blooming carob trees that guarded the entrance to the school. She hated how those trees smelled—it was an artificial, almost antiseptic scent that shouldn't come from trees. It didn't help that they produced a poor replacement for chocolate that tasted as offensive as the blooms smelled.

She was running away again, but only for the evening. Her feet ached in anticipation of the long night, remembering her fourteen-hour adventure three years ago. Ma had thrown the nightgown she'd been wearing that night in the trash. She'd said it was because it was ruined. What she didn't know was that Doris had snuck out a second time the morning of trash pickup and fished it out again. She wasn't sure what instinct made her do it, but on nights like tonight, she was so glad that she did. The grittiness of the fabric, the tears and stains were all a comfort to her. They were like stamps or tattoos; they marked her. She kept pieces of it on her always, usually in a pocket or stuffed in her backpack. Then when she eventually did leave for good, she could leave it out like a letter, saying all she ever wanted to say but couldn't, and imagine her mother eating crow.

Beyond the middle school was another cluster of homes and then the elementary school. About two blocks ahead, she could still hear the kids playing on the playground. The school closed at four, but kids climbed the fences and played anyway. She headed there, toward the noise, because she had nothing else to do.

By the time she reached the playground, the school had nearly cleared out. A couple younger kids stopped playing and stared at her as she slunk toward the swings, and she wondered if she knew them. They seemed to know her, because as soon as she sat down, they dropped from the monkey bars and skipped away, giggling. They looked back at her over their shoulders until they were out of sight.

The lights surrounding the playground were dimmer and fewer than the military-grade spotlights of the middle school, so she twirled on the swings in the dark, as she'd done many times before. Sometimes a janitor or a teacher would spot her out there by herself and shout at her to go home. Most of the time that's all they did, because they didn't care if she went home or not, and a complacent nod from her would satisfy. Once or twice there'd been a stubborn adult who would sit and watch until she got off the swing and began walking away, but she knew the shadows better than they did—she'd hide in the darkness underneath the acacia trees near the bus pickup at the back of the school.

There was no one there tonight, though. She had the place to herself.

Thea would like it here. The dark wouldn't scare her. Doris could push her as high as she wanted on the swings, and Thea would laugh.

She started swinging, pretending Thea was on her lap. Sand sprayed as her feet skidded against the ground. She was too tall for the kiddie swings, but she didn't care. She'd push until she was so high the chains went slack and the weight of her slammed down as she fell back to earth. It was what flying must feel like—total weightlessness, touching nothing but air. The creak of the chains rocking to and fro was the most comforting sound she knew. She dreamed of it. It crushed her to leave them behind when she started middle school.

She stayed on the swings until the moon sat atop her head—a few hours at least. There was no one around to stop her. Her legs were wobbly and sore on the walk home, and by the time she reached her front door, she was exhausted. She didn't even bother trying the knob; everything would be locked.

A large boulder by the back fence allowed her to hop into the backyard without opening the squeaky gate, then she crept to her bedroom window. The shades were drawn, but she knocked anyway.

It only took a moment for the window latch to lift with a click. Doris slid the window open from the outside and was greeted by her sleepy-eyed sister.

"Hi, sissy," she said.

The comforter on Doris's bed was rumpled into a ball from Thea's restless sleep. Kicking off her shoes, she straightened the covers and slid underneath, still in her clothes. Lifting a corner of the blanket, Thea scurried into bed after her. Within minutes, both were fast asleep.

There weren't many things Doris hated more than hearing the words *we're going shopping* on a Saturday morning.

Ma stuck her head through her bedroom door. "Get dressed."

Pulling the covers farther over her head, she wished her mother would let her sleep late just once. If it wasn't shopping, it was chores or prayer or family breakfast. She often chose to go to church service alone. It was one of the few things she couldn't bully Dad into doing with her. Not that there was anything wrong with going to church. Doris wouldn't mind attending herself if her mother wasn't involved.

She didn't even consider pretending to be asleep. Last time she had, Ma had torn the covers back and dumped a cup of ice water on her face. Good girls didn't loaf.

Thea was already up and squawking about the house. As Doris dressed, she heard her break into a shriek that permeated the drywall.

"Not those!" she screamed. "*No ruffles!*"

Ma mumbled back a threat that Doris couldn't hear through the walls, but whatever she'd said hadn't resonated because Thea streaked down the hall naked. Ma hobbled after her, heavy bangles clanking with indignity.

She might have gotten another slap if they weren't going somewhere. Thea knew it, too. She was always at her worst right before it was time to leave the house. It was generally the highlight of Doris's morning. That is, until she took it too far, as she often did, and it suddenly became Doris's problem. And once the Thea train got going, it was almost impossible to stop.

They ate quickly, Thea through defeated tears. She looked like a marshmallow in her fluffy dress, a flower girl with nowhere better to go than the corner grocery store.

Doris wore her khaki knee-length skirt and a white collared shirt underneath a navy knit vest. She pulled her hair into a bun and placed a single black barrette above her ear. Ma appraised her appearance with a snort, but thankfully said nothing further.

They loaded into the car, both girls in the backseat, and drove wordlessly to Kroger. Aside from Ma's recent dabble in Christianity, this was her religion, and everyone had their parts to play.

It was the usual weekend fare at the grocery store—busy

and angry. They parked, and Doris silenced Thea's incessant ruffle-scratching with a firm grip to her wrist. She grimaced, but otherwise did as she was told.

They walked to the entrance. It hummed like the airlock, threatening to consume her.

Like always, they entered by the produce. Doris pulled her arms tight against her sides and breathed through her nose. Thea burst toward the flower display and pointed. Like always, it was Doris's job to chase her down.

"What's wrong with those flowers, sissy?"

"They're just flowers."

"They look mean."

Doris reached for the tag to see what they were.

"Vulgar things," Ma said.

"Actually, it says they're Stargazer lilies."

Ma scrunched her face. "Go get strawberries. And make sure you turn them over first and—"

"Check for mold, I know." Engulfing her sister's hand in hers, she headed toward the berries.

Thea insisted on touching everything, and Doris simultaneously swatted her away and checked the plastic bricks of strawberries for bruises and mold. Most were fine, but not fine enough, and she had a small hill of rejects to the right of her before she found a good bunch. She was turning it over in her hands when she saw her—Colleen Simpson. She and Ma were lowkey rivals, but Colleen's daughter Jennifer was Doris's worst fucking nightmare. Jennifer was charismatic and witty, as vicious as broken glass, and maintained Doris perpetually in her sights. She wanted nothing more than to kick Jennifer's perfect teeth into the back of her perfect head, but whenever the opportunity arose, Doris always found herself missing a backbone.

To make things worse, Colleen was nothing if not wonderful, forcing upon Doris a mixture of fury, envy, and admiration that made her act like more of an idiot than everyone already thought she was.

She tried to duck away, dragging Thea behind her with one hand, but it was too late.

"Doris!" Colleen waved her over.

She wished she hadn't flinched, hadn't paused. Then maybe she could have pretended to not hear her. Grinning, Colleen pushed her cart toward them while Doris forced a smile that made her cheeks burn.

"Oh, hi."

"Don't you two look nice. Such good daughters. You should give Jennifer some tips. I couldn't drag her out of bed on a Saturday morning for a tornado, let alone to help her mother get the groceries."

Doris might have cackled in her face if Thea hadn't piped up before she'd had the chance. "I *hate* ruffles."

Colleen smiled, the real kind that happened when a person thought something was funny or cute. "Well, they look darling, anyway. Where's your mom off to?"

Like always, the mere mention of her made Ma manifest like a demon.

"Colleen! Hi, how are you? Hope the girls are behaving for you." It wasn't a threat, but a declaration. She wanted Colleen to confirm it out loud.

"Of course!"

The women leaned in for a perfunctory peck against the cheek and smiled. Ma placed a hand on Doris's shoulder and left it there.

"Did you find the strawberries?"

"Yeah."

Ma hissed through clenched teeth. *Yes.* The correct answer was *yes*, not yeah.

"I was just saying how nice it is that the girls come with you to shop every weekend. I couldn't bribe Jenny to come if I wanted to."

"Oh, you know. Sometimes a girl just needs to do girl stuff with her mom. I'm sure you and Jenny have plenty of little things to do together."

Colleen nodded, gaze fading into the background before she returned with her usual white grin.

Doris watched her search for words. She started to speak, if anything to break the spreading awkwardness, but Ma gripped her skin and tugged.

"My little miracle baby, this one. I have a hard time letting her out of my sight. She hates me for it sometimes, I swear." Ma laughed and laughed, even though it wasn't funny.

She continued, and Doris turned away, watching as a breeze blew through the parking lot, whipping up abandoned bags and other garbage. She squeezed Thea's hand while her mother went on and on for the thousandth time about how Doris had been born blue and not breathing.

"Two full minutes to get her to breathe . . . We thought we'd lost her . . . When I touched her, that's when she started screaming."

Doris always smirked at this part of the story. Ma claimed that she'd leapt out of the hospital bed when her baby wouldn't breathe, that the nurses had tried to keep her down, and that Doris had started breathing only at her mother's touch.

This may have been true, but not for the reason's Ma liked to think.

"But look at her now."

Ma nudged her before releasing her shoulder, pulling her close to her side in a half hug.

"A great girl," Colleen said. "Two great girls."

"No!" Thea said, agitated like a caged puppy. "I hate ruffles."

Ma dropped her grip and clamped onto the handle of the

shopping cart. "Can't have it all, I guess. Can we?" She cackled again, a little too loudly. A teenager restocking the bananas turned to look at her, and Ma pinched her lips together.

Doris imagined all this bottled crazy going home to the Simpson house like rotten takeout—Colleen opening it up at the dinner table so the family could poke at her life like maggots and mold.

"Didn't you say we needed milk?" Doris said.

"Yes, we do."

"I suppose I should finish my shopping, too. I'll tell Jenny you said hi, okay, Doris?"

"Oh. Sure. Great."

Colleen sprang away from them as if her shoes were biting her, carrying with her another week of torment at the hands of her crappy daughter.

The three of them marched alongside one another toward the deli.

"What did you say to her?"

"Nothing."

"I saw you talking. What exactly did you say?"

"Nothing. Just hi and stuff."

Thea ripped her hand away from Doris and scratched at her dress. "I hate ruffles!" she said again, louder now and with more urgency.

"You aren't lying to me, are you? Because I need to know."

"I didn't say anything, Ma. I swear."

Thea looked up at them. "Mama."

"I saw the way she was looking at you is all. Like a nosy deer. She loves to sniff around you."

"Mama!"

Ma didn't even face her youngest as she chastised her. "You will hush when I'm speaking to your sister."

"Maybe she just likes me." Doris desperately wanted to

believe that this was all it was.

"She looks at you like you're abused."

No one said anything after that, and neither of them noticed that Thea had fallen behind. Doris was too far in her own head, thinking of all the satisfying things she could say to her mother. Ma had busied herself studying price points of varying brands of Swiss cheese when a hundred thuds of a falling display jerked them both out of the stupor. Thea had taken hold of a banana gondola and was shaking it.

"Earthquake!" she said, screaming it louder and louder while store staff sprinted toward her like an oil spill.

It would have been funny—and in fact, many people did laugh, because it's funny when other people's kids are assholes but not yours—but the blood drained from Doris's face with such vigor she expected to see it pooling at her feet.

Ma was a guided missile. It was a true feat of physics that landed her nose to nose with Thea before the child could take a breath. Doris positioned the shopping cart between herself and the debacle.

There was apologizing while Ma hefted yellow bunches back onto the display. A clerk helped her while Thea flung herself onto the floor in a tantrum, having inherited Ma's incendiary temperament and none of her sense of social propriety. Once or twice Ma cast a glance over her shoulder in search of Doris, who, much to Ma's chagrin, would not be coming over to help.

People moved on, stopped watching, and after what could only have been a minute, Ma had returned, dragging Thea behind her. Doris pulled her fingers from the handlebar of the shopping cart as if frozen—bones cracking, muscles and skin sore.

Doris waited for Ma to regain control of the cart, but instead Ma pushed it into a corner and walked away, leaving Doris to figure out for herself that they were, in fact, done shopping and would be leaving the store empty-handed.

Thea had calmed considerably by the time they reached the car, confused more than anything. "Mama. Mama. Mama!" She beat the word into the back of her mother's head but was ignored enough to know to stop trying.

Not even Doris reached for her hand now, as if doing so admitted complicity. Thea wiggled in her booster seat, but quieted.

The ride home was silent and felt constrained, like when there were too many people in a small space. Doris breathed in through her nose and out through her mouth and counted the blocks until home. It was a short ride, but still she breathed in deep when they stopped.

Ma turned off the ignition and fiddled with her purse for a few moments before exiting, slamming the door behind her.

The girls stayed in the car until it was certain that Ma wasn't returning.

Thea asked if they were going back to the store, and Doris could only shake her head while unbuckling her seatbelt. There wasn't much else to say. They were both in the deepest of shit.

"Why did you do that, Thea?" She wasn't even sure her sister would understand what she was talking about, but Doris couldn't help herself. "You know you can't play earthquake around Mom."

Thea stared at her, expression flicking between confused and accusing.

"No more earthquake."

Thea clamped her mouth shut, so Doris got out of the car and held open the door as she stomped past her with a childlike emphasis of feet that could never be as loud as she wanted.

Doris trailed behind, feeling eclipsed, dreading the hell sure to pay. But she waited and waited more, and nothing came. Every moment of silence ticked by heavier than the last, like a spring-wound trap overdue to strike. Even Thea sulked herself into a corner, turning her back to Doris every time she neared her.

Ma kept to her room, leaving only once to loudly make tea—

so loud Doris swore the teacup was seconds from shattering from the force of her mother's stirring. The clanging echoed in a house so perilously silent.

For Doris's part, she desperately wanted to leave—hit the swings and let the moon swallow her—but something rooted her in place. She wasn't sure what it was, but every time she grabbed the door handle, a pit of nausea in her gut began to bubble.

There was no dinner that night. Dad folded his paper in his lap, the disturbance too thick in the air for even him to ignore. Doris held a sliver of hope he actually went into the bedroom to confront her mother, but the conversation was shockingly one-sided—his side. Ma didn't say a word. He emerged, square-shouldered, and skulked into the kitchen. All hope of any regularity dimmed when she heard him cursing over a jar of pickles.

Thea joined him, sprinting toward the commotion in the kitchen. Dad handed her a pickle, which she promptly dropped onto the floor because it was slippery and then she cried. Shame rolled over Doris—Thea hadn't eaten since breakfast. Doris, with all her worry and mounting dread, couldn't even think of food, but Thea was only three. She had to be starving.

Annoyed, Dad fled the kitchen, leaving his littlest daughter to cry alone, and got into his car.

When Doris tried to go calm things down, Thea kicked the pickle at her and stuck out her tongue. The tears had stopped, and her little toddler rage consumed her hunger, at least long enough for Dad to return with a pizza.

The food seemed to perk her up, and by the end of her first piece, Thea was setting the pizza on top of her head and giggling in her small, infectious way. Even Doris, who felt obligated to remove the pizza from her hair, allowed herself to laugh. The release was palpable. Surely Ma was conjuring up some dire punishment for what had happened earlier, but whatever it was appeared to be waiting until tomorrow.

So she thought. The evening passed as uneventfully as the day, and Doris was just on the verge of considering herself lucky. She and Thea brushed their teeth, changed into their pajamas, and curled into Doris's bed like always to read another story out of her Brothers Grimm anthology. When they were done, Doris clicked off the light while Thea burrowed under her comforter like a giggly little mole. Ma had been suspiciously absent from all of this, where she usually would breeze by with the laundry or yell at them for not wiping the toothpaste from the sink basin.

That was, until the lights went out. Like a game of Bloody Mary, Ma appeared in the doorway at the sound of Doris pulling the chain on her ceiling fan light, casting a long shadow that consumed the bed.

"Not tonight," she said.

For a moment, Doris thought she meant sleep. She wouldn't put it past her mother to keep her up all night as punishment. But it was quickly apparent that she was after something far more devious.

"Go to your room, Thea."

Giggling and hidden, her sister missed the fatal seriousness of Ma's expression. Instinctively, Doris drew an arm over the bed—a role reversal that was not lost on anyone.

"Now." Ma delivered the judgment with zero emotion. It was not a discussion—this was the law.

Thea refused to appear. "No."

Doris felt the small, whispered word ripple through the room like dynamite. She was so little. She just didn't know any better yet, and Doris was too slow and too stunned to do anything about it.

Ma lunged forward, a machine, as if following instructions laid down by a god. She ripped the blanket to the floor, its ends whipping in the air from the force. Yanking Thea by the ankle, she dragged her out of the bed so that she thumped to the floor with a sound that made Doris wince. Thea kicked and kicked, hitting Ma square in the gut more than once, but it didn't change anything. Ma just grated her toddler against the carpet faster and harder with every act of defiance.

Before she could process what was happening, Ma was out the door with her sister, and just as Doris reached them to pull her away, Ma slammed the door in her face, locking it from the outside.

Thea's room was just across the hall, a handshake away, but locked inside, Doris was useless to help her.

Thea screamed. Then she screamed again and again, wails of unimaginable intensity as their mother beat her—slapped her repeatedly—for her insolence. Doris pounded on the door. *Stop STOP STOP*, she silently begged. *It was all her fault, not Thea. Not little Thea.*

She rammed her fists against the door until they were stamped with blood. She cursed. She said everything she could think of to ignite Ma's fuse and draw her toward her. She might have killed her that night if it'd worked. The hinges wobbled, but never gave, and soon the slapping and the screaming stopped and all that was left was her own raspy breathing and condemnations.

I fucking hate you.

Fuck you. I hate you. I hate you.

Poor Thea. Her baby. Her sister. Poor Thea.

She slid to the floor. The noises ceased from Thea's room, and Ma eventually retreated into her bedroom after an exhausting evening of delivering judgments against her children. Doris listened for her sister, not daring to call out to her. It bothered her that she couldn't hear anything, not even a whimper. Silence was so out of character for Thea that for a brief moment, Doris despaired that she might be dead. There was slim comfort in the fact that Ma would never allow such a social faux pas to occur under her own roof.

She never left the door that night, sleeping against it in spurts when exhaustion overwhelmed her fear. Every click of the air conditioner jolted her alert, and she'd press her ear against the door just in case it was Thea. Surely she was locked inside her room too, but her sister's ingenuity never ceased to amaze Doris.

I'm still here.

Doris chanted it silently, pretending that her sister could hear her.

I'm right here. Don't be scared.

She wasn't sure how long she sat on the floor, but before she knew it her bedroom door swung open and banged against Doris's head. Ma told her to get dressed and then disappeared.

Before anything, she sprinted into Thea's room only to find it empty. The bed was made, the room immaculate. If she didn't know any better, she'd say everything about it was picturesque, which only served to inflame her further.

Doris charged through the house, calling out to her sister. Not in the bathroom. Not in the hall. Not in the living room. She found her in the kitchen, sat at the table with a heap of eggs and toast on her plate. Eyes meeting hers, Thea began to cry. Eggs flew out of her mouth.

Ma wrapped herself around Thea, calmly shushing her as if she hadn't beaten the shit out of her just hours before. Doris grabbed Ma's arm, taking extra care to dig her nails into her skin. "You get away from her," she said, breathless with fury.

But Ma simply *tutted*. "I wouldn't do that if I were you."

The calmness of those words was quiet as barbed wire. Doris understood immediately what they meant.

For a moment, she gaped at her mother as if she was someone else, *something* else. She couldn't believe that she was human, let alone a mother. Weren't moms supposed to love their kids? Colleen sure seemed to love Jennifer. Perhaps Doris was switched at birth, but then she'd look at Thea with her upturned nose and slight freckles just like Ma and feel guilty—if she had been switched at birth, then that meant Thea wasn't her sister. The conflict of emotions tore at her, leaving her speechless.

Ma reveled in the silence of her victory, eventually setting out another plate at the table for her husband, but none for Doris. There'd be no breakfast today.

The rest of the day played the same—threatening *tuts*, little amounts of food, and a constant wall erected between Doris and Thea. Whenever one of them would balk or sigh or squint or breathe or exist, Ma would quiet in a way that reminded them who had all the power. Her face turned to glass; Doris began to form the fake expression she'd later hone to perfection. But even absolute compliance could not satiate Ma. She knew they were faking it.

"If you'd just listen *for once*, you'd see that it's not so bad. What teenage girl doesn't want her own room anyway?"

She wanted to scream. It wasn't just a room she wanted—it was an entire life. How many times had she thought about stealing away in the night, Thea in tow? And every time she figured it would be best to wait. Now it was too late. If they were caught and returned home, Ma might finally finish what she'd started. She might not be able to control herself.

But instead of screaming, her glass face cracked around the lips, revealing the only smile she'd ever wear—the same soulless smile over and over.

That night, after Ma had presumably fallen asleep, Thea came into Doris's room. The edge of the covers lifted like they always did, and her tiny body easily found its usual spot right next to her sister. Thea did her very best to stay quiet, but toddler quiet and Ma quiet were on two very different levels.

Doris threw the covers off before either of them could get comfortable.

"You can't sleep in here tonight," she said.

Thea pretended to ignore her, but the tenseness of her back indicated that she'd heard her just fine.

"Ma will hear."

And she'll hurt you, again.

Doris touched her shoulder. Thea flinched with pain.

"You have to go, Thea." It killed her to say it, killed her worse than hearing her scream through the door.

"No, sissy."

Nothing moved. Ma hadn't come. Maybe she could let her stay, just for a few hours. Maybe if she drank a bunch of water, she'd wake up early to pee and could get Thea back to her room before Ma noticed. Or maybe she could just stay up all night, letting her sister sleep in peace.

But she couldn't. Ma said as much.

I wouldn't do that if I were you.

Doris scooped her up, avoiding her bruises as best she could. "Come on," she said. "Your bed is so comfy anyway."

She wiped her tears away with her shoulder as she laid Thea in her own bed for the first time since she was a baby. Rolling her blankets over the top of her and planting a kiss on her head, she lingered just a second to stroke her hair. "I love you, Thea."

Thea rolled toward the wall. "Night night, sissy."

A glance toward Ma's room revealed the door was ajar, but she couldn't tell if Ma was watching or not.

She cried herself to sleep that night, and every night for months after. Thea would never again share her bed. She cried that night for herself, for her sister, and for the future that suddenly became a lot scarier.

———

It had been a month and a new routine had begun to form— every night Doris would kiss the top of Thea's head after brushing their teeth and wish her good night. Every morning she'd wake thirty minutes before everyone else. She'd start the coffee pot for her parents and decide what to make for breakfast and try not to seem as exhausted as she was. She hadn't slept a night through in a month. Nightmares were a regular thing for her, but never this intense, and never nightly as they were.

The first few mornings she'd wanted to get up and watch television just to have something to drown out the lingering unease, but Ma seemed to have a sixth sense for when someone touched the remote when they weren't supposed to. Ma had a sixth and seventh and eighth sense for just about everything.

Instead of sitting around thinking about how shitty everything had become, she decided to distract herself with tasks, and tasks soon evolved into breakfast and coffee. Even Ma, who generally played dictator of the kitchen, seemed to relax to the thought of being served by her daughter. And Doris was keen to do anything to keep Ma from losing her temper again.

Like every morning for the past month, Thea rose last of everyone and plopped in her seat at the table, still rubbing the sleep from her eyes. The sight of her frizzy bed head used to make Doris smile, but now all she could think about was how far away her sister seemed.

"Good morning, sleepyhead," she said.

"Hi, sissy."

Hi, sissy. That's all she seemed to say to her anymore.

"Pancakes or waffles?"

A resounding *yes* to waffles later, Doris was pouring the pre-made batter into the waffle iron, thinking about how the clattering of her cooking was the only noise in the house. Dad had already left for the hardware store after announcing that he needed some screws. He always needed screws or nails or bolts or some made-up something for a made-up project that would never be completed. Unless his project was to collect various thingamabobs from Home Depot. He was acing the hell out of that.

Ma had eaten her whole wheat toast with one shave of margarine and retreated to her room to "fix herself up."

It was just Doris and Thea and a mountain of unsaid apologies.

The urge to just sit next to Thea and watch her eat was overwhelming, but Doris was afraid that Ma would catch them. She'd begun treating them like illicit lovers instead of siblings, as if their closeness was somehow immoral. Maybe it was the exhaustion, or maybe the silence had finally broken her, but Doris couldn't hold it back anymore. She wanted her sister back; she wanted everything back. She wanted to sleep through the night again.

Chair squealing against the floor, Doris sidled next to Thea at the table, as close as she could get without suffocating her. Content to simply sit and watch her eat, she'd have managed some semblance of decorum if not for Thea's smile. Not saying a word, the three-year-old grinned with relief, as if she was thrilled to finally be breathing again after a month of constant smothering.

Thea's cheeks were sticky with syrup, but Doris pinched them anyway. It was good to be close again.

It was good.

Neither girl spoke, just smiled and poked each other. Thea stretched her face in weird ways and giggled a little too loudly. Doris let herself laugh too, just a little, while picking up the remains of Thea's waffle massacre.

Good waffles, she thought, congratulating herself. Ma's waffles were always too crispy. Thea batted Doris's hand away from her plate even though they both knew she wasn't going to eat any more. They giggled louder.

The moment must have lasted only minutes, and to an outsider might seem like nothing more than a regular morning. But how precious were those regular mornings? Didn't everyone else see how lucky they were to have them?

She was just settling into their old routine when the clicking of Ma's shopping heels set the room on ice. Doris couldn't help but flinch, whipping her hands away from Thea and into her lap.

Thea swirled a finger in the syrup pooling at the edge of her plate. Turning the corner, Ma eyed them, zeroing in on Doris's hands. She was squeezing them together so tightly that her knuckles went white.

Of the many things to be expected, what actually happened was not one of them. Ma smiled—the real kind—and waltzed toward the kitchen sink as if her reaction was totally normal, as if her mere presence hadn't frozen the laughter of the room to the ceiling. Pulling on blue rubber gloves with a snap, Ma leveled her gaze at Doris.

"Why don't we do the dishes together today?"

"Really?" Her response emerged too quickly, too eagerly, but shock overrode her composure. Never once had Ma offered to do something *with* her, as opposed to *to* her or *for* her, let alone a chore that Doris was regularly tasked to complete by herself.

The joy she felt quickly dissolved—this felt like bait. Even Thea had the presence of mind to snort, her ability to detect bullshit still elegantly honed despite her age and recent beatings.

But Ma's sincerity continued unabated. "You know what? I think I'll just do them today. Why don't you girls go wash up?"

What was this? "I'll do the dishes, Ma. Really."

"No, no. Just go get dressed. I promise it's okay."

This was uncharted territory, and Doris hadn't a clue how to proceed. "How about I help you, then?"

And, oh, how Ma smiled. "That sounds lovely."

Dutifully, Doris collected the leftover dishes and arranged them on the counter by the sink. Thea wrapped her arms around her plate, unwilling to give it up. Doris let her keep it to avoid the inevitable tantrum that would destroy the weird calm permeating the room. Not that she trusted it quite yet herself, but it was better than the alternative.

The water scalded her hands, but she wasn't about to complain. They worked in silence, Ma plunging the dishes in the soapy lava, Doris rinsing and drying. It wasn't long before they fell into a quiet routine. Ma scrubbed faster than Doris could dry and put away, and an assortment of breakfast dishes collected on the counter. Ma said nothing, knowing full well that her daughter would have it cleared up before she was done draining the sink.

Her head felt overstuffed—as if the moment passed in slow motion. She didn't want to feel so good about it. All her instincts collided into a soup. In her haste, she accidentally dropped a plastic plate on the floor. Ma clicked her tongue but asked for the dish back. "We'll just rewash this one."

"What?" Doris couldn't stop herself.

Ma didn't hesitate, repeating herself with a deadly calm usually associated with anger. "Just a quick wash."

All this time Thea hadn't spoken a word, observing the display as if the syrup on her plate had glued her in place. When she eventually broke free from her chair, her shuffling made Doris jump, having forgotten that the little girl was there at all.

It startled her even more when a plate came crashing into the sink, flinging suds and water all over the counter and the floor.

"Thea!" Ma said. "Look what you did."

"I want to clean too."

Ma unraveled the dishrag from its place on the over handle and threw it at the floor. "You can clean your mess."

But Thea pointed steadfastly at the sink. "No, that."

"You can clean your mess and then go to your room."

Doris knelt for the rag, but Ma stopped her with a palm. "*She* will do it."

As it turned out, Thea would not do it, instead slapping a bare foot into the puddle so that it splashed all over Ma's pantyhose.

Ma's demeanor switched in an instant. It was frightening

in its swiftness and subtlety, nothing but a steel glaze in her eyes to indicate that she was milliseconds from ruining your life. But Thea persisted, screaming every inch that she was hauled off to her room.

By the time Ma returned, Doris had already wiped up the floor and begun putting clean dishes away in the cupboards.

"Thank you, Doris," Ma said.

"You're welcome."

They finished the task in silence.

———

She'd sworn she heard something. Ear pressed to the door, Doris strained to hear through the two-inch wood. Thea had been crying, she was sure of it.

Doris had spent most of her day pacing up and down the hall. Thea hadn't been allowed to leave her room except to use the restroom, and even then, Ma timed it so that Doris was distracted whenever allowing Thea out of her confinement.

It was after midnight and Doris couldn't sleep. At first, she thought she imagined the whimpers, but they had become too loud to ignore.

Thea cried often, but usually out of frustration. Sad tears were a new development. The shiny calm of the day evaporated with the sun. Now it was dark and all she had was the dread calcified in her gut.

She wanted to run to her, but Ma was listening. She was sure of it. Ma was always listening.

Thea didn't understand. Poor thing was only three years old. How could she?

But Doris did.

Doris was older. She was wiser. She was doing the right thing. She was doing the right thing.

Palming the door, she whispered to her sister through it,

understanding with an acuteness beyond her years that a piece of them was dead and gone. At the time, shuffling back toward her own room with its lonely bed, she imagined their slow recovery. Their adult reminiscence. Their eventual rekindling was all that allowed her to sleep at night. Doris was patient, even when Thea was not. All it took was a few years under their belt and Ma wouldn't be such an imposition. They would find their way back to one another.

They had to.

They must.

***

There were monsters in her dreams. There were monsters everywhere. There were monsters in her house.

The world was full of growls and sharp teeth.

Doris swore she'd have no part of that.

She would be stealthy. She would be clever. She would be love and patience. She would absorb pain like a sponge. She would hold it for both of them. In her dreams, she had so many arms, and each of them held a different piece of herself.

But there was too much pain, and soon the reservoirs would begin to leak.

***

Thea appeared at her door in the morning, dressed and ready for the day. Doris had been allowed to sleep.

"What time is it?" she asked.

"Time for breakfast, sissy," Thea said before disappearing down the hallway.

"Hey, wait!" Doris called to her, hoping she would come scrambling back in a fit of smiles. She wanted to say she was sorry. She wanted to hold her and check her over for bruises, kiss her boo-boos and tell her that Ma couldn't do this forever. Just a small moment to explain to her what was happening and why they had to stay farther away. It was for their safety. It was for the best.

But only for now.

Doris sat tangled in her bed for minutes. Then minutes more. Part of her imagined Thea hiding just around the corner, hands clapped over her mouth. But more time passed, and then more, and she knew Thea wasn't there. She wouldn't have been able to keep quiet that long.

Still, dragging herself from bed, she peeked down the hall.

It was just as she thought.

Shutting her door, she climbed back under her covers, wondering how long her mother would let her be. The sounds of breakfast kicked around in the kitchen—the toaster popped, a dish rattled, and little Thea mumbled something low and soft. Then it was quiet once again.

CHAPTER ELEVEN
THE FLOOD

DORIS WAS ON a boat. An honest-to-goodness boat. Blood and yellow bile soaked the bottom. Thea hovered over her. There were other eyes, too, but they kept just out of sight. Doris could feel them on her, though. She could feel them.

"They picked us up," Thea said.

"Help?"

"Just people like us. He had a boat."

Doris couldn't focus, couldn't see. "I was dead."

"Don't say shit like that. You're alive. You're on a boat."

Thea repeated it as if it might make it truer. As if she didn't believe it herself. The motor sputtered. Gas smog lingered over her head. "How did you find me?"

"Floating."

There were people on all sides of her. A man driving, a woman clutching a kid to her chest, Thea, and an old man with gray hair and yellow eyes. He stared at her, muttering in a Slavic-sounding language, maybe Russian.

Thea caught the exchange. "He was here when they picked us up. No one knows what he is saying. Another straggler."

A survivor. So far. The man tossed his hands around, miming the inflection of his words, shoulders sagged and relaxed. One of many disasters in his lifetime. He saw right through the fear—her fear and Thea's fear and everyone else's fear—and talked and talked. Another day. Another problem.

All of them looked at her, and she wished they'd stop. "Where are we going?"

"We're just going."

"I want to see."

"You need to rest."

"Thea."

There wasn't any anger in her voice, but she wasn't stoic either. Thea removed the hand that held Doris back and instead helped roll her upright, even though her own limbs were on fire. It was the least she could do.

It was a small pontoon boat, already at capacity with five adults and a child. Doris's blood was everywhere. The boy watched it spill from her torso as Thea jostled her to the fiberglass edge of the boat.

Water lapped up the sides as they puttered along. As far as she could see, they were the only ones on the water. It seemed more like a weekend lake trip gone sour than an end-of-times flood. Doris looked for a dock, for a sheriff's patrol boat, for other beleaguered boaters spinning about aimlessly in the din but saw no one. The tops of streetlights were totally submerged by this point. There was nothing but water above and water below, daylight sandwiched between two ominous entities. They would suffocate soon if one of them didn't let up.

Releasing the edge, she slid along the side and back into a sitting position. Thea hovered next to her, blocking the stares with her body while she sat figuring out what to do next. Her face was a waxy calm, and for a moment, it made Doris feel a little better. It felt good to know something for certain. She could jump right into Thea's head and hear the tumbling thoughts spin like a broken washing machine. *Heroin stop the bleeding who are these people blood we need food fuck fuck shit heroin heroin I am sorry.*

Doris had the urge to stroke her cheek but resisted. Too late for apologies, far too late for love now. She felt a dark pull at her back—the ring of all her senses telling her that they weren't going to escape this. Keeping things familiar, even if familiar was cruel and distant, was the smallest measure of comfort she could think to provide for them both. It was easier, anyway.

The entire boat of people trembled; the boat vibrated with it. The man at the helm had yet to glance back at her. His gaze remained vigilantly toward the horizon. Occasionally he would cup his hand over one of the gauges and grunt. The Russian rambled on and on with the immutable structure of a prayer. They stayed that way for a while.

The woman held her son and cried. The boy did not. He stared, soaking in his surroundings. Of any of them, he was the only one to hold Doris's gaze. He made her uncomfortable.

Haphazard tarps were strung atop the boat's canopy frame, tied with zip ties. It was all that was keeping the rain away.

Thea crouched next to her, head resting against a bent knee. Rain splattered against the platform at the rear of the boat. Doris could crawl over to it and be at eye level with the water.

Her sister didn't budge as Doris dropped to her hands, nor did anyone else acknowledge her elbow-crawl across the floor. With every move, she expected Thea to pop awake and start ranting. She waited for someone to grab her from behind and pull her back, but no one did. The Russian kept chanting, the man kept driving, and the boy kept watching her. His stare felt like eels all over her.

She dragged herself toward the edge, collapsing in the rain just far enough for her hand to reach over and touch the surface of the flood. It was warm or she was freezing or both, but it felt good.

Scooting closer, she hung both arms in as far as her elbows, ever cautious of the motor whirring just below her. The rush of water tickled her fingertips as the boat sped through it. She was tired, but instead of sleeping, she stared at the muck and tried to guess where exactly in the city they were, which direction they headed, where they might end up. Hopefully north toward the mountains. They needed to get to land, and she had a feeling that this storm wasn't going to stop any time soon. The way it hammered down on them, she had a hard time imagining it ever stopping.

Something touched her. She yanked her hands out of the water and pulled her nose to the edge of the platform. There was nothing there. She turned toward the other people aboard and saw nothing but eyes. They all stared at her without blinking or speaking, just dilated black eyes. She blinked, and everything was as she remembered.

The boat slogged on. Thea's chin touched her chest as she slept. Doris wanted to wake her now and ask what she had seen. Had she ever seen the monsters? The one that strangled them both, the one that lingered in windows, baring vicious teeth? Are these things in the water what those old monsters had become?

But then she saw her—really saw her sister for the first time in years. The way she curled into her own body. The way she cradled herself. The way she covered her face so that nobody could know what she was thinking, but Doris knew. Her terror oozed all over the floor as red as the blood that covered it. She was hunkering down, shielding herself from the hopelessness that would consume her if she allowed it.

She was a little girl that had grown up all alone, and Doris was the person that had failed her.

A tingling in her fingers turned her attention back to the muck swirling around her wrists, lapping up her skin like brown cuffs. It was impossible to see anything.

Aside from the boy's stares, the rest of the passengers ignored her. Every time she faced them, nobody else so much as glanced her way, but every time she faced the water, she felt their eyes crawling up her neck. She waited for it—the thing, whatever it was—to reach for her again. She wouldn't flinch a second time.

It'd been minutes. More. Less. She didn't know, but nothing was there. It had fled or was afraid or was nothing at all—a dishrag, a shoe. Just debris. She was crazy and exhausted and imagining things.

Thea whispered gibberish in her sleep, and Doris's stomach dropped at the thought of her waking up. The boat had gone quiet. The Russian leaned against the rail, catatonic at this point. The man at the helm cursed under his breath, propelling the woman into a panicked series of *what* and *why* and *what's happening*. Something about fuel. *Something something we're out of gas*.

Thea jerked, head shooting up from her knees like the pull of a cannon. Her gaze settled immediately onto Doris as if watching her in her sleep, but Doris nodded her away. *What's wrong? Go see*.

Thea *would* go see, because she was insatiably curious and always needed something to do. Because Doris was there at the back of the boat, watching. Because having something to do would make it easier for Thea to pretend everything was okay. Doris placed herself right smack in between her sister and danger, as best she could. She'd been doing it her entire life, or trying to do it and failing miserably at it. How many times did she throw herself into the fire just to blot it out for Thea's feet? She didn't know. How many times did she think she was sacrificing herself for Thea, but in reality was crumbling under the weight of her own baggage? She didn't know that either.

Doris stared at the water. *I know you're there*. She swatted at it as if to clear it away like smoke, but it only made visibility worse. Her body agonized over every movement, the trauma of the past few hours—or was it days now?—finally setting in.

The presence of her sister cloaked her, shadowed her sight. Blinking it away didn't work. And for a moment, the water didn't seem so dark and murky. The sky vomited all over her, the boat reeked of fumes as the engine sputtered out, and a shriek from the other passengers cut through all of it like a bullhorn. Steps toward her. *Step step step* came Thea.

"They're out of gas," she said. And then the floor beneath her popped, smoke billowing from the seams of the hatch. Thea leapt back, smoke curtaining between the sisters. And down in the water, shooting up a mass of outstretched gray limbs, was exactly what Doris had been looking for.

It was there—that monster, her monster, screaming toward her with new outstretched limbs. It broke the surface—one gleaming tentacle, so fragile and wispy at the ends. No one had seen it. Thea was caught in a whirl with the others as the boat rebelled.

They froze in place—she and her monster, deep in consideration.

Then it snatched her, wringing her by the neck and pulling her down into its deep.

Doris heard her name and a splash, but it all seemed so distant now. She couldn't see, but she felt the spastic rush of movement that meant her sister was in the water. Everything bubbled, the water a simmering pot on the verge of boiling over.

The sisters sank.

The sky seemed so bright in comparison to the black water. It rolled over their heads, tangled their hair. Neither could see the other.

It became darker and darker. Nowhere to go but down, an effortless fall. Doris let it consume her, let the drowning wrap her up. The pain snuffed out nerve by nerve. Glancing up, she imagined her sister tearing at water, fighting everything about it, hating it, hating her. And Doris was sad, but there was nothing she could do to make her sister okay. She knew that now. There wasn't anything she wanted to do anymore.

Nothing but sleep.

But the car flipped.

The car flipped.

She flipped, and here she was. Here in the hospital. Water everywhere, filling it up.

James was there. He turned his key in the lock of the front door. She was waiting, back pressed against her couch. She asked him what he had done as tentacles sprouted from her body. They lunged for him. *She* lunged. Then there was black and red. She closed her eyes, and when she opened them, she was in the hospital again, floating on a cot. James slept in a chair by the door, head dangling at an unnatural angle. She was glad he was over there and not next to her. She loved the swish of water, the density of it. The solitude was a comfort. He would have to swim to her side and pat her hand and brush the sweaty slap of bangs out of her eyes. He was never a strong swimmer. He drifted in his chair, the current dragging them apart.

Her mother had been there, perhaps still was. Her mothball perfume hung cloyingly about the room.

A doctor informed her of her condition. It was a nurse who explained to her what had happened.

"Why were you driving so fast?" she asked, so genuine in her execution that Doris set aside the accusation. "Where were you going? Did you really think you could help her? You're stupider than we thought."

The nurse smiled. "Are you in pain? Do you need anything?"

No.

But the nurse didn't wait for her to answer, just checked her IV drip and smiled her way back under the water as if melting.

The car flipped.

It had been a Friday. She'd gotten an alert that their checking account was low. It was strange; James was meticulous with his money. He'd pulled a penny out of the trashcan once after she'd accidentally swept it up. But wasn't that always how it was when a wife stumbled upon things that she shouldn't?

She'd pulled up to the house one day. Thea had been out front with James. At the crackle of her tires on the driveway, he'd taken two giant leaps back from her and Thea had just smiled and smiled.

Doris had asked her what she wanted, and Thea had said, "To see you, sister."

James had stared at the mailbox.

"I'm not giving you money."

"I didn't think you would."

James had returned to the house, looking back as Thea left shortly after.

Doris had known then exactly what had happened and spent the next few weeks trying to talk herself out of the idea.

He'd given her money. He promised he wouldn't, promised he hadn't. But he had, and Thea was closer to the grave than ever.

"What did she say to you? Did she ask for money? Do you think she'd stay in rehab this time? What do you think? What the fuck do you think, James?"

She'd lobbed sticky questions at him over the course of weeks, trying to draw it out of him. Kept bulleting Thea's name into the back of his guilty head. Each time, he'd deflected back at her with his "I don't know"s and "Can't we talk about something else"s.

And then their bank account had been low when it shouldn't have been.

James had been at the hardware store getting hinges for the cabinet door she'd *accidentally* bent when she finally put the whole of the story together. He'd withdrawn cash. A lot of it. Too much for her to not notice. Then she'd gone back and back and there'd been so many more.

Months of withdrawals. Maybe years, but she couldn't bring herself to go back that far.

Doris had waited for him to return home.

Memories of it floated back in flashes.

"How many times?"

"How much?"

"Howmuchhowmuchwhereisallourmoney?"

Then she was driving—she was going to find Thea and end this shit once and for all—but the black street rose over her head, and then she was here.

The low glow of all the machines keeping her alive washed her in a sickly white, or maybe that was just what her skin looked like now. Pushing the bedside button, she raised the back of her bed more, more, more, until it stopped. She hadn't sat upright in days—too drugged, too exhausted, dreaming in between invasive procedures and needles.

There was no ceiling to this hospital, just black storm raging where a ceiling should be.

"Stop, Doris. You'll hurt yourself." James's face hovered over her.

"You had an accident," his face said. The lips that she had loved, the mouth she had kissed—it lingered out of reach.

"You had an accident. You have to try and calm down."

"Don't fucking tell me to calm down. Where is my sister?"

His lips pulled in just so slightly, his jaw squared below clenched teeth, but his eyes never left hers.

That damn nurse slid in through the door, fumbling like a manic idiot at the closed curtain. Metal rings clanged together as she swung it open. "Everything okay in here?"

Doris couldn't bear to even look at her.

The nurse faced her shoulders toward James.

"She's just tired."

"Are you listening to me? Tell her what you fucking did, *tell her what you did*—"

There were hands on her—*calm down, it's okay, oh please hysterical lady, keep your voice down*. Doris wanted to fight them, but she didn't have the strength. Instead she watched as her husband backed through the commotion, fading away.

She was in a bedroom. She was in her bed, covers drawn tight around her. Something squirmed around her feet, then her calves, her thighs, her stomach. It reached her hands. It touched her face. It giggled like a small child and Doris giggled back, not realizing she was choking. It hugged her and she hugged it back, until it was impossible to tell them apart.

The ripples of the surface faded until there was nothing but a solid wall filling her body, making itself apart of her. She felt herself going down and down, deeper and deeper. Her fingers glanced against something—another set of fingers. She reached up as she sank; those fingers reached down. She'd never know whose they were.

———

Thea shrieked as her natural buoyancy pulled her up too close to the boat, too close to the people aboard it that were shouting at her. It felt like she'd traveled leagues, but every time she surfaced, she hit her head on the hull, always right there no matter how hard she fought and screamed. Eventually, a pair of hands gripped her by the hair and yanked her out of the water enough for someone else to grab her arms. A collection of hands and fingers and elbows heaved her onto the boat platform, then dragged her toward the prow. They performed like headless marionettes, as if they had a job to do and they were going to do it whether she liked it or not.

"That water's not safe," a man said. "There's something big in it."

They were never going to find her sister. Thea could jump back in, and they'd simply pull her back out again. She could dive in again and again, and even if they left her to drown, she would never find Doris. Thea had seen it happen, despite the smoke and the commotion. Doris sitting there, then something lashed around her neck, and then she was gone.

Now, as she paced the perimeter of the boat waiting for her sister's body to surface, she knew it wouldn't. She'd finally turned to stone and had plunked herself on the bottom of the stream, content to tumble along with the other forgotten pebbles. Not even physics could bend Doris's will.

The driver kept a suicide watch over her. The lady and her kid clung together and stared seaward; it was truly an ocean now. Rain scattered itself, slowing, but not stopping completely for another three months.

Before he died of fever, the Russian leaned over to Thea, resting a hand on her shoulder, and said, "Sestra." More a proclamation than anything. Thea could only guess at what it meant. What she always had been—*sister*. He didn't live to see the rain stop.

She sat in one of the ripped-up bucket seats of the boat, floating, hiding from the rain for days. After the Russian died, she helped roll his body into the water while the woman and child, the driver's wife and child, stared in silence. The man watched them until his eyes went bloodshot. No one ate, no one moved, no one spoke. Thea felt the tautness of muscles, as if the entire boat was about to capsize. The tendons in the woman's neck stuck out, as if to be plucked, and the boy pointed ahead of them, behind them. Pointing at nothing, but it wasn't nothing. It was that thing, that big thing that'd continued to follow and torment her.

Sleep draped over her like a fog, so that she was never sure if what she remembered was real or a dream, and often she'd wake calling out to her sister without realizing that she'd even been asleep.

"No!"

She woke up as water splashed over the sides of the boat. The driver dove overboard. The mother and son were gone. How long had it been? Weeks? Hours?

Thea watched from under the tarp as the man scrambled in the sea, digging through it and screaming names Thea didn't have the energy to commit to memory.

"There's something in that water," she said. The driver didn't hear her. "It's not safe."

They were gone. *Bloop*—gone under. They would never be found.

The man slogged his way back to the platform of the boat and curled his arms around the top rung of the ladder. He didn't hear Thea approach or see her hand extending toward him. Covering him in her shadow as she loomed over him, she wrapped her hands around his wrists.

"Come on," she said.

He did not come, not at first. He languished in the water, wailing for his family. Thea didn't have it in her to feel bad. She should have but didn't. He wanted to find them and die with them, but Thea knew as soon as she saw his screaming head surface above the water that he would live (for now). Doris had gone down like a stone. Bobbing only meant that it wasn't his time yet.

Both plunked into ripped-up bucket seats and searched their own corners of the water.

"Who are you?" the man asked.

"Call me Sestra."

He said to call him Rob. Then they floated.

CHAPTER TWELVE
THE AFTER

ROB HAD HER cornered in the cabin. Mijo sat next to her, careful to keep his hands to himself.

"What really happened?" Sestra asked. Again.

"I already told you." A quick flick of the eyes toward Mijo, and Rob repeated himself. Again. "You were going nuts. I knocked you out."

He was fucking lying. She knew he was lying, and he knew that she knew he was lying and yet here they still were, repeating themselves for the third time.

She'd ask Mijo, but she didn't trust him much either. The way they kept glancing at each other could only mean that they were in cahoots. But what neither of them understood was that her not knowing was far more detrimental than anything they might tell her. Had she hurt one of them? Tried to hurt herself? Did she try to jump? Rob, for all his saltiness, would never lay a hand on her without serious cause. His style was stealthier than that, like black mold growing behind the drywall. Sestra figured this was why they'd gotten along so well all this time. Or at the very least, hadn't thrown each other overboard.

And though they had never expressed it aloud, she felt betrayed, as if Rob had severed a bond between them.

"What are you not saying?"

His body clenched; he was a diamond-compressed with anxiety. "What does it matter? Doesn't change things."

She wanted to throttle the bastard, but God help her, she restrained the urge. "You know why it matters." There was so much that she didn't know—wouldn't ever know. For him to withhold something as important as this felt spiteful. It felt like a lot of things, and her composure quickly faded.

Apparently, so had his. "You want to talk? Then talk!"

"Talk? About what? You knocked me out!"

Dismissing her with a wave, he said, "It was only a few minutes."

"And you haven't let me topside since." Two days, to be exact.

She must have tried to jump overboard. Shit, this sucked. She looked to Mijo and he nodded. Sestra couldn't help but detect a little satisfaction in the way he grinned.

What was it about these posies? She'd thought she'd understand it better once it happened to her, but all it had done was make her irritable and gassy from not pooping for forty-eight hours.

Her legs were weak, but she stood anyway. She squared off at Rob. "I'm going up." No *needs* or *wants* this time. It just was.

Rob palmed her chest. "No, you ain't."

That was all she needed. Instincts that had all but shriveled suddenly bloomed. She swung at him, clocking him good in the jaw. But he had instincts too.

The pair went feral, unleashing a year's worth of grief all at once. Though not meant for one another, they delivered it all the same. Scratching, biting, screaming and cussing—they were well matched, what with his age and deterioration, and her penchant for conflict. If anyone had listened, they'd have detected the audible snap of their sanity.

Due to an error of judgment on Thea's part, Rob managed

to pin her on her back. He screamed at Mijo to help him while attempting to hold her still.

For her part, Sestra hurled every clever insult she could recall. "You pussy. You fucking pussy, *let me up!*" Annoyed at her own redundancy, she switched tactics. Poignancy gave way to volume, which ended up being more effective anyway.

Rob yelled louder at Mijo, and louder still, until he couldn't muster anything else. "Shut up. Shut up now!" He covered her mouth with his hand.

She bit him, tasted his blood, but still he didn't remove his skin from her mouth. That only made him hold her down harder.

"You need to shut up." His regular voice disappeared. He only spoke in growls.

She'd have gone on and on forever if not for little Mijo, waving his arms behind them in a way that suggested he was either panicked or trying to direct a Boeing 747 onto the tarmac.

Rob seemed pretty pleased with himself as she quieted, not seeing Mijo's desperation fanning out behind him.

"Let me go, Rob." He relented slightly, but not enough for her to move.

Mijo flailed in a blur. He spoke softly in Spanish, and even though she couldn't discern the words, she could tell it was a prayer.

"Rob!" She was screaming again. Whoops.

Then Mijo was gone. His steps sounded thumped up the stairs and he was gone. Only then did Rob release her, scurrying after, begging him to stop.

There wasn't time to think There wasn't even time to catch her breath. Off she was, absorbing the fresh air like osmosis. The pleasure didn't last long. It never did.

Mijo craned over the bow of the boat, staring at the water. Sestra didn't need to join him to see what he was looking at—the water glowed, just like before.

Floored, she didn't assist Rob in yanking Mijo away from the edge. She didn't move much at all. These definitely weren't any kind of shrimp or krill.

"Do you see what you did?" He pointed to the water as if it were her doing.

She switched her gaze between the toxic-colored water and Rob.

"It's listening to you." His voice was softer this time.

"What the fuck are you talking about?"

"It gets brighter when you scream. It hears you."

"And what is 'it'?" The morning was warm as usual, quiet as usual, but today carried with it an eerie undertone that plucked at all the hairs on her body.

Mijo signaled outward. "El monstruo."

"Bioluminescence," she said.

But even Mijo shook his head. "No."

"What am I supposed to do about it? Really, how is this my fault?"

"You tell me," Rob said.

A crack widened between them, each of them positioned on opposite sides. "This is nonsense."

"Oh, is it? You have always been strange about these things. You like them. You talk to them. I hear you whispering like I'm not there. Well, now the things are listening and listening only to you. Maybe you don't know what they want, but I don't think that matters."

The fight had left her—she didn't have it in her to be indignant anymore. What if he was right?

Really, what if he was?

She still had to poop, but the thought of hanging her bare ass over the edge of that neon ocean was enough to stifle the urge.

Without another word, she fled back into the cabin, suddenly exhausted beyond all functioning. It was like her body knew to conserve itself, to shut off her brain. If it didn't, who knew what she might do?

———

Knock knock. She mouthed the words, realizing a while later she hadn't actually knocked on the door.

James answered once she did. She made sure to come when Doris wasn't around. He seemed shocked to see her. He shouldn't have been.

"I need some money."

Realization dawned on him, his pasty jaw shivering at the indignity. "You stole my wallet."

"Of course I did. Now I need more money."

Blocking the doorway with his body, he leaned toward her as if he meant to shake her. "Where's my ring?"

"Why was it in your wallet?" she asked. It'd been bothering her since she found it.

"Where is my ring, Thea?"

"It's odd for a married man to keep his ring in his wallet during clandestine meetups with his sister-in-law. Very, very odd, if you ask me." It was so easy to toy with him; his emotions reeled against his features.

"Where is my ring?" He was getting angry now.

All the better. Angry people were the least reasonable of all people. "Some people might get the wrong idea."

"What wrong idea? What the hell are you talking about?"

She shrugged. "You know what I mean."

He was fit to explode, but somehow buttoned it up just in time. "You don't have it anymore, do you."

The pawn shop had paid handsomely for it, but he didn't need to know that. Yet.

"It'd look awfully bad for me to show up with your ring on my finger. Who knows what people might think?" She laughed.

God, he was the easiest mark on the planet.

But he laughed too, as if the idea of them together was too ludicrous to take seriously. "Doris wouldn't believe that for a second and you know it."

"She's probably the only one to not underestimate the depths of my shittiness. I'm sure she'd figure it out. But the rest? Jesus, can you imagine what my *mother* might say? Can you imagine how tiring that would be? Especially for Doris."

His body went rigid, to the point that she could have rung him like a bell. "You truly are a psychopath."

No, she wasn't. Of course she wasn't. She was smart and he was dumb, and this was all too easy. She wasn't a psycho—she just needed money. And he was going to give it her.

She smiled. "Small bills, please." Then she waited.

James stood in the doorway, stunned. It was all too easy. Too easy.

Then he backed away from the door, moving at an odd slant that had her wondering if he was fainting or was just too upset to function properly. Slipping into the dark of the living room, she grabbed at the edges of the door and peered after him.

"I don't have all day, James. And if I know Doris's schedule like I think I do, neither do you."

But he was gone. The shades were drawn and the lights off— the room was completely empty. No furniture, no pictures on the wall. The archway into the kitchen was black as tar.

"James?"

When had they moved in? It was years ago. She remembered their housewarming party—Ma had been adamant that Thea show up *and be presentable for the love of God.* There was champagne, and she'd stolen an entire bottle for herself, boozing it up in the corner of their yard while pretending to smoke. Ma had found her, and she'd been spitting mad.

Where was all that shiny new furniture now? Where was

James?

She was about to step inside when a low gurgle echoed from the black space where the kitchen should be. Then came the water—a slow trickle at first, like runoff from a leaky cooler.

"Doris?"

No one responded.

The water picked up, churning into the living room and spilling through the doorway. Where was all this water coming from? It just kept coming, more and more and more. Thea wanted to back away, to run, but something rooted her in place.

"James!" Her voice cracked, springing from her throat in a panic. "What the fuck is going on, James?"

A voice—so familiar and so strange and so not possible.

"I told you they were coming, sister." The noise oozed from the black space. "Now look what you've done."

She spoke delicately, so that Thea had to lean in to hear.

"Doris?"

There was no answer.

"This isn't funny. Fuck this, I'm leaving." Her body wanted to bolt, to get the fuck out of there as quickly as her feet would carry her, but the moment she stepped back from the doorway, a wail erupted from the house. Something monstrous and huge shuddered and shook the walls apart. The floors began to rock, splashing against the drywall in waves.

Before she could run, a tentacle sprung out of the black. It snatched her around the waist, crushing her organs between her bones with ease. She tried to scream or fight or do something, but it gripped too tightly.

It pulled her down and down and down. Down under the house. Down under the waves and water. She could do nothing as the house sealed up over her head, her breath pressurizing in her lungs.

Down she went.

Down she stayed.

Sestra startled out of it, unsure what was real and what wasn't.
The boat moved. She wasn't on a boat. She was in the water, or
on a raft, or in the clutches of a monster, or getting high behind
a dumpster. She settled into a fog, never quite sure if she was
awake or asleep or dreaming or just seeing shit like it had always
been—gray and mean and indecipherable. There were times when
she was certain that there were other people on the boat besides
Mijo and Rob, but then she'd snap out of her funk and realize that
it was just her, acting a fool all by herself.

Past and present stretched and snapped together, her mind
circling itself like an ouroboros—a snake eating its tail—she was
consuming herself whole.

More than once she felt the warmth of a small hand laid
across her cheek. She was rather certain that was real.

She heard crickets and the soft rapping of knuckles against
the window.

And then she woke up for real. There were no crickets. The
room was empty and dark. She was alone.

Her mouth felt waxy and parched. How long had it been
since she'd bothered to drink anything? Where was everybody?

By now she had gotten used to the sound of lapping water
against the side of the boat, but just then it slapped a little too
loudly. Every shift of the boat knocked her legs loose. Aside from
the water, the boat was suspiciously devoid of noise, and a knot of
panic congealed just beyond her tonsils.

Where was everybody?

It felt like the first time she stepped foot on this boat.
Shadows jutted out at devious angles; she bumped into steps
that she'd memorized weeks ago. Sestra couldn't orient herself.
Everything was foreign and new all over again.

She found Rob and Mijo at the back of the boat. Mijo draped a makeshift fishing pole over the rail, tugging at it a little too vigorously. Rob calmed him with a hand to his shoulder but snatched it away the second he heard her coming. They'd been at it awhile from the looks of it—tangled fishing line clotted the deck.

Rob must be high or dying or some shit, because he would have kicked her shins out if she'd been the one to waste all that line. And although it was a good thing the two of them had finally broached their callous distrust of one another, it panged her to see how seamlessly they'd done it in her absence.

Moonlight shone against Rob's patchy baldness, turning his skin gray. Scars creased his skin. Her own hands were unrecognizable—cracked and sallow and missing a fingernail or three.

Only Rob faced her.

"You look like dog shit," he said.

"Well, I feel like a million bucks." She scratched at a rash on her arm, shaking off a couple of scabs. "Catch anything?"

"Problems, I suppose."

"Well, I hope you threw them back. We've got enough of those."

He nodded and looked away.

"Where's the water jug?"

"Gone."

Fuck. "Gone?"

"Lost it."

Lost it in their game of Twister with a sea monster. The latent accusation of those two little words wriggled at her feet.

Lost it because of you, you fucking sea harpy.

Mijo glanced at her, and immediately back to the water when she met his gaze. While Rob's lips were chapped to hell, Mijo's were the pinnacle of smooth hydration. One of those sneaky fuckers had water. Or at least they used to.

Wouldn't do a whole lot of good to press them about it now.

"Too dark," Rob said. "Dark and empty."

Only then did she realize that the lights in the water were gone, and it panged her in a way that she didn't dare admit. Even the goddamn monsters were tired of her.

"I'll leave you to it, then," she said, *it* meaning distracting themselves from their shitty, inexorable death with homemade fishing poles.

Choosing a spot as far away from the pair as possible, she hunkered down, cross-legged, just how she and Mijo used to do.

Agua. That's a whole bunch of agua, kid. El sol. Sun. Caliente as fuck.

She stared at the dark water rolling endlessly around her, groggy as hell but unable to sleep. She watched for lights while listening to the *bloop*ing noise of Mijo's fishing line tugging hopelessly at the water. None of them would find what they wanted.

———

They must have assumed she was asleep, and to be fair, she hadn't budged in a few hours. Maybe they thought she was dead.

She might never have known they were talking about her if not for deep timbre of Rob's voice that made it impossible for him to keep quiet. Nothing at all like Mijo's, so slight and wispy a gentle breeze would snuff it out.

Rob was offering assurances. "I know. I know. We'll figure it out."

Then the absence of noise indicating Mijo's turn, and Rob would be at it again. "I know. I don't want to either."

The exchange was brief, and no matter how much she strained, she never could pick up anything more than that.

She kicked the rail, for no other reason than to be a bitch.

It had been two more days, and the cleave between them had been thoroughly salted. Nothing would ever grow back.

She passed her days at her end of the boat and they at theirs, occasionally hurling pleasantries when passing the canteen—the one Mijo had kept hidden from her until now—between them.

The totality of everything that had happened loomed over them. No rain, drinking water reduced to drops, and no food for days. Things were souring rapidly.

Sestra hadn't given much thought to what she planned to do about it. Crappy things happened all the time; what was there to do besides add it to the agenda and continue about your day? That was the plan until it became clear that the plan was terrible, which occurred about forty-five seconds after concocting the damn thing.

She was getting stir-crazy and restless, and by the second day began pacing.

"Would you just stop, Ses?"

"I'm staying on my side, okay?"

"What do you mean, your side?"

Then she remembered that she never actually explained the whole side thing to him. "Just...nothing."

"Then stop pacing. It's making me insane."

Sestra stopped, but only so she could yell more effectively. "I'll walk however I want."

Niceties were out the window at this point, and Rob squared off as if he'd been living for the day. "You'll stop or I'll make you stop!"

Mijo positioned himself within their sight, yet far enough away to avoid an altercation. He leaned back and watched, perhaps hoping they'd throw each other overboard and shut up for good.

"You aren't going to do shit, Rob. And you know it."

"I'll throw your ass in the damn floor if I have to."

She could tell he meant it, and so stomped down the stairs with him at her heels. It didn't take much effort, what with the sea-rotted hinges and aged wood, but even so, she felt badass ripping that door out of the floor and tossing it against the wall.

"You're losing it," he said, calmly yet loudly.

She stared at him. "I know." Because she did. Although she'd argue that she never had *it* to begin with.

Sestra didn't follow Rob as he marched up the stairs. She just fell to the floor as her resolve left her, staring at the hole in the floor and the door she'd just destroyed.

She spent the rest of the day down there, and sometime in those few hours she decided what she was going to do. There was no epiphany, no master plan, just a subtle knowing that this was her best course of action. It may as well have been laid out for her like a storybook, big baroque letters spelling out her doom.

And then she flung her crazy ass into the sea and lived happily ever after.

That wasn't exactly how it went. It happened sometime after her argument with Rob and before nightfall—a calmness floated over her. It reminded her of the first blush of heroin as it hit her bloodstream. It draped over her, heavy and thick. Her chin dipped; she was nodding off just thinking about it. The serenity of it. That's all she ever wanted anyway, just a little bit of peace. A moment to *not* think, because thinking is what got her into trouble.

She reached for her back pocket, a habit she'd developed that only appeared in her more desperate moments. Maybe she forgot something there? After Rob had picked her up, all that time ago, she'd reached back to that pocket in search of her sister's ketamine. It was gone, lost after so many dives underwater. She'd spasmed and cried at the realization. Maybe the others thought it was because of Doris, about the flood, about literally anything that had happened to them, but it wasn't. It was about the drugs, how just when it didn't matter if she was high or dead or what, they were gone. The drugs were gone. The sheer hilarity of it was too much to bear.

It was all so tiring. Existing was tiring, but she didn't want to die. Drugs would have helped immensely, but there weren't any. Being left to her own devices was worse than anything. Having Mijo and Rob surgically extricate themselves from her was more than she could bear. That was always the worst of all the things— being alone. And somehow on a boat of only three, she managed it again. If the others had to choose between nothingness and her, they chose nothingness and locked her in the cabin.

She was stir crazy, probably delirious, but the sensation of having to do something, having to go somewhere or be somewhere, anywhere other than here, consumed her. She used to wander the streets in search of a cure for it, but it always returned. The desire to wander, to not be pinned down by anyone or anything, is what made her. She was never comfortable, never satisfied, and never calm. She had that feeling now but had nowhere to go. She could go up and face the stares and whispers or stay down here in the dark alone. Those were the options.

She hated those options, and she hated the way Mijo stared at her. She hated her own behavior, too, but that wasn't anything new. The time for bettering herself had long passed, but that didn't mean she couldn't change. It dawned on her sometime during the twilight hours, after catching herself gripping the skin of her chest every time Mijo slunk by. At first, she wondered if Rob had instructed him to check on her, knowing that if he did it himself they'd start shouting again. But after the tenth or so time of him pretending to stretch his little legs, Rob called to Mijo, asking him what he was doing. Each time Mijo grazed by her, he'd sneak the smallest of glances, only daring to meet her eyes for the briefest moment before scuttling back to Rob.

And then it struck her. Her wasn't checking on her, he was wishing for her. From the moment that boy leapt from the floor he'd been at her side, and now they were drifting. He was afraid of her. He wanted her, but was terrified of her.

The realization crashed into her, more painful than she thought possible at this point in her existence, because she knew exactly how Mijo felt. She'd been that kid, wide-eyed and innocent and needing someone to hold her. She understood the ache it created when no one came. She was well-versed in longing stares, in being surrounded by people she was too terrified to approach.

Mijo came around again, braving a longer look this time. Sestra held it, and the two sized each other up. His chin jutted out, defiant. He wanted to come nearer, but now that he had her attention, he didn't want her to know that. Sestra couldn't help but make comparisons to herself. Desperation and loneliness had a way of shaping people that way. It left people scarred.

She flashed an easy smile at him, and he grimaced. She knew he would. A smile isn't what he came here for, but a smile was all she had to give.

It was night again by the time Sestra decided to enact her plan. It had been creeping up on her for a while now, but she'd always found a reason to ignore it. Until now. Until Mijo. She'd been running away from things for so long that she wasn't sure knew how to do anything else, and the thought made her ill. A new type of exhaustion had seeped into her, released by Mijo's frown. She felt more anxious than she had in years, maybe decades. She had to act before time and starvation and thirst and insanity acted for her.

Sestra waited until she was as certain as possible that both Rob and Mijo were asleep. As if sensing a wrongness, Mijo had decided to sleep below deck with her, although still more than an arm's length away. It was the first time they'd been this close in days. She wanted stroke his hair but thought better of it.

Taking the door she'd ripped from the hinges, Mijo's hidey hole now destroyed, she emerged topside both triumphant and terrified. Rob slumped against the wall, seemingly unconscious. Tiptoeing to the bow, she glared at the watery horizon. It was moments like these that people in movies comment on the beauty of things, but to her it still looked like an evil, black swamp.

For once in her stupid life, she thought about what she was about to do. There wasn't any turning back. There wasn't any coming back. The sea and the sharks and the sun were all deadly on their own, but that's not what scared her. Nor is it what motivated her.

She was going to find a posy, and she was going to kill it.

Or die trying.

Or just die.

But if that was her fate, she wasn't about to do it quietly in the dark, letting little Mijo help toss her corpse overboard. If she was going down, she was taking a fistful of flesh with her.

So she flung herself in the water.

If she'd bothered to look back, she'd have seen Rob on his feet, watching silently as she fled.

———

The water was repugnant. It itched at Sestra's skin, but she was determined anyway. She found her posy. She floated her happy ass out here on a damn door and she found it. Arms ahead of her, she dove deeper down until she could no longer see. Still she kept her eyes open. That fucking posy was waiting for her, and even if she couldn't see it, it could see her, and she was going to face it with her eyes open. It was easy to get disoriented; open eyes brought with them the expectation of seeing. As long as it stayed dark, she knew she was going the right way.

It was only seconds before her lungs faltered, too weak to hold her breath much longer. She feared she'd lose the thing having to surface for air—as if it would know she was weak and turn away in disgust. Soon there wasn't much of a choice as her chest seized, struggling to find air. Up she went, letting her natural buoyancy carry her. The water thinned, navy to cerulean to aquamarine to the yellow of the sunny surface.

Up she arrived, and down again she dove. Light to dark and back to light again once it became too much. Down and down and nothing to show for it. It was fucking insane. Others were snatched and stolen and were just gone. Even this she had to work for. She was tired of the sun and the way it flayed her skin. The door she'd arrived on was gone. Up and down, up and down again.

She'd been at it enough and was becoming quickly accustomed to the idea of just drowning and calling it a day when a burst of coolness blasted against her bare feet. The surface churned and settled again.

"Finally. Goddamn." She spoke slowly, but inside her body melted at the thought of a posy being so close to her. But this was what she came for. This was what she fucking came for. She wanted to rip it to shreds, to defile it somehow, but the pressure encapsulated her. Her arms didn't have the range, and like all her well-laid plans, this one too imploded before it even got started.

There was no fighting here. She couldn't even give the fucking thing a paper cut.

So down she went.

Down and down and down.

It had snaked a tree-trunk tendril around her torso. In the water, no one could see how much she cried. It felt like electricity, like a shock up and down her body, and it clamped on with exposed-wire tenacity.

Water slid up her face and into her nose as it pulled her down. Pressure pounded at her temples until her head felt ready to burst.

Her lungs filled up. She choked and gagged, but there was

only more water to choke and gag on. She did this until the urge to try faded and she was content, just going to ride it out. Maybe she'd died? It was okay if she had.

Then it stopped. There were shadows here where before it had been a wall of ink. Things moved in front of her. Fine hairlike strands grazed her cheek.

She was delirious from the struggle, her body shutting down part by part. She shouldn't be able to see so far down, and yet she could. She couldn't feel her fingers but was aware of every ounce of water crushing into her. The shadows moved too much, flicking up and down, side to side, closing in on her face and then pulling away. Tendrils slipped by her again, this time snaking around her shins before disappearing again.

Shadows were getting darker—no, wait, there was light. The tentacle gripping her midsection began to glow. The posy itself was glowing. Faint at first, but soon it lit up like a cheap glow stick. Blue-green shimmers rolled up its body, sending cracks of light along its massive tentacles. She searched for the head, the mouth, imagining a beak bigger than her head ready to snap her in two, but only a tangle of tentacles was visible, coiled together like a nest of twigs.

That tickling sensation grabbed at her again, reaching down her arm. When it hit her palm, she grabbed at it, caught it between her fingers.

It came easily as she pulled it closer. It felt like hair . . . closer . . . and fuck, it *was* hair. She'd grabbed a body. Caught around its middle was another tentacle. The face was female, and if Sestra could have, she would have screamed, instead of kicking the thing away with her one leg that could still move.

It should have been rotted away, but under the glow, the lady appeared to be only sleeping. A great sweep of water brushed against her as another tentacle unfolded itself from the mountain of knots. Brighter than the last, in its grip was another body. The glow crawled all over it, painting its skin blue. Even at a distance, it too looked as if it was asleep. A male this time.

More and more, it unwrapped itself, presenting her with claimed souls. She never got much of a good look at any of them, each one resembling someone she used to know while still being a total stranger. Never again did the posy allow one to fall within arm's length of her, breezing them in front of her, taunting her with their existence.

Sestra assumed she was dead now. Her lungs no longer stung; her temples no longer throbbed; her skin was loose around her bones instead of wrinkling at the edges. She was one of them now, she guessed. Another trophy. Another soul.

But her eyes weren't closed yet. Unlike the others, she could still see.

More and more tentacles unraveled until there was more posy than not. It overwhelmed her vision, like standing too close to the television as a kid. The glow brightened as its center was slowly exposed.

Through a slew of fingers and hair and blue-lit skin, she saw a new tentacle pull itself free. It was smaller, thinner at the base, and tucked closer to the middle of the beast. It held its body by the neck. A male.

She didn't realize it at first, but she was moving toward it. It was pulling her in.

How quickly she recognized him once she was close, though she shouldn't have. Bloated and purple as he was, rotted with water before the posy could claim him, Sestra still noticed his long chin and the horrible paisley tie that he always wore. It was James. She imagined him stuck in his car on the freeway as he tried to get home to his wife. Or maybe he'd been trapped in the office and drowned pressed up against a window overlooking the parking lot. How had it found him? Why did it bother?

Is this why it chased her? Following the tendrils floating

in all directions, she searched each of their faces. Were these all people she'd once known or fucked or fucked with? A conglomerate of her bad decisions all stuck together until it had no choice but to become a monster.

Next to James's corpse, another tentacle billowed out—so small, small enough to hold its tiny hostage by the hand. Oh God, she didn't need to see the face, fearing who it might be. The child bobbed so peacefully, his free hand reaching out. Whatever bit of her still lived died on the spot. This was just a kid. Kids weren't supposed to be down here, frozen in the deep with a corpse-monster. They didn't deserve this, but did any of them?

This was bullshit. She tried prying herself out of the posy's grip, but it wouldn't budge. She didn't want to see any more, but the weight of the water crushed her body into submission. Every move was sluggish and thick, and the creature held her like a vise. Too late to change her mind.

She stopped fighting it, but that didn't stop her from trying to hurt the fucking thing. Digging her nails into the flesh, she tried ripping away at the skin, but it was like oil and rubber and no matter how much she sank her nails into it, she couldn't bring anything up. Fuck it. She just wanted to hurt it now.

Another body presented itself to her.

It looked like Rob, but it couldn't be him. She'd left him safe on the boat. He watched her go. The illusion of him sitting on the deck catching big, fat fish shattered. She reached out to him, couldn't stop herself. Was he even real? His cheeks still burned with memories of life. He was cold, like everything else, but *looked* warm. No one would be the wiser if he changed his mind and swam back to the surface.

Whoever it was, he hadn't been here long. Maybe that was why it had taken so long to find the damn thing. Maybe it had been busy snatching up her friend.

No one can see you crying down here.

For a moment, it seemed the posy had finished. Its limbs paused now, frozen people dangled at the ends of their monstrous tethers, and Sestra waited for anything else to happen. But nothing did. The posy glowed and glowed while serving up her past on a platter.

It glowed so brightly, so wildly. The sight of it stung her eyes. *The monsters are here.*

She couldn't bring herself to look. The sight of it stung. It was too bright. Her skin felt like worms. Or was it tentacles? She didn't want to look. She didn't want to be here. She regretted everything. There was so much to regret, and she did. Oh, did she.

Everything.

The stillness ached. She wanted her sister.

It had everyone else. It had everything. It had gone and found them and tucked them into its breast, and now it stopped?

Where is she? Where the fuck is my sister?

She waited for the last reveal. There had to be one more. She had to be one more.

After all of it, Sestra still didn't get it. She might not ever. So the posy reached into its clutches and flung out one last body.

The world melted into alien hues of green and blue and black, and then she was alone.

But she wasn't.

A gentle hand landed on her shoulder. Thea knew it immediately.

"Where the hell have you been?" she asked.

"Here. I've always been here," said Doris.

"Oh really? Just been having a rest with a posy, have you? Having a grand old time while the rest of us are up there dying?" The very sound of her sister's voice was like a reset, immediately dropping her back on the streets, back into the rage and sorrow and rejection.

"That's exactly what I've been doing, Thea. Exactly it."

Thea wanted so badly to grab her, squeeze her close until her head popped off. She had missed her so much. She hated her and missed her and was so fucking sorry. But she couldn't bring herself to look at her. God only knew if it was even really her. Doris was dead. Thea probably was too.

"Sorry," Thea said.

"Still stubborn as hell, I see."

She shrugged. "I guess."

"Will you look at me, please? I hate talking to the top of your head."

Hesitant, she did as her sister asked. It scared the shit out of her to imagine what Doris had become, but she looked just as Thea remembered. She wore the same shirt and pants as the day she died, and her body was rigid with pain. Ever here she was not free of it.

"Are we dead?" Thea asked.

"You aren't. Not yet."

"Then where are we?" She tried to see beyond Doris, but nothing would materialize. The space around them shifted and warped whenever she tried to focus. It was as if they were still sinking, monstrous things slithering around them in the dark and deep.

"I'm not sure. I've been down here a long time. It's hard to tell how long."

"I saw James. The posy has him."

"I know. I found him." Her expression was distant, as if still deciding whether to keep him.

Does that mean that she found her too? That she was searching for her all this time? "You always told me to run. To hide. You always told me there were monsters out there and I thought you were fucking deranged."

She expected a fight but received nothing but a smile in return. But even that was fleeting—her usual consternation swallowed it up as soon as it began.

"Not that it did any good."

"Your training was pretty piss poor, considering the circumstances."

Doris dropped to her knees, taking both hands to Thea's cheeks. It was her gentlest gesture since childhood. Maybe because they both were dead, and this was just the final, desperate sparks of Thea's psyche flickering one last time. Maybe because this was what she always wanted and wished and prayed for. All those times she'd wandered and wandered, completely convinced that wandering was for the best, that she was a wild, uncaged bird not suited for the traditional trappings of love and comfort. Deep in all those places she tried to delete sat this demented and human wish for someone to hold her the way Doris held her now.

That was the thing too—it had always been her sister she thought of. That had always been the only loss that mattered. She wondered, in those rare times she allowed herself to reflect on it, if Doris mourned too. Honestly, she would never be certain. Not even now.

Doris gazed at her, eyes endless pools of water. She was fading. "We always were better storms than we were people, weren't we, sister?"

Thea returned the gesture. Doris's cheeks were frail and soft, not cold or warm. Empty. Fleeting.

"Like the stories," she said.

"I shouldn't have filled your head with such scary things."

"You were little. A kid. It didn't do much harm."

"It didn't? Did you forget where we are?"

For a moment, she had. It was just her and Doris. Two sisters. It wasn't cold or hot; she wasn't tired or broken; she was just Thea again, listening with rapt attention to the coos of the only person that'd ever mattered to her.

It was fleeting, but enough. It would have to be.

Thea closed her eyes, clinging to the image of her sister as it slipped out of her grasp like sand.

A flurry of emotions coursed through her—she wanted to yell at her for leaving the way she had, yet hold her forever, if only to remember that she'd been real once, that she'd really lived.

She wanted to tell her that she was sorry.

Even now she couldn't bring herself to say it. She should, but she wouldn't.

A weightlessness took over, and she was suddenly aware of being moved around. The tentacle around her waist tightened and went slack, as if to jolt her back to the present.

The present of being underwater, of not breathing, of never seeing the sun or the sky or Rob or anyone ever again.

The blue glow of another tentacle slid in front of her, one so small it may not have been part of the same creature. She reached out; it was right there. Her arm wasn't even fully extended before she bumped a knuckle into it.

It was cold.

She opened her eyes. It was cold.

A hollow skeleton glared back at her through a fog of water.

It was empty, a shell. It could have been anyone—Doris, her mother, Death. It was all of them.

It was herself. Or someone just like her.

Is this what her family had seen every time they looked at her? Every time they pleaded and begged for her to change? Was she nothing more than a hollow corpse just wearing her skin, waiting for the moment to be free of her saggy existence? She'd been on the bumpy road to overdose. She'd been closer than she'd ever thought.

She despised the thought of Doris remembering her this way.

And Thea laughed. Was this the ghost that had haunted her so? Since her lungs were full and her body a sinking stone, she thought about her cackle spitting across this thing's face. The bones paled under the blue. Instinctively, she massaged her arms, her inner thighs, her toes—all the places she'd used as gateways for heroin, the hot rush of it settling over her body like an electric blanket. Pure comfort. Total satisfaction. She'd always miss it, but she didn't miss it as much as she thought she would.

The posy released her a moment before tightening its grip once again. She was face to face with the skeleton now, body to body. Its ribs jabbed at her gut, prodding at her like some sort of joke. Still, she threaded herself through its bones, so that once she rotted, no one would be able to tell the two apart. It could have been anyone, but she was sure that it wasn't.

Her thoughts slowed. Everything slowed. She'd always been a hurricane of a person, her body a crumbling dam unable to contain it. Doris had tried her best to keep her safe from herself, but all that ended up doing was destroying them both.

A little girl had run away. She was barefoot and cold.

The girl tried to hide, but the things—the thing—found her anyway. The monster came after the girl.

It watched her.

It was always watching.

It had a dozen hands and sharp teeth . . .

. . . little sister crying . . .

. . . no matter how hard you try, your monsters always follow.

So we started playing the monster game.

Lights shimmered around her, dimming, creeping closer. Color throbbed messages at her that she couldn't understand, looping around her tighter and tighter.

It wasn't long before the posy smothered her. Completely cocooned, maybe she'd emerge as something new. Maybe she'd stay right here and rot, though that didn't scare her like it should have.

She closed her eyes, hearing once more a voice she thought

had been lost forever. Her sister's voice.

Oh, how she had missed it.

ACKNOWLEDGMENTS

Where do I start? So many people over a span of so many years have nurtured my writing in ways that made this book possible. So I suppose I'll start from the beginning. To Laura, my first creative writing professor, thank you for cradling my insecure writer ego as I learned. Thank you for assuring me I could do it, even when I wasn't sure I could. Thank you to all my writing friends, most notably Eshe and Amy, of which were subjected to years of me talking about drafting and rejections, and somehow still wanted to be my friend. Thank you to Kate Brauning, you beautiful soul, for championing my work and simply being an all-around class act. Thank you to my mother, my most fervent, proud, an enthusiastic supporter. You have no idea how many times you kept me afloat as I waded through publishing's choppy waters. Thank you to my husband, who has treated my writing with more respect than it probably deserved. You are a saint. To my kids, I finally did it despite your constant distractions (love you, boys!). Thank you to those that I neglected to mention here. Trust me that it is not from a lack of gratitude, but instead the pressure of actually writing my acknowledgements making my brain seize. I'll most certainly write you a very emotional apology once I realize what I have done. And finally I'd like to thank Lindy Ryan and the entire Black Spot team. Thank you for taking a chance on me, for encouraging me, for working with me as I panicked my way through revisions and edits. Lindy, you are a rockstar, and I am forever blessed to have crossed paths with you. Here's to more adventures!

ABOUT THE AUTHOR

Tiffany Meuret is a writer of monsters and twisted fairy tales. Her publications include Shoreline of Infinity, Luna Station Quarterly, Ellipsis Zine, Rhythm & Bones, and others. When not reading or writing, she is usually binge watching comfortable sitcoms from her childhood or telling her kids to put on their shoes for the tenth time. She lives in sunny Arizona with her husband, two kids, two chihuahuas, gecko, and tortoise.